Russell Tho⌐
1885-1972

My father, Russell Thorndike, was born in 1885 in Rochester, where his father was the vicar of St. Margaret's; from an early age he wanted to write and to act; his first study was a chicken shed at the vicarage, where, as a young boy, he wrote religious dramas. After being a leading chorister at St George's Chapel, Windsor and schooling at Rochester, he and his sister Sybil entered the Ben Greet Acting Academy and later joined his Shakespeare company playing all over America. It was while touring there that he divulged his idea for the plot of Doctor Syn (see Sybil's preface)

The book was eventually written in his Dymchurch study, a boat house on the sea-wall, near his mother's cottage, and published while he was serving in the Gallipoli campaign in 1915; he was invalided out after being badly wounded, but as soon as he could walk, he resumed his acting with his sister Sybil at the Old Vic in the early Shakespeare seasons under Lilian Baylis. Thereafter he had a long and di⌐ ⌐ ⌐ ⌐ ⌐ ⌐ an actor and his writings included the seven Doctor Syn ⌐ ⌐ eneral books. He died in November 1⌐

DOCTOR SYN
RETURNS

*

'Terror of the American Coasts, Pirate of the High Seas,' This is the reputation which Doctor Syn conceals when, shipwrecked on the Sussex coast, he becomes the worthy Vicar of Dymchurch. Mipps also wants to forget a pirate's past and settles in the village as Sexton and Undertaker.

Less careful than his master, Mipps becomes involved with local smuggling and is caught red-handed by a regiment of the Dragoons. It is then that Doctor Syn decides to take a hand; and though by day he continues to occupy the pulpit and win the love of the Squire's beautiful daughter, by night he rides the Romney marshes captaining his Demon Riders.

DOCTOR SYN
RETURNS
by

Russell Thorndike

ROMNEY PUBLISHING

First Published by
Rich & Cowan 1935

This Edition published
under Licence from Rhona Thorndike
by Romney Publishing 2011

ISBN 978-0-9533726-3-8

Cover Illustration by
Charles Newington 2010

CONTENTS

FOREWORD

This is the second volume in the Saga of Dr. Syn and follows chronologically upon *Doctor Syn on the High Seas*. The third book in the series is *The Further Adventures of Doctor Syn.*

CHAPTER I

THE WRECK OF THE BRIG ON DYMCHURCH WALL

NEVER in the history of Dymchurch Rookery that sways above the church and court house had the black-robed inmates such cause to fear the snapping of their fighting tops as during the soul-shaking tempest that swept the English Channel on the night of November 13th, 1775. The giant elms creaked and groaned as the racing wind shrieked in their bent riggings. Far beneath on the flat grass of the low-lying churchyard the headstones of the graves were torn from their sockets and in some cases hurled and splintered against the church. The roof of the old Manor Farm house opposite, through the weakening of a beam, rained tiles upon the road, while all along the straggling village street chimney tops crashed down. It was braving death to pass the strongest buildings on that ghastly night. And yet two men were daring enough to attempt it, and that when the storm was at its height.

They had been regaling their spirits in the company of Mr. and Mrs. Waggetts, the proprietors of the Ship Inn, and consuming a vast quantity of excellent French brandy. Then they had heard the gun. It echoed above the storm from the desolate pebble nose of Dungeness. A ship was in distress. Simultaneously both men had risen and buttoned their coats.

"You're never going out in this," protested Mrs. Waggetts.

"There's no call for Merry to, but I must," answered the shorter of the two. "If a ship's coming ashore, it's my duty to see what manner o' ship she be."

He was the Preventative Officer. A dogged, bitter man, and most unpopular in the village by reason of his trade. He knew that no throat in Dymchurch was in such constant danger of being cut. He also knew that no one was more likely to cut it than his drinking companion who was, like him, buttoning up his coat.

This Merry belied his name. He was sullen, intractable and cross-grained. Tall and cadaverously thin, he was strong, and could pick up a living at most things that came his way.

"Why was he leaving the snugness of the 'Ship' parlour to court disaster outside?" the Preventative Officer asked himself.

A terrific crash near at hand.

"There goes our chimney stack," whined Mr. Waggetts, who

7

sat propped up with pillows in a wheel-backed armchair by the fire. Waggetts was a sick man.

His wife was the reverse. Large, ugly, vain, but capable. She it was who steered the Ship Inn and made it the profitable concern it was.

"Well, I says, it's one of them nights when one must take the crashes as they come. Besides," she went on, "the inn ain't going to come down. Ain't it stood all these years?"

The officer turned in the door and said 'good night', and, when they both got outside, these ill-assorted companions had to negotiate their way over the branches of a great tree that had been blown across the road from the Grove House, the comfortable residence of Dr. Sennacharib Pepper, the local physician and surgeon. Lights were burning in the Grove House. Evidently, Dr. Pepper expected the storm to give him a duty call, and was not yet abed.

At the corner of Grove House, the road turns and forks into an upper path which runs up a bank and snuggles its way immediately below the sea-wall. Up this path the two struggled, making their way towards a snugly-gabled house known as 'the Sea-Wall Tavern'. The events of this night were, however, destined to change this name. The two adventurers looked up at the bedroom window, where in the light of a candle a good-looking young woman was peering through the diamond-shaped panes. Behind her loomed the figure of her husband.

Making a trumpet of his hands, the Preventative Officer shouted: "Ahoy there, Abel Clouder."

In a vivid flash of lightning Abel looked down over his wife's shoulder and recognized the two men standing on the gravel path beneath the window. At the same time his wife pointed out to sea and uttered a frightened cry that was echoed by what seemed like the wailing of lost souls.

Abel made a sign to the men below and disappeared from the window. In a few seconds they heard the chains being taken down from the door, and it suddenly opened inwards. The two men dashed into the passage and turned to help the owner close his door. Against the fury of the wind, it took their combined force to do it.

"There's a ship in distress, ain't there?" asked the Preventative man. "Do you know her?"

"No," answered Abel. "Come upstairs and have a look. There'll be lightning again in a minute."

Mrs. Meg Clouder left the window as the men came in, and sat down on the side of the big bed.

Her husband dragged the Preventative man to the window, where they waited for the next flash. Merry stood just inside the door and turned his cadaverous eyes upon the girl's clear-cut, almost classic, features, her broad honest brow with the light brown hair that crowned it and fell in a provocative kiss curl upon her firm young breast. Her eyes had the green of the sea in them, and he was afraid of them, but the suspicion of freckles under them somehow stirred his blood. She was dressed in an orange-coloured frock of rough cloth, open at the neck. His eyes that had been devouring Meg's face and figure, shifted to her feet. They were bare, and he had a mad desire to crunch those beautiful little bones between his teeth.

As the lightning flashed he saw what the others had been watching, a sturdy brig with broken masts and fallen sails being hurled nearer and nearer to the sea-wall.

"She's no doubt striking the sand already as she dips," said Abel. "But she won't stick, not with that power of sea. It'll lift her off every time. She'll be broke up within the groyne. Maybe she'll get hoisted on to the wall before she breaks her back. By gad. She's on fire, too. Look."

The sky had gone black as the thunder crashed, but a dull red spot suddenly leapt into a fierce tongue of orange flame, and once more arose the wail as of lost souls. And that their bodies were lost there was no doubt. That flame, venomous and spiteful, had the ship. It was as though one element were striving with the other for the victim. Fire and water fought for the doomed vessel.

"Oh, poor people," murmured Meg, trembling. "Can we do nothing but watch?"

"I fear that's what it will amount to, lass," replied her husband. "It's no use trying to launch a boat, because it couldn't be done. But a line might help 'em."

The shrieking wind seemed to scoff at his words, for a sheet of water struck the lead-rimmed panes. Once more the lightning lit up sea and sky.

"She's nearer now," said Abel. "But every time the waves drop her she sticks. When she stops shifting, if she does, I'll risk it."

Meg stood up and said firmly: "You are not to go, Abel. It is madness."

Abel, however, had decided that he must go. He turned and laid both his hands upon her firm young shoulders.

"You ain't going to make me unworthy of your love?"

"Mrs. Clouder, that ain't a sea to swim in, I allow," said the Preventative Officer. "There's but two men on Romney Marsh that might attempt it at a long hazard, and your man's the stronger swimmer of the two."

"And is the other one a married man?" asked Meg.

The Preventative Officer shook his head. "It's the young vicar, I mean, Parson Bolden."

"But look at that sea," protested Meg.

"Why, there is the parson," exclaimed Abel. "See him, crouching his way up by the boat-house wall. He's a dare-devil for all he's a parson."

"There's quite a crowd of the lads collected," said the Preventative man.

"Where?" asked Merry, going for the first time to the window. He had a purpose for doing it, too. He dropped his dark scarf upon the dark floor-board. The light of the flickering candle did not betray this fact, as Merry leaned against the casement.

"On the lee side of the boat-house," was the reply to Merry's question.

"Then it's time we joined 'em," said Abel. "Have you got the key of the boat-house, in case them rescue ropes are needed, mate?"

"I've got it," answered the Preventative man, making for the staircase. "Come on, Merry."

Merry followed down the stairs. But one look he shot as he went, and he saw Meg in her husband's arms, and he hugged his hatred to his soul.

"Give a look to the parlour fire below, lass," said Abel, "and keep a kettle going. We may get one or two of 'em ashore in spite of all, and they'll want reviving."

When Abel had his hand upon the bobbin of the front door, Merry put his hand up to his coat collar. "You go on. I'll join you," he said. "I've left my scarf up in the bedroom."

"You'll never pull this door to by yourself," laughed Abel. "Here, Meg. Mr. Merry's left his scarf up there. Heave her down, will you?"

But this didn't suit Merry. He had a word to say to Meg alone and he meant to say it. He was up the stairs before Abel realized he was going, and he entered the bedroom without a word.

Meg had evidently neither heard her husband call nor Merry's footsteps, for she was kneeling beside the bed with her face buried in her arms. Feeling a heavy hand upon her bowed head rumpling her hair, she imagined that her prayer was answered and that her husband had returned to tell her that the seas were too high to adventure.

Smiling through her tears she looked up into the cadaverous face of the miserable Merry.

Meg found herself suddenly afraid.

"What do you want here?" she asked.

He turned away, muttering: "My scarf." He hovered round the bed, pretending to search for it.

She rose from her knees, dashed the tears from her eyes with the back of her hand, and in a business-like way went to the window-sill and picked up the candle. Her quick eyes immediately saw the scarf where he had dropped it. With her other hand she pointed to it.

"There it is," she said, but made no attempt to stoop for it.

The voice of Abel jerked him into action:

"Can't you find it, man? You're wasting time."

"Got it," answered Merry, as he shambled forward awkwardly and picked up the scarf. As he straightened himself up, he seemed surprised to find himself so close to her. There was only the candle which she held between them. Now, he decided, was the time to give her his message.

"Should anything happen to him," he whispered, jerking his head towards the stairs, "I shall be here to take charge of you, see?"

Meg looked bewildered, as indeed she was. "I don't understand you, Mr. Merry," she said.

"No?" he queried. "Well, you've made me understand something. you have. I see now why them damned fool moths get caught up in the flame."

As he spoke his fingers had fluttered in tiny circles above the lighted candle which she held between them. Then suddenly they had dropped, extinguishing the flame and plunging the bedroom into darkness. Before she could cry out in her astonishment, her head was clenched in the crook of his arm and she was half suffocated against the wetness of his coat. As he held her there, she heard once more a wail of agonized terror from the ship outside.

"Come on," cried Abel, climbing the stairs.

She felt herself freed, and as the lightning flashed again she was alone.

"Have you got a light to rekindle the candle for Mrs. Clouder?" said Merry from the top of the stairs. "The draught blew the damned thing out."

Abel produced a 'flasher' from his pocket, and passing Merry on the stairs went into the bedroom. 'Flashers' were small pistols without barrels, about four inches long in all, with flintlock and pan to hold about a quarter thimble-full of powder. 'Flashers' were used by the Dymchurch men to signal night messages to one another across the Marsh, or perhaps to the crew of a lugger awaiting a 'run' on Dymchurch Bay. They could also answer the innocent purpose of a tinder box.

Presenting the flasher at his wife's head, Abel growled in mock sepulchral tones, "stand and deliver," and then, as he flashed the powder and lit the candle, he added, laughing: "And how's that for your handsome Jimmie Bone?"

Jim Bone was the notorious highwayman who transacted a brisk business on the busy Dover Road and periodically went into hiding upon the Marsh when the chase became too hot. Though a hard man to cross, by reason of his calling, he was a good friend to his friends, amongst whom the Clouders were numbered.

"The seas are too high for you to attempt a rescue, Abel."

"That's for the other lads to decide," he answered. "If they think it's possible, I shall have to attempt something."

Meg, who was seething with anger against Merry's madness, turned her temper against the villagers who took her young husband's strength and daring so much for granted.

"But why should you risk so much for others, for strangers? You forget you are married, Abel."

"Not I," he contradicted. "Why, that's the reason I'm married to you, and it's because I love you that I have to do more than the rest."

Meg smiled. "You're a clever old flatterer, Abel, and as obstinate as you are good-looking. But for all that, I want you to do something for me."

"Why, anything, except to be a coward, and you wouldn't ask that I know."

"I want you to take care of that man Merry," she said solemnly.

"I reckon he can more than take care of himself, but why——?"

"I mean avoid him," she corrected. "Keep clear of him. He hates you, Abel."

Abel laughed. "Now why should anyone take the trouble to hate a good enough natured fool like me? I haven't an enemy in the world, please God."

"Perhaps there are some who are jealous of your good nature," she said.

"Jealous?" he repeated. "My faith, the only jealousy I shall meet in life will be your fault. Everyone's jealous that I happened to win you, Meg, and quite right, too. But you can take it from me that Merry ain't that way. He's altogether too sour and selfish to be taken up with a pretty girl."

"You may find you're wrong, husband, and later I'll tell you my reasons."

"I must go, lass. I wouldn't have 'em say that Abel Clouder hung back. I love you too well, Meg."

"Thank you, Abel," she answered with a smile. "And as I love you, watch Merry."

"Trust me," he nodded, and with her kiss on his cheek, he went down the stairs and gave the sour Merry a hearty clump on the back which made him look the sourer.

"Now lads, open the door, and let's see if we can cheat the devil and snatch a few souls from his grip. Ready? Then out into the lightning and the waves."

A splash of spray in the passage, a gust of wind that set every beam and floorboard creaking, and then silence, told Meg on her knees beside the bed that they had gone.

The three men reached the fast-gathering group under the shadow of the boat-house. They were joined by the parson with the news that the burning ship seemed to have stuck fast in the sand and that the waves breaking over the well deck kept the fire in the after hold beneath the poop deck cabin, and prevented it from spreading amidship. He agreed with the fishermen that it would be impossible to launch a boat, but he did think that a strong swimmer might reach the wreck with a rope, and he stoutly maintained that he was quite willing to attempt it.

Accordingly, the necessary tackle was brought out from the boat-house. However, since both tide and wind were driving into the bay, it was doubtful whether a single swimmer would be able to make headway with the weight of rope hampering him. Abel immediately suggested that if another line were fixed to the rescue rope and each end attached to a cork jacket, that he would then adventure with the parson.

Both men accordingly stripped off their coats and boots and buckled on their life preservers to which the line's ends were fixed, and then with practically the whole male population of the village assembled to pay out the slack, the two heroes climbed the sea-wall, arm-in-arm, and waiting for a favourable backwash of a gigantic wave, they plunged in side by side, and were swept out to meet the oncoming seas.

Meanwhile, the news of the wreck had spread through the village and reached the Court House, so that by the time the swimmers, fighting for every inch of progress, had cleared the end of the stone groyne which was about half-way to the ship, the helpers on the rope were augmented by the squire himself, four or five gentlemen who had been his dinner guests, and Dr. Sennacharib Pepper, whom they had collected on the way. With these extra strong and willing hands, it was simple for Merry to move away without being missed, for while his colleagues were busy over the living, he decided that it might be more to his advantage to get busy with the dead, or nearly dead.

By calculating tide and wind in relation to the wreck, he imagined such bodies would come ashore near the flight of steps built into the sea-wall opposite Sycamore Farm, so he scurried away under the shelter of the sea-wall till he reached his coign of vantage, and, crouched down in his strong recess like a wild beast scenting prey, he waited for what the devil would send him from the sea.

Crouched over the rope as they paid it out inch by inch from hand to hand, the villagers wondered what was happening at the other end, and whether both, or one, or neither of the men would effect a landing on the ship.

While the rolling rotundity of the resounding thunder was drumming up to its last grandeur, a strong stench of sulphur swept down across the sea and hung in spreading fumes upon the sea-wall, until with a sharp crackle as percussive as a square of muskets, another fire, a ball of flaming gas enveloping a thunder-stone, darted across the sky and dashed with a hissing explosion into the sea.

Then up—and right above the sea-wall line rose the waters, lifting the ship into the sky and carrying it onwards, down the liquid hill that swept towards the wall.

Out went the sky as the thunder cracked, but not even that, nor the mighty roaring of the waters, could drown the great thud as the ship's bows cut into the masonry of Dymchurch Wall like a battering-ram.

Now although Meg, in a vain endeavour to catch sight of her husband, had braved the flashes of the lightning, the terror of the fireball as it burst across the sky made her involuntarily clap her hands over her eyes, and during the destructive seconds of the storm's ferocity that followed, she felt the house shake violently, give a sickening tilt and then shiver, as joists and beams groaned and creaked in their shifting. Built as it was upon the lower level of the sea-wall, the foundations slid with the soil as the waves, bursting through the cellarage, weakened it. The front door was torn from its hinges and blown bodily against the staircase, as the sea water gushed through the passage, silting up the floor with a loose deposit of gravel, sand and shell. At the same time the diamond-paned casement through which Meg had been looking, crashed inwards, its heavy leadwork striking her on the head and bearing her to the floor beneath its weight. This was the last wicked prank of the hurricane before departing. There followed what, in contrast to the noise, seemed almost a silence, broken only by the accustomed sound of waves against the Wall.

How long Meg lay there beneath that pile of twisted lead, glass panes and broken plaster, she could not tell, for the injury to her head had left her senseless, but when she recovered she still found herself looking through the casement, and for some time it puzzled her that she could only see the sky—a wild sky of fast-flying clouds lit with the full radiance of the moon. Then she realized that she was laying on the floor with the window resting upon her face. She remembered the storm. Its violence had gone, but in her heart it had left behind its terror, and it was not the thunderbolt that had made her cover her eyes, nor the noise, nor the rocking house which made this terror so paralysing, but the thought of what it had brought, the thing which she had seen between her fingers, in that awful moment. It was the huge form of a giant, a devil of the storm, who with staring eyes had rushed towards her at the window. She had seen its face plainly, with its great eyes and black beard; as it rushed, it waved a great lantern above its head, and this swaying light had revealed the horrid face. The devil himself made manifest in the shape of a wooden giant.

Meg roused herself from the old oak floor, which, though never straight at the best of times, was now canting at an alarming angle. With all this calamity, no wonder she had imagined a wooden devil which was nothing more than a frightening dream. She could soon dispel that by looking out of the open space where the window had been. Comforting herself with the suggestion, she looked out.

Though her fears had been acute, they were as nothing to the overwhelming horror that now possessed her, for there, right opposite to her and leaning over the lip of the broken sea-wall, his lantern still alight, was the enormous head and shoulders of the wooden-looking giant. Its staring eyes regarded her with a fixed expression of contempt and hatred, and as she gazed, she listened too and heard a voice beneath her window saying: "Here's a shutter. Help me wrench it off." There followed a squeaking of iron and a bump of wood, and then the slow, regular tramping of men's feet.

The malignant face told her to come and look at what was going on beneath her window. He swung his lantern invitingly.

She was powerless to move, but she knew that they were carrying her Abel away on the shutter, and she guessed he was dead, for she heard a voice which she recognized as the squire's say: "Wait, while I break the news to his wife." She heard him enter the passage and wondered why his footfalls sounded as though they trod a beach. Then she heard him say: "I'll want a hand there. The stairs are all but gone under this door." After much whispering and mumbling, and the noise of wood clearance, followed by the effort of someone climbing, she knew the squire was clinging to the crooked doorpost of the bedroom. She was unable to turn round, for the wooden man had her hypnotized, but she knew it was the squire before he spoke, which he did with difficulty

"My poor Meg, I've got the worst possible news to break to you. Look at me, please, Meg, won't you? It will help me to tell you."

"But I have been told, Sir Tony," she answered. "I've been told in a cruel way, not kind, like you would do. He told me. Look. He's staring at me. He's killed my husband and destroyed my home and he's gloating on me there, leaning over the sea-wall. It is the devil. He told me so. And he sent that other brute to warn me. He looked at me with fixed eyes, too. He stared at me like that, before he put out the light and seized me. Don't let him get me, Squire, oh!"

The staring eyes, the monotonous, metallic tone of her voice frightened the squire. He had imagined that he would have to deal with a weeping, hysterical young woman, whom he could have taken home to his wife to be mothered. But the deathly still horror which possessed Meg was a symptom altogether more alarming, and he feared that her reason might be affected permanently.

He answered her calmly: "Why, Meg, this devil on the sea-wall, as you speak of it is no devil at all, but has, no doubt for years been the pride of every honest sailor behind it, for it is nothing but the wooden figure-head of the ill-fated, broken brig, *City of London*. Your heroic husband and our no less valiant vicar had almost reached it with a life-line, when a great tidal sea wave lifted the ship above them. It is some comfort to know that their death was quick. It is a great comfort to know that their death was heroic. Now, Meg, I have come to take you to the Court House."

"And leave my home?" she asked, bewildered.

"It is unsafe to stay in it, Meg," replied the squire. "I will undertake to see that it is guarded by responsible men answerable to myself, and tomorrow we will repair the damage."

For the first time she cut the spell which the wooden figure held on her, and turning to the squire, asked in a matter-of-fact tone: "Where is—Abel?"

"They are carrying the—they are carrying him," he corrected, "to a shelter for the night. It is customary to use the barn at Sycamore Farm in cases like this. Come, Meg, it is something to know that you bear the name of a man whom the whole of the Marsh will always be honouring. Let me take you to her ladyship."

Meg took two steps towards him and then turning suddenly looked once more at the figure-head. Then with a pathetic moan she collapsed into the squire's arms. He carried her through the door and lowered her unconscious body to willing hands beneath the broken staircase.

And so in solemn procession were the Clouders carried towards the rookery where the party divided, those bearing Abel's body turning into the Farm Lane, and the squire's party, who carried Meg, going on to the old Court House, where Lady Cobtree and her three daughters busied themselves in preparing a guest-chamber and making ready such remedies as Dr. Sennacharib Pepper prescribed for the unconscious young widow.

Meanwhile Merry, soaked to the skin from salt water, peered out along the base of the sea-wall when the black thunder clouds rolling away across the Marsh uncovered the moon, and showed him the dark huddled body of a man lying face downwards on the stones. The ghoulish wretch approached the body cautiously, and perceived at once that the survivor was dressed as a sailor of rank, with long sea-boots, and his fingers were clasped around an oilskin package. Merry had some difficulty in wrenching it from him, and when he had ripped open the waterproof case, found that it was of no value to him, though of the greatest import to a conscientious captain for it was the log book and bills of lading. The gallant captain of the brig had to the last preserved the good name of his ship.

A last wave of the full tide surged up and all but drew the body back with it, but Merry clung on, and when the water cleared, he dragged his find up the sloping stones beneath the shadow of the Wall. He then turned it over on its back, and in so doing heard the chink of gold. Of course, this would be the ship's money. With greedy fingers he unbuttoned the sea-coat and found, sure enough, a waist-belt fitted with many pouches. Fumbling for the buckle in order to transfer this to his own waist, the corpse of the captain, to his utter astonishment, opened his eyes and regarded him with an expression of wonder.

The captain was alive. What was more significant to Merry, the captain looked a man of iron, broad shouldered, and with hands hard and hairy. It was no time to hesitate. His victim was recovering his senses, for with a protective gesture, his hands moved to the belt. Better for him had he feigned death, for Merry flashed the knife out of his pocket and drove it into the captain's heart.

This cold-blooded murder did not upset Merry in the least, for what more likely than that the captain had been stabbed by a member of his crew. He drew out the knife and cleaned the blade upon the dead man's soaking clothes, and then dragged the heavy belt from the corpse and fastened it securely beneath his own coat.

Then he saw to his delight that another body was lying a few yards away.

Leaving the captain, he approached his second victim with every degree of caution. The body lay on its side dressed in a suit of sober black. Despite the rough passage of the waves, this survivor had managed to keep on his shoes, which were fastened with handsome silver buckles. Beneath the heavy but well-cut top-coat, he saw long, spindly legs in black hose and breeches. It seemed incredible to the murderer that this body had not only retained shoes but also a large, imposing three-cornered hat, which fitting tightly to an intellectual forehead, had yet been tilted to a rakish angle during its journey across the stones.

With his left hand grasping his knife, Merry's right explored the corpse cautiously. To his great delight, he found that this one had also a money belt, which by the size of its well-filled pouches promised a greater return than the one he had filched from the captain. He also noticed above the collar of the coat a lanyard, the ends of which disappeared beneath the white cravat, and wondering what valuables the man thus secured around his neck, he tugged it out and found a large handsome silver key. That was of no use to Merry, for it was no doubt the key of a sea-chest which would by now have been consumed in the hold fire. He then saw that a rope was fastened round one of the wrists. The other end was trailing in the water. The man had most likely been lashed to a spar which had broken loose.

On the whole, the belt interested Merry more than any other detail, but before transferring this to his own waist, a perverted sense of humour which this knowledgeable villain possessed, prompted him to a course of action which would save him the exertion of returning the bodies to the sea that brought them up. He resolved to stab this corpse as he had stabbed the other, and then lock them arm-in-arm upon the stones as though they had perished in a fatal fight.

He thereupon drew out his knife, and for greater caution glanced back over his shoulder to make sure that he was not being observed. That movement was his undoing, for as he turned his head he received such a violent crack over the skull that for some time he knew nothing.

The first thing he discovered on coming to himself was that the situation as he slowly remembered it, had been woefully reversed. In other words, he was now lying on his back while his intended victim was sitting upon his chest and grinning at his discomfort.

"So you've decided not to rid the world of yourself as well as of the captain, eh?" asked the survivor of the wreck. "Not that you would have journeyed together, for if ever a sea captain was sure of a berth in heaven, he was, and from the little I have observed of you, I should suggest that hell flames would not be hot enough. I say 'the little' I know of you advisedly, because here's to our longer acquaintance," and the speaker, producing a silver flask of large proportions, tilted a dram of good brandy down his throat. "No doubt you could do with a drop yourself?"

Merry could, and moved one hand, which in a mysterious way drew the other with it. He glanced at his hands and saw that his wrists were tied very efficiently with rope. He looked at the rope and saw that one end stretched away into the fast receding waves.

"What's the idea?" he grunted.

His captor took another pull at the flask and sighed with satisfaction.

"You ask me what is the idea?" continued the survivor, "I will tell you. To stick a knife in a helpless man as you did to that unfortunate captain merely to steal a belt of money which is now round my waist—no, my friend! And, by God, unless you comply with my terms——"

"And what are the terms?" growled Merry. "To say nothing about the money belt, I suppose."

"My terms are first of all obedience," replied the other. "Open your mouth wider."

Into his open jaws he poured a few drops of brandy on to the tongue, then took another generous pull of it himself.

"And now," he continued, "speak up smart and true. Your name?"

"Merry," replied the unfortunate.

"Your name belies you, then. Occupation?"

"I do odd jobs."

"Very odd jobs, it seems. Where do you live?"

"Here in Dymchurch, by the great sluice gates. I've a room in the long white cottage that lies alongside, and what's more, I've lived there all my life."

"And what's more, you'll go on living there all your life," retorted the stranger, "until such time as it pleases me to send you to the gallows, for if you try to slip your cables without my leave, I'll have the constables on your heels for this night's murder, and get this clear in your head. Just as you have lived here all your life, so am I going to live here the rest of mine, and since I am all for peace and quiet and we are likely to be neighbours, you can take it that I shall keep a weather eye upon you, Mister Merry Murderer."

"But what are you going to do now?" asked Merry.

"My good and murderous friend, it is not the magistrates you tried to murder, but me," replied the stranger. "A dead man, swinging, is only serviceable to the crows and rooks that nest above the gallows. To see you as a picked corpse is small compensation to me for the shocking reception I sustained at your hands, but as a strong living slave, as one who must willy-nilly do my bidding—why, there is every chance that I shall exact full compensation for your wrong-doing? And now, tell me. Does a Cobtree still rule at the Court House here?"

"Aye, Sir Antony Cobtree. He's chief magistrate now."

"Then Sir Charles is dead, I take it, for he was never the man to retire."

"That was his trouble. He wouldn't retire even from hunting. Broke his neck after the fox he did."

"Well, there's a worse way of breaking your neck than that," replied the stranger with an ominous gesture. "And how long ago was this tragedy?"

"Ten or twelve years," explained Merry.

"Well, with all respect to the late squire, I rejoice to learn that my old college friend Tony is now the King's Authority upon the Marsh, and the sooner the tide allows us to visit him the better shall I be pleased."

"But there's no need to wait for the tide," corrected Merry. "Here's steps up to the sea-wall."

The stranger pulled the rope attached to Merry's wrists. "But here's my baggage, on the end of this cord. The captain helped me to heave it overboard. It is waterproof, but I was not so sure of it being fireproof. The silver key which you ignored belongs to it. When the water goes out a little further you will wade in and lift it from the sand. And now up on your feet and let us wind in this rope till it's taut. You're wet enough, and so am I, to bid defiance to further wading. But I'm hungry, thirsty and tired, and I dare swear you can say the same and can add 'disappointed'. When my sea-chest is safe at New Hall of the Court House, I'll expend one of the captain's guineas on you, which will give you the price of a good hot supper, plenty of drink, treatment for your head, and payment against loss of a good knife."

Merry got to his feet with some groaning occasioned by the wound to his head and the black hate in his heart. He followed his new master across the rough boulders to the level beach. At the water's edge the stranger stopped and gathered in the slack of the rope.

"The great wave was a help to you," said the stranger, as soon as the rope was taut. "It carried the chest further than one could have hoped, otherwise, you might have had a long vigil before reaching it. But we must wait even now until the water is only to your waist."

Merry was thinking quickly now. Never would he be safe while this mysterious stranger lived. And never would a safer opportunity arise than now for killing him. He was the only one in Dymchurch who knew of his safe landing. The beach was deserted, for between them and the villagers was the wreck, and they were waiting to board her from the further side. The stranger dead, Merry would win back the captain's guineas as well as the stranger's money belt, which promised to be the more valuable, and then there was the rope attached to the submerged sea-chest with the silver key around his victim's neck. Such a chance was a gift from the devil himself and he must take it. The thought of a hand-to-hand fight was dismissed. The stranger had taken his knife, but the devil showed him a handier weapon. This was a broken billet torn by the waves from a wooden breakwater. In size it resembled a belaying pin, and its end was weighted with an iron plate from which protruded a heavily studded clamp bolt.

Covering his movement with a blasphemous oath against an uncomfortable sea-boot, Merry stopped, pretended to adjust the boot in question, and rose up again with the likely weapon in hand and hid it in the fold of his coat. The moment was ripe, for the stranger had not turned round, but was engrossed on the hidden sea-chest, flapping the rope upon the surface of the waves in an endeavour to locate its lie. Merry approached behind his back, slowly and stealthily.

Reasoning that the stranger had not got eyes at the back of

his head and was therefore ignorant of his silent advance, he ignored the fact that the 'likely weapon' had not escaped his eye. Indeed, the stranger had expected that Merry would stoop for it, and smiled grimly to himself at the string of oaths against the innocent sea-boot. Although he had not got eyes at the back of his head, his alert instincts told him just exactly when Merry was crossing the danger line, and then changing the rope to his left hand, he whipped Merry's knife from his pocket and balanced it in the palm of his hand, so that the moonlight shone on the blade.

"Nice knife, this of yours, Mister Merry," he said, without turning round. The glint on the blade and the suspicion of a threat beneath the words made Merry stand still. "Sharp, and on the whole well-balanced, though a trifle heavy in the blade to my thinking. But not bad. Oh no, damme, not at all bad." And as he spoke he sent it spinning up into the air and caught it neatly by the handle. This he did not once but many times, and at each toss the knife seemed to soar a trifle higher than the last, and each time the knife was in the air Merry did some quick thinking and mental timing.

"The devil save us," laughed Merry, with what affability he could muster. "That's a pretty trick, mister. And where did you come by that?"

"A keen eye and a quick hand," replied the other pleasantly.

"And about how high can you toss it?" asked Merry, scarcely able to conceal the pleasure at his own cleverness.

"In the sunlight I have caught a knife falling from the height of a church steeple," boasted the stranger.

"I can hardly credit that," scoffed Merry. "It's easy to brag in the light of the moon about what you do in the sunlight."

"I'll not be accused of bragging without an attempt at proving my words," retorted the other, with some annoyance. "As you say, there's moonlight, and it's clear enough. I have been something of a thorn in your flesh so far, Mister Merry, that I feel it would be scurvy of me not to amuse you. I can't promise to judge exactly the height of a steeple, but I'll throw it as high as I can, and your eyes shall judge whether I catch or no."

The stranger took off his three-cornered hat, much to the satisfaction of Merry, who had not liked the look of it covering his target. The stranger dropped it on to the sand beside the rope and then looking up began to move the knife up and down.

"Keep your eyes skinned on it, Mister Merry," he enjoined.

"I will," laughed Merry, coming nearer as though in interest.

"One, two, three and UP." The stranger had crouched and shot up, and away went the knife into the sky. Merry saw it go and then forgot it. He was watching the other's bent-back head. A perfect target.

Gripping the iron-loaded billet with all his strength, he swung it up when the stranger whipped around like lightning and the astonished Merry was being driven back with a long blade pricking into his chest.

"Drop that, you dog, or I'll drive this knife out through your back."

Merry dropped the billet of wood and retreated gibbering with fear from the point of the knife.

"So you thought I was going to follow your knife up to heaven did you? It never occurred to you that I had another of my own already to send you to hell. I seem destined to upset your plans, Mister Merry."

"All right," grunted Merry. "I'm beaten. Let me go and pick up your hat for you, sir."

The stranger shook his head. "Not yet, Mister Merry, for your knife is sticking in the sand but a yard away from it, and it might tempt you to be foolish again, and I am going to show you just how foolish. Since you interrupted one knife trick, I am about to show you another. You see the post behind you. It is about your height. Put your hat on the top of it."

Merry sullenly removed his hat and walked towards the breakwater, only too glad to escape from the pricking knife. He put the hat upon the six-foot post.

"Very life-like, upon my soul," laughed the stranger. "Let me introduce you, Mr. Merry that shall be, to Mister Merry that for the moment *is*. A man of your perception, Mister Merry that shall be, will realize that this Mister Merry that *is* has little to recommend him. He is at the best as stubborn as old oak and iron, but the oak is rotting, and the iron eaten with rust. Twice has he tried to murder me tonight, and he is thinking hard how best to try again. Let me show you how I deal with such a stumpy idiot. Ha!" The stranger made a quick movement.

The knife whistled past the live Merry and stuck deep and quivering in the centre of the post a foot beneath the hat.

"Right through the neck, Mr. Murderer. Right through the neck. Now pluck it out and give it back to me."

Once more Merry saw a chance, a faint chance, and leaping to take it, he worked the knife with difficulty out of the post. But when he turned he saw that the stranger had retreated and while settling on his hat, was also balancing the other knife which he had picked out of the sand.

"And now," he said, taking up the slack of the rope and giving it a spin on to Merry's wrist, "drop that knife in the sand in front of you and step in after my chest, for this little diversion has filled up time while the water dropped, and don't fear at being carried out by the tide, for I have the rope as a reins with you as one horse and the chest as the other."

Merry strode desperately towards the waves and then stopped.

"Is this chest a big one?" he asked.

"Very big, and very heavy," smiled the stranger.

"Then how the devil do you think I can carry it with my wrists lashed together?" he demanded.

"I don't for one minute. If you will come here, I will free you."

"Then you'd best pick up your own knife," advised Merry. "It seems handier for cutting rope."

"I have been brought up to believe it a crime to cut rope wantonly. I'll untie it."

Merry watched the stranger's long, sensitive fingers working, and he realized that any man possessing such hands and such penetrating eyes must be someone above the average. In a few seconds his left wrist was free, but the rope's end still held his right firmly.

"I noticed that you are left-handed," remarked the stranger. "You killed the captain, at least, with your left. And in my own defence I should like you to realize that the first thing I remember after my buffeting on the stones, was the descent of your knife. Had I recovered sooner I should have saved your victim's life."

"Don't make another speech about it," growled Merry, striding off into the waves.

He picked up the other section of the rope and, lifting it from the water, waded along it.

The chest lay in deeper water than the stranger thought, for as Merry stooped to up-end it, a wave broke over his shoulders. This discomfort irritated the baffled Merry beyond all bearing, and he expended his rage upon the chest. He would anyway show the stranger that he was a man to be feared for his strength, and with a superhuman effort fed with rage and wounded pride, he somehow got the breaking weight upon his back and staggered with it from the water.

"Splendid," cried the stranger, with a great show of admiration as Merry passed him.

'And when I have a knife in your shoulder-blades, I'll say

"splendid" too,' said Merry to himself. Aloud he grunted: "To the Court House, you said?"

"I did," replied the stranger, "where I intend to spend this night unless Tony Cobtree be much changed from the gallant lad he was when I knew him."

As they climbed the steps cut in the sea-wall, Merry rested the chest upon the ledge of masonry, for the stranger, who had coiled the long slack of the cord over his arm, had given Merry's wrist a pull as he stopped and regarded the captain's body.

"Yes," ejaculated Merry, as though blaming the stranger for the dead man's plight. "What are you going to do about that? Best thing is to give him a sea-burial, eh?"

"No, we'll lay him to rest in the churchyard with full honours," said the stranger. "I happen to know his wishes on burial. We discussed it. I was for sea-burial, having witnessed one, and he, the sailor, said not for him. So we'll respect his wish and cheat Davy Jones. I'll take his papers and report his death."

"But the wound?" muttered Merry in interrogation. "They'll find that and wonder. Unless they think the fire aboard spread panic and it was a case of every man for himself. I've known cases where sailors run wild against authority. Now, if you, being a survivor, could tell them some such panic took place——"

The stranger, who had stowed the oilskin packet in his pocket, silenced Merry with a gesture, then straightened out the dead man's limbs. A sea-gull screeching and hovering overhead, then caused him to lay his kerchief over the face. Having concluded the last service of respect, he removed his hat and with bowed head uttered a prayer. Then, signing to Merry to proceed, he climbed the steps and fell in at his side, saying quickly:

"As to what they will think of the captain's death wound, I cannot say, but you can be sure of this. Cross me but once, and they shall know the truth, for just as surely as they will believe my words against yours, I shall denounce you for tonight's murder at the next assizes."

They walked on silently save for Merry's heavy breathing. It was slow going, for the rough road was littered with branches of trees, and bricks and tiles. At the corner of the churchyard the stranger stopped and gave a little tug on the rope. Merry stopped too and eased the weight of the chest on the low churchyard wall.

"Yes, a moment's rest before we ring at the door, I think," said the stranger. "The old church, eh? Looking very beautiful in the moonlight. But I see that you are more interested in the gallows and the rags and bones that swing there. What was he? A smuggler?"

"No. Sheep-stealer," growled Merry.

"And to think that a love of mutton should bring a poor fellow to that," philosophized the stranger.

"It was other people's mutton, you see," grunted Merry.

"Oh, I am not excusing him," replied the stranger. "The law of the Marsh must be kept, just as the Wall must be maintained."

"It seems then you're no stranger to these parts," said Merry. "Since we are to be further acquainted, it might be as well if I knew what your name and occupation might be."

"All in good time, Mister Merry. This is Friday? Very well then, on Sunday you will attend morning prayer inside there.Then you may learn something, if you keep awake."

"I don't attend church. I ain't a hypocrite," growled Merry.

"Nevertheless, you will be there," continued the other. "It is a command. Understand? And one thing more, before we part. To insure your good behaviour, your guilty secret will be made public at your first legal offence. In plain words, if Mister Merry appears for any misdemeanour at the Petty Sessions, he will appear also at the Assizes for the captain's murder and attempted murder on me. Now, up with the chest again and follow me."

As the church bells were pealing out their danger summons to the Marsh, the stranger and Merry had not heard the ringing of the Court House bell, but as they crunched their way across the gravel to the front door, they saw that they were forestalled, and that another man was being admitted into the hall. The footman was about to close the door again when the stranger called out to him.

"I wish to see Sir Antony," and then, without waiting for the footman's reply he turned to Merry and added: "You can bring my chest in here and put it down. Not on the rug, but against the wall there on the flagstones, where the sand and wet won't harm."

New Hall, the residence which surrounded the Marsh Court House and legal offices, in those days kept up a great show of state, all the Cobtree serving men wearing scarlet liveries and powdered hair. Although taken aback by the strangers unexpected entrance and air of command, which assured him that he had to deal with a gentleman above the ordinary, the pompous young footman was not so impressed when he recognized that the bearer of the chest was none other than the infamous Merry. Also, the stranger's clothes of solemn black were sadly deranged by sea water and sandy mud.

Before the footman could utter a word, the stranger continued: "I take it that the squire has not departed from the Cobtree habit of sitting up o' nights. However, if he should be abed, I fear that the occasion demands you to call him."

There was a something about the stranger which made the footman realize that if he tried any browbeating he would fare the worse. But the presence of Merry demanded that he should demonstrate his own dignity.

So, avoiding the stranger's gaze, which disconcerted him, he looked at Merry down his exalted nose as he replied: "The High Lord of the Level is at present engaged in the company of several local gentlemen. One of the villagers who arrived just before you, and is the bearer of grave news, has been admitted, so that for a time the squire is fully occupied. No doubt, he would see you by appointment in the morning if your business is urgent."

"Urgent?" repeated the stranger. "It would seem so, I think, in that I have successfully negotiated fire, tempest and sudden death to transact it. When a man sets out from New England to Old in bad weather even those more exacting than yourself will admit the urgency, I think. As to the villager you mention, I rather gather that his bad news concerns myself, since I have now swum from the brig, *City of London,* which lies with her back broken on Dymchurch Wall."

"Are you then a survivor of the wreck, sir?" asked the footman.

"Unless you can convince me that I am a ghost," smiled the stranger.

"I was about to say, sir, that if you are a survivor, Sir Antony will see you, and immediately, for such were his orders, though he had small hope that any could live."

"Then that bad news you spoke of," continued the stranger, "was no doubt a report that no survivor had reached land, eh?"

"It was somewhat worse than that, sir," replied the footman solemnly. "It was the report that the body of our vicar, who had attempted with another to swim out with a life-line, has been recovered. He is dead."

"The vicar of Dymchurch is dead?" repeated the stranger.

"Aye, sir. Parson Bolden. He went out with young Clouder. Both lost. The young widow Clouder has been brought here. Going on something shocking till Dr. Pepper give her something to quieten her. She's asleep now."

"Poor lass," said the stranger.

He undid his coat and his long sensitive fingers felt in one of the many pockets of the captain's belt. He took out a guinea piece and dropped it ringing on a table.

"And now, my very young friend of the scarlet livery, be good enough to carry that coin to the man Merry there."

"A guinea, sir?" ejaculated the astonished footman. "For a porter's fee? We can change this at the bursar's office and he can call for a shilling."

"Give him the guinea, sir, and have done with it. The money is mine and the chest is heavy. I will give you the same if you can carry it up to my bedroom here later."

The footman eyed the stranger with a puzzled look, something between admiration and suspicion. Who was this man who came from Boston, referred to the squire as 'Tony', and boldly talked of his chest being carried to his room for a guinea? If he were a survivor of the wreck, then it was probable that the squire would offer him hospitality, and since he wore such a well-filled money belt and was obviously a gentleman of importance, it would be wise to show him attention in order to gain, perhaps, another guinea at his departure.

So he picked up the guinea and carrying it to Merry, handed it over with some disgust. Merry, however, showed no sign of moving.

"Well?" asked the footman. "Why don't you hop it now that the gentleman's treated you handsome? You ain't wishing to stay the night, I suppose, for the only time you honour us is on a pallet bed in the cells. So get along with you."

"How can I get along when I'm lashed to the gentleman's chest?" asked Merry with a scowl.

"You have at least two free hands to unfasten the rope from the chest," suggested the stranger. "I shall not need the rope any more, I think, and I daresay you can find use for it, if only as a reminder that a knot at the wrist is better than a noose round the neck."

It took even the strong fingers of Merry some time to loosen the knot attached to one of the iron handles of the chest, for it had been tied by one who knew something of knots and cordage. But at last it was undone, and with a snort of disgust from the footman and a quite a cheery "good night and keep Sunday in mind" from the stranger, Merry was shown the door and barred out.

As he clutched his guinea he was reminded again of what he had missed. The two money belts and the contents of that chest. With a little luck, he should by now have been a rich man, and then Meg would have been his for the asking. The exasperation at such a failure sent his blood racing in red rage, and he vowed that, somehow or other, he would find the means of settling scores with the mysterious stranger. Cudgelling his brain how best to accomplish this, a magnetic curiosity, common to criminals, compelled him to make his way towards the scene of the crime.

A glance showed him that so far the corpse had not been discovered, and it occurred to the murderer that it might be worth his while to go through the captain's pockets. No horror of what he had done assailed him. Only an increasing black hate that he had not accomplished more.

The white silk handkerchief placed there so reverently by the stranger had at least preserved the face from the greedy sea-gulls, who walked around it suspiciously, afraid of one of its flapping corners. As he appeared they flew off screaming.

Realizing that he must not be discovered lest his story of discovering the corpse might not agree with whatever it pleased the stranger to tell the squire, he went through the pockets rapidly, becoming the richer by two crown pieces and three silver four-pennies, a brass whistle and a clasp knife, which he used to sever the rope around his wrist. It was then that he noticed particularly the flapping corner of the stranger's kerchief that had successfully kept the sea-birds at bay. It was worked. Now, although not claiming to be a scholar, Merry at least had this superiority over many—that he could write and read. A silk kerchief was, as he knew, of sufficient value to safeguard, especially to a traveller who did not know his washer-woman. He ripped the kerchief quickly from the dead man's face and read by the light of the moon the owner's name. Yes—there it was. Beautifully worked in violet silk thread. A large 'D' and a small 'r'. That, he knew, stood short for 'doctor'. So, he thought, this arch-enemy is none but a bloody saw-bones. Then followed a capital 'S', a 'y' and an 'n'. 'Syn.' 'Doctor Syn.' . . .

And just as the murderer spelt out the name and committed it to his memory, the footman in the hall, turning back to the stranger, added: "Oh, and what name shall I say, sir?"

"Syn," replied the stranger.

His answer astonished him. At first he thought the gentleman was giving way to an oath, and resentfully he said: "Well, I must know the name in order to announce it, sir."

"Syn," repeated the other. "Doctor Syn. Not s-i-n- but s-y-n, and I rather imagine it will astonish the good squire more than it has you."

"I beg your pardon, sir, but the name is unusual."

"I beg yours, but 'tis none of my fault," smiled the owner of the name. "All we can do for our names is to hold them in honour as well as we can." He then repeated: "Doctor Syn."

CHAPTER II

DOCTOR SYN RETURNS

A R O U N D the great fireplace in the dining-room the squire and three or four gentlemen of the Marsh were sitting, and had been gravely discussing the tragedy of the wreck. On a small table stood an enormous punch bowl full of steaming 'bishop', from which Sir Antony kept ladling generous allowances in order that his friends should recover from their exertions on the rope. The depression they had felt through dragging ashore the dead body of Abel Clouder was now increased at the news of the parson's death.

"So history repeats itself again," he said gloomily. "As you know, Sennacharib" (for the doctor was of the party) "my father was just as unfortunate in the bestowal of the living. Just as soon as he got a man he liked, he was preferred elsewhere, and it has been the same with me. I really did think that since poor Bolden liked the place that we were settled with him for life, and now his life has been sacrificed in this heroic, tragic fashion. If you are visiting patients Burmarsh way tomorrow, Sennacharib, you might ride to the vicar and ask him to conduct our service on Sunday morning, for there will be no time to get anyone else at such notice."

"I'll do that," replied the doctor. "Have you no one in mind that you would wish to appoint in poor Bolden's place?"

"I shall have to depend upon the choice of the Archbishop, I suppose," said the squire. "There's only one man I can think of—but whether he is alive or dead, God alone knows. It was an understood thing that he should become vicar of Dymchurch, for he loved the place as we all loved him. He used to stay here during the Oxford vacations."

"I recollect the man surely," said Sennacharib Pepper. "He was an undergraduate with you at Queen's."

"That's the man," nodded the squire. "He was given a Fellowship, which he vowed he would hang on to till the living here was vacant."

"I talked with him often," said the doctor. "A brilliant young man."

"I should think he was," agreed the squire, turning to a glass-fronted bookcase at the side of the chimney-piece. "There's a book here somewhere—yes, here it is." He opened the glass door and drew out a leather-bound volume, which he opened at the title leaf. *"A Solemn Discourse on Religious Assemblies and the Public Service of God, According to Apostolical Rule and Practice.* What it all means, I can't explain. It's beyond me. But the book made such an impression upon Oxford that the University, despite his youth, conferred on him the title of Doctor of Divinity," added the squire.

"He was a fine horseman, too. He hunted here," added the doctor.

"And as magnificent with the sword as with the pistol," went on the squire. "He winged Bully Tappitt, the Squire of Iffley, in Magdalen Fields one morning. Fortunately, Tappit was a notorious duellist, and we were able to prove that he had offered the affront, otherwise it would have gone hard with our friend."

"What happened to him then?" asked another of the party.

"He went to America under distressing circumstances," said the squire. "But that was a few years later, after he had married the most beautiful girl you ever saw. Unfortunately, her beauty was but skin deep and she ran off with a blackguard, named Nicholas Tappitt, the nephew of the man he'd killed. I never heard what happened, for after telling me that he found life in England unendurable, he went abroad. I never heard from him again, but it is believed he was killed by Indians, for after much inquiry I learned that he went amongst them on a mission and has never been heard of since."

"What was his name?" asked Dr. Pepper.

The squire's eyes were filled with tears, and to hide his emotion he pointed to the fly-leaf of the volume and handed it to Dr. Pepper, who read the name of the author and nodded. "Of course, yes. I remember now. A good many years ago."

"What was his name?" asked one of the other gentlemen, as they both got up to look over the doctor's shoulders at the book.

The squire, after clearing his throat, said: "His name was——"

"Doctor Syn," announced the voice of the footman.

The squire spun round as though he had been shot, while the others looked up sharply from the name on the book, the name which they had just read, and which they had simultaneously heard announced.

In contrast to the bright livery of the footman who stood against the white panelling of the door which he held open, the sombre figure framed in the dark doorway seemed unreal. A shudder of superstition passed through the blood of everyone in the room as they gazed. No one moved, for concentration was riveted upon this tall, slim stranger. He had removed his heavy overcoat and thrown it over one shoulder, where it hung like a cloak. One long arm hung by his side and held a large, three-cornered hat, while the other was bent so that the white hand with its long, tapering and sensitive fingers rested lightly against his heart, as though he were about to bow in greeting. But he did not move, and until he did no one else had the power to. They looked at his face, pale and long, with fascinating lines cut into it, each one challenging the onlooker to respect his romance. A face carved by that master sculptor, Experience. The lofty brow, the queer but shapely head framed in a mass of raven hair. Eyes deep and piercing that seemed to each man in the room to be searching out the secrets of his soul. The nose was high with an aquiline droop. The cheeks hollow. Gaunt jaws that seemed to hold the whole decision of his destiny. A thin upper lip and fuller under one gave to the mouth an expression of alert determination. The strong neck and full throat were shapely, exactly right to the carriage of such a living head. Though standing deathly still, every limb conveyed quick and splendid movement momentarily arrested at the man's iron will. Showing no embarrassment at the silence, he showed no intent to break it, only allowing a gentle smile to twinkle in his eyes and gather at the corner of his mouth. It seemed almost as though he enjoyed their consternation and relished the thought that he was master of their sudden helplessness.

It was perhaps natural that the footman, being the only one not in a position to grasp the significance of the situation, should be the means of breaking the spell.

"The gentleman seems to be the only survivor of the wreck, sir."

"And consequently must ask your indulgence, gentlemen, for his appearance," added the stranger. "It has been a nasty night to swim in."

That he was still a stranger as far as the squire went was obvious, for all he did was to stare and mutter such phrases as: "No—no. Impossible. Asking too much. Incredible——"

"I hardly expected you to recognize me immediately," went on the stranger. "We have so many years to span, and a hard life alters most men. Although Time has dealt most generously with you, I have not yet quite captured from your features the gay and pleasant Tony that I knew. But I shall get him any moment, just as you will suddenly get me."

The jolly face of the squire was all puckered up into a vast frown as he once more shook his head. He looked again and said: "Yes, it's more years than one imagines. But it would be too strange. Yet, wait, there is just something reminiscent. Of course, the room's confoundedly dark. Suppose we light another candle sconce."

"The room is light enough," protested the other gently, "the last time I was here your father stood where you are standing, and I asked him to accept a book of mine. He stood there glancing at it, then sat me at that table and told me to inscribe it. Being my first inscription, I remember it. 'To Sir Charles Cobtree Baronet, of New Hall, Dymchurch, from his humble servant and admirer the Author.' He put it there, next to the *Odyssey of Mr. Pope*." He crossed to the bookcase. "Yes, there it is—the Odyssey —but where my book was—a space."

"We were but now admiring it, sir," said Sennacharib Pepper.

Mechanically the physician handed the volume to the squire, who passed it to the author. He, in his turn, looked at the title-page with a grim smile. "My faith, I must have been in a solemn mood when I penned this."

The squire could never decide afterwards whether it was the extra light supplied by one of the gentlemen carrying a candle-abra from the further end of the room or some trick that the stranger had in handling a book, but it was certain that he suddenly brought his fist crashing down on the table.

"Gad," he thundered, "I see him now, my old friend, Christopher Syn, mercifully restored. My dear friend, welcome home."

But feeling the wetness of his coat he became immediately the bustling host. "My poor fellow, you're wet through. Positively soaked."

"I've been swimming, Tony," smiled Syn.

In a few minutes the whole house appeared to be alive with people hurrying this way and that on various errands, but on tiptoe out of respect for the invalid, and by the time Dr. Syn had been taken with his chest to a comfortable bedroom, had been arrayed in a dry shirt and breeches of the squire's and wrapped in a red quilted dressing-gown, had been presented to the Cobtree family, especially to Charlotte, who was his godchild, and whom he remembered as a baby, and had insisted that the new baby should not be awakened, a magnificent cold supper was awaiting him in the dining-room, where he did full justice to a game pie and a bottle of claret.

Dr. Syn had told the squire that he had seen the body of the

B

captain lying on the sea-wall, and as he was eating, news was brought that it had been carried with other bodies they had recovered to Sycamore Barn. Maintaining that his own story could wait, Dr. Syn wanted to know all the news of the village, merely satisfying their curiosity about his own doings by telling them he had been in the wildest parts of America preaching the gospel to the Indians.

"And none of your experiences could be stranger than the shipwreck," went on the squire. "A very strange thing. Here we are, talking of you, and in you walk. And there you were wondering when the living of Dymchurch would be vacant, and the living vicar swimming out to rescue you is killed."

They all nodded gravely, and Dr. Syn said: "Yes, it seems like Fate."

"Seems? It *is*!" exclaimed the squire.

Charlotte nodded. She was the eldest, a beautiful blonde of nineteen.

Maria, of seventeen, fair like her sister, and Cicely of fifteen, somewhat darker, were both thrilled with this strange man who had come up from the sea.

Charlotte felt a strange thrill in the presence of this newcomer. The pale, tragic face, the sad smile that was so ingratiating. 'Yes,' thought Charlotte, 'here is a man, a sad lonely man, of whom any woman in the world would feel proud.'

Dr. Syn surprised the look that such thoughts wrote upon her guileless face, and he read an interest there, an admiration innocent enough, but yet a warning to him of something which this girl, the daughter of his friend and patron would never know, and it was this look that influenced him that very night to take a certain course. But this was after the household had settled down to quiet after the excitement of the storm. The physician had left his patient in Lady Cobtree's care, who had arranged to share the watches with Charlotte and the old housekeeper. After another bottle of port between the three of them, Pepper at length went home and the squire carried Dr. Syn's candles into his room.

"It's strange, too," said the squire, "that the servants got ready *his* room. I didn't mean to tell you, but I see you would have found it out."

"You need not think that I am afraid of his poor ghost, if that's what you mean," replied Dr. Syn. "But how should I have discovered it?"

The squire pointed to a wig and gown that hung behind the door. "He brought home the wig to have it dressed, I suppose, for he would only wear it in the church, and there only as a badge of his office. But why did he bring the Geneva gown? He always put that on just before preaching."

"He tore it on the chancel rail last Sunday, Papa. I noticed it and told him to bring it back for me to mend."

They turned and saw Charlotte standing in the doorway with a black coat over her arm.

"And what are you doing here, miss?" asked her father.

"I have been mending the sleeve of Doctor Syn's coat. I noticed it was badly torn when they were drying it, so I thought I had better do it at once. You will find the rest of your clothes hanging up. They are dry."

"That's very kind of you," said the doctor, taking the coat and examining the damage. "Now that is very beautifully done, Miss Charlotte. I have had to learn to work with a needle myself out of necessity, so I know when I see a thing done better."

"So you are starting in already to mother the Doctor, are you, miss?" laughed the squire.

This had been a daily joke with the squire over the young parson, and it had never affected Charlotte. So that she was the more puzzled and perhaps annoyed that the same old joke with reference to Dr. Syn should make her blush. To hide this, she walked away to hang up the coat which Dr. Syn had put down on a chair.

"It seems that someone must mother the poor gentleman," she laughed, "for he very cleverly thinks of a way to save his sea-chest there, and then forgets to unpack it. I suppose you know, Doctor, that your clothes in there are most likely to be wringing wet."

The doctor shook his head. "I suppose my nice new young mother will be very disgusted to hear that my sea-chest is full of old books. My clothes, other than I swam ashore in, I am afraid were all destroyed in the fire, for they were hanging in my cabin. But I have a few guineas that will take me to the tailors."

"But your precious books?" she asked.

"All wrapped round in oilskin, my dear," he chuckled. "Besides I can assure you that this is a sea-chest worthy of the name. I have known it dropped into a river, and when rescued the contents were bone dry."

"What things you have seen," whispered Charlotte with awe.

"Well, yes, but there's not much to see in an old chest being fished out of a river. I'll perhaps tell you a real story one day. An exciting one."

"Do," she answered. "Were there crocodiles in the river?"

"And now off to bed," commanded the squire. "If you are not sitting with the invalid, you ought to be sleeping."

"Good night, Tony's daughter," said Dr. Syn, bowing over her hand. Then he straightened himself and laying both hands gently on her firm young shoulders, he smiled, and kissed her on the cheek, saying: "Good night, little mother."

Once more Charlotte found herself blushing, so with a hurried curtsy she left the room.

"You have nice children, Tony," remarked Dr. Syn.

"Wait till you see young Dennis in the morning," replied the squire, glowing with pride. And with fervent 'good nights' and 'God bless you's' the squire went to the door.

"God bless you," replied Dr. Syn, and after listening to the retreating footsteps he tiptoed across the room and very quietly locked and bolted the door.

The squire went off to his room and did not notice that the outer door of Dr. Syn's powder closet was wide open, and as for the doctor, he never gave it a thought, but it was the means of giving food for thought to Charlotte Cobtree for a long time to come.

Charlotte had taken over her mother's watch at Meg's bedside, pleading that she felt strangely awake and could not sleep if she tried, so on the understanding that she would awaken Mrs. Lovell, the housekeeper, in two hours' time, she had been allowed her wish.

Outwardly she busied herself with feeding the fire and creeping to the bedside whenever the poor girl stirred in her sleep, but all the time her inward thoughts were far busier, and it was the new guest that filled them. He was a romantic figure. He had lived a romantic life. Why did she think of him with such a swift beating of her heart? Why had she blushed when he had praised her needlework? And why had she blushed when he kissed her? Why did this extraordinary joy that she felt in his arrival override the sadness for the young parson's death and Meg Clouder's tragedy? Had he thought of her at all? If only he were thinking of her now.

And he was, but not quite in the way she wished.

He thought first of all about her advice concerning the contents of his chest. She was right. Everything should be taken out and dried. He was alone, and could not be disturbed till morning, and a splendid wood fire burned in the grate. He slipped the corded key over his head and fitted it into the lock. It turned easily and he blessed the locksmith whose work had not been damaged by salt water. He pulled the chest towards the fire and raised the iron lid. Inside was a second chest of teak, reinforced with brass, and the inner one did not fit to the iron sides but was held in place by iron springs that gripped it tightly, and the small space between iron and wood was packed tightly with oakum, so that should any damp get through the outer iron case, this caulking would absorb it before reaching the wood. A second lock on the top of this lid was unfastened by the same key and two doors could be lifted and opened out sideways. The interior of this second chest was packed tightly with various compartments, and in all, the packing was worthy of the chest. Carefully covered with a velvet pad and lying taut in a grooved tray was a pair of silver-hilted long-swords with magnificent scabbards and carriages. In another corner, a case of pistols. Of the books he had spoken of so much there were but a few, and all bound round with oilskin to preserve their bindings. A Bible. The plays of Shakespeare. A volume on navigation. The works of Don Quevedo in Spanish. A book of Tillotson's sermons, and a Homer. All these he carefully spread out upon the hearth-rug to dry, though there appeared no sort of dampness on any. A brass telescope and a boxed sextant had their own departments, and when all these had been removed, a tray of clothes, neatly strapped in place. This he propped against a chair close to the fire. The lowest department was tightly packed with bundles and bags. Dr. Syn's sensitive fingers tapped them one by one, as though recalling their contents to his mind. Lifting out one of the bags in order to get the end of another package clear, a pleasant chink of coin came to his ears. The package was heavy and he weighed it lovingly in his hands, but he did not remove the piece of red flannel that was wrapped round it. In shape, it resembled a long brick, but was vastly heavier. He turned it over, patting the flannel and, satisfied that it was bone-dry placed it back again.

Dr. Syn stood up and surveyed his property. It represented all his worldly goods, but having reminded himself of the contents, and being assured that nothing was missing, his face bore a look of infinite satisfaction. His next employment was to examine the Geneva gown of his predecessor. Slipping off the quilted dressing-gown he put the gown over his head. Although quite full in the body, it was too short in the arms and legs, but he thought that for a village pulpit this would not greatly matter. By the open door of the powder-closet there stood a tall pier glass. Holding the lighted candle, he surveyed himself, and appeared dissatis-

fied. Not with himself—for Dr. Syn had his vanities, though in
company taking pains to hide them—but in the general effect
towards which he was working. There is no colour that can
compare with black or white for a striking effect, especially when
contrasted with those of brilliance. Amidst the garish court of
King Claudius, the inky cloak and suit of solemn black rivets all
eyes upon the solitary Hamlet. So thought Dr. Syn as he surveyed
his pale face and raven locks that fell upon the shoulders of the
Geneva gown. "My appearance like this in the Dymchurch pulpit
will be too striking. People will be curious about me and talk, and
if I preach as I know I can, the authorities will be preferring me
to a pulpit of more importance. No, it won't do, my dear friend."

Thus he addressed himself to his reflection. True, a doctor of
Oxford can reasonably be expected to cut a figure above the
ordinary, but as he told himself in the glass: "In my case, it is
dangerous!" The thought of his degree gave him an idea, and he
went to the tray of clothes that had been warming by the fire. He
unpacked his scarlet hood which had accompanied him on all his
travels, put it on, surveyed it critically and shook his head. "It's
the hair. It suits the face too well. It gives a romantic environ-
ment to the owner." He criticized his reflection as though it were
a second party. "Tony's girl, Charlotte, gave me the warning of
it, for the sweet girl had not the skill to disguise her thoughts, and
it won't do. There must be no romance. Nothing of note beyond
the ordinary. My degree will raise me dangerously enough above
my fellow vicars, therefore I must tone myself down to keep the
balance. If I am to lie low here, I must not be too conspicuous.
I must be a leaf lying in a forest of leaves, a stone upon a stony
beach. Above all, there must be no women to play Delilah to my
Samson in the time to come. My secrets are too dangerous."

He picked up the dead parson's wig, and put it on his head.
He looked once more in the mirror. The incongruity of the raven
locks escaping from below the rigid white line of the formal wig,
made him smile. He took a pull at the jug of small beer and smiled
again. From the chest he took his toilet case, and with a pair of
scissors he cut away the rebellious hair that hung beneath the
wig. He threw the cut hair into the fire, and as it fizzled, he found
his dark-tinted spectacles that he had used in the tropics and
pushed them on his nose. Once more he regarded himself in the
mirror and was so elated by what he saw that he took a deep pull
at his silver brandy-flask. He then discarded the wig, the hood
and the gown and began to dress himself in a fine suit of scarlet
velvet trimmed with silver braid. The coat, which was full-skirted

in the fashion that had already passed out of England, he bound round the waist with a silver sash into which he thrust his brace of pistols. Before fastening one of the swords to the carriage, he pulled on a long and elegant pair of thigh boots, and then attached the sword. Into his hat he clipped a fine ostrich feather, and then picking up the silver flask with one hand and fingering the hilt of his sword he yet again approached the pier glass and favoured his magnificent reflection with a bow. Just then the stable clock struck three.

"Captain Clegg," he whispered, "I regret to inform you that we have reached in safety the parting of the ways. If I do not discontinue your company, it is as like as not that I should accompany you to Execution Dock. By reason of the many services you have done for me, and for the fact that the name of Captain Clegg is known and trembled at over the seven seas, I rest your humble servant. Let me in parting present you to your successor, Dr. Syn—Christopher Syn, D.D., of Oxford University and Vicar of Dymchurch-under-the-Wall, in the County of Kent."

Drawing his sword he picked up gown and wig upon the point and made it bob up and down before the mirror.

The same three strokes of the stable clock reminded Charlotte of her promise to her mother, so after seeing that Meg was still under the influence of Sennacharib Pepper's sleeping draught, she gently opened the door and crept along the gallery to awaken Mrs. Lovell, the housekeeper. There was no need for her to carry a light, as the moon, riding now in a clear sky, shone brightly through the landing window. Her mind, so running on the guest who had been cast up by the sea, it was only natural that she should look across to the door of the room she knew he was occupying. It was shut of course, but she saw suddenly that the door of his powder-closet was open. After his fearful experience of the wreck, she felt it would be too cruel if he were kept awake by a creaking door, so very quietly she crossed the landing to close it. Small as this service was, she found so much pleasure in doing it that her heart was beating so loud that she was afraid someone might hear it.

It was not until she reached the door that her heart-beats stopped in sheer terror, for there, standing in a most unearthly light, she saw a vision of her father's guest, the man who had so disturbed her heart.

There he stood looking at her, yet not seeming to notice her. She had heard tales of ghostly visitants that looked through one

and there was nothing real about this figure. It certainly resembled
the man she so admired in feature, but the clothes were those of
a swaggering gallant. True, she could not see too plainly, for in
front of him there flickered a veil of light, a sheen that shimmered
so that the face seemed to be hovering in airy darkness beyond the
moving radiance. But why should a living man appear to her? It
was then that she saw the dead one. A second form, vaguer than
his, seemed to be dancing beside him, and she recognized the
white wig and shiny, black silk preaching gown of the dead
parson.

Then in sheer panic Charlotte fled along the gallery.

Hearing the rustling of her silk petticoats and knowing it
would never do to be caught in his present finery, Dr. Syn quickly
divested himself of hat, pistols, sash and coat. Then laying his
sword upon the bed, he slipped into the quilted dressing-robe,
and picking up a candle quietly unfastened the door of the powder
closet. The door leading to the landing was wide open. There was
no one in the powder-closet and all was still and quiet on the landing and galleries. But just as he was about to close the door, his
eye caught something white upon the carpet near the wall. He
saw it was a small lace handkerchief, and picked it up. The faint
odour of roses which it held, rolled back the years and he felt
young again, romantic and in love.

With the same whimsicality that he had betrayed over his
sea-chest, he allowed himself not to do the sensible thing, which
was to drop the little lace handkerchief where he found it. Instead,
he held it to his lips, and when he heard footsteps and whisperings
approaching round the gallery he took it with him, when he
quietly shut the door and locked it.

He went back to the bedroom and began stowing all his
property back into the chest. Then throwing a towel around his
shoulders, he sat in front of the dressing-table and cut his hair
short. Having done this to the best of his ability in the candlelight and promising himself to better it in the morning, he made
up the fire, consigned a handful of black locks to the flames, put
out the candle, and then, after opening the casement wide, so that
he could hear the sea grinding upon the beach, a soothing lullaby
to one who had spent so much of his life upon it, he clad himself,
by the light of the fire, in a nightcap and gown of the squire's
providing, and took himself and the lace handkerchief to the
sanctuary of the great four-poster bed, where, holding the handkerchief close to his face in the hope that its gentle fragrance
might breathe into his sleep sweet dreams of long-forgotten

innocence, and thanking God for having preserved him through so many dangers and for bringing him home again he heard the stable clock strike four and fell asleep.

The next thing he knew was the same clock striking eight.

Dr. Syn swung himself out of bed and crossed eagerly to the window. There across the red roofs of the farm and the Little Manor rose the sharp grass bank of the sea-wall upon which a party of men were at work repairing the damages of the storm. Observing the eagerness with which they toiled, Dr. Syn repeated to himself the slogan of the Marsh, "Serve God, honour the King, but first maintain the Wall".

A door beneath him opened and the charming vision of Charlotte appeared, dressed in a green velvet riding habit trimmed with fur. It was her habit to go riding every morning with the squire. Looking up she saw the doctor in his very ludicrous nightcap and shirt.

"You'll catch your death of cold," she called. "Why, you want looking after. Would you care for some hot chocolate now or later?"

"Now, please."

"I'll send Robert—he's the footman who opened the door to you last night. Oh, and if you would like him to shave you, you needn't worry. Father says he has not met a barber to equal him in London."

"Ah, then I will put my life into his hands and save myself the bother of cutting my own throat," he laughed.

She laughed too, but not at his facetious remark, but at her own exclamation of: "So you've got it all the time, and I've set all the servants looking for it. I suppose I dropped it in your room when I brought your coat."

"What?" asked Dr. Syn.

"Why, my lace handkerchief that you are holding so tightly," she answered, pointing up to his right hand.

Up to that moment Dr. Syn had been unaware that he had been doing any such thing. He now realized that he must have clutched it all night and risen with it still in his hand, but he had no intention of confessing this to the charming young lady below.

"If you drop it down, I'll catch it," she said.

"If I were twenty, nay, ten years younger, Miss Charlotte, I should not think of giving up this kerchief. Although, were I younger, as I say, I should find it hard to refuse you anything. Catch."

He dropped the kerchief and she caught it, giving him a

curtsy of thanks, which he returned with a bob of his night-capped head.

Charlotte went in to send Robert up with the chocolate. Upon the tray was a single rose with pinky-white petals. Dr. Syn picked it up gently, laid in on the palm of his hand, and slowly raising it to his face sniffed at it audibly.

"Very kind of you, Robert," said Dr. Syn.

"The gift of the rose is not mine, sir," answered the stately young footman, who was honest enough not to accept thanks that were not his due.

"I meant for preparing this excellent chocolate," explained the doctor.

But yet again Robert insisted on being strictly honest. "I fear, sir, that I merely had the honour of carrying up the tray. The chocolate was prepared by Miss Charlotte herself, sir, and there is no better hand at making it, sir, believe me. The rose was also her idea, sir. Seeing that your reverence has been absent so long from England, she thought that you should be welcomed by what she was pleased to call 'the heraldic flower of the realm'."

"Very kind," said Dr. Syn. "I hear, Robert, that you are an expert with the razor. The ministry in America is not the same as it is here. I wore my own hair there for convenience. But in England it is meet and right that I wear the orthodox badge of my calling—a parson's wig, so if you'll shave and polish my skull, Robert, I'll be ready for breakfast at half-past nine. I am sure my predecessor will not grudge me the use of his wig."

"But, sir," pleaded Robert. "You will put on a great many years if you shave your head and wear a wig of this kind."

"My good Robert, that is just what I require," replied Dr. Syn quietly.

At half-past nine, Dr. Syn entered the old dining-room to find the three young ladies in possession.

"Good morning, young ladies," he said, bowing in the doorway.

They all turned and looked at him, and it was obvious that they were struck dumb with surprise.

"Have I changed then so much?" asked Dr. Syn.

"Utterly," exclaimed Cicely.

"And grown older?"

"Years and years," replied Maria.

"Dear, dear, how distressing," sighed Dr. Syn. "And what does Miss Charlotte think?"

"That my sisters are being very personal," she answered smiling.

"But have you no criticism to add?" he asked.

"Well, then, I think you must give me your wig to dress."

"But surely," he argued, "one seldom sees a parson in a well-kept wig."

"One seldom sees a parson with a gay rose in his lapel," she answered mischievously.

Dr. Syn was saved from further attack by the arrival of Lady Cobtree and the squire, who immediately became a new target for his daughters' criticism by reason of his being dressed in his bright red hunting coat, to which he was very partial.

"You mustn't be seen in that with the whole village mourning," said Maria.

"But I was going riding, and I have nothing so comfortable," pleaded the squire. "I thought Charlotte might stitch a black ribbon to the sleeve."

"I don't believe it entered your head, Father," said Charlotte reprovingly.

"On my honour it did, at least, I think it did," retorted the squire, attacking a large plate of home-smoked ham. "It's like old times. Seems only yesterday, Doctor, that you and I sat next to each other in college and ate as hearty as we're doing now."

"Yesterday?" repeated Dr. Syn. "It seems longer to me, my dear Tony. And during the time between, I have daily looked forward to the possibility of this home-coming. When I look round your table here and see you surrounded with so much goodness and beauty, not forgetting the son-and-heir upstairs in his cot, why I can see that looking back is to you nothing but pleasure. But I prefer to look forward to the pleasant times coming amongst you all. The past has not been so pleasant that I wish to dwell in it. Rather do I thank God for this hour."

"Quite right, Doctor," cried the squire. "I applaud your sentiments. Let us help you to forget the past by making your present life as jolly as we can, eh? For my part, I never remember feeling jollier in my life." And he smiled at another round of toast which Charlotte had brought smoking from the fire to plaster it with rich home-made butter.

"I know you do, dear, and do see what can be done about the 'Sea-Wall Tavern'," said Lady Cobtree. "From all I hear the place is uninhabitable. Poor Meg has got it into her head that it is left unprotected and that Merry, of all people, is rummaging about amongst her treasures."

"Tell her that I've put responsible people in charge," replied the squire. "You can also tell her that I shall make it my business to see that the house is restored. We'll all do what we can to make it a great deal better than it was before, and if she intends carrying on the business, why, we'll see it's well stocked with saleable liquor."

This idea strongly recommended itself to the villagers, who one and all, and most readily, promised that, as the squire was ready to bear all the necessary expense, they would at least save him the cost of labour, and bind themselves voluntarily under the most fitting foreman, to be elected, under whom they would carry out all the necessary labour.

A suggestion made by one Josiah Wraight, master builder to the works of the Lords of the Level, was that since the same storm which had destroyed the tavern had also wrecked the brig and brought the two in such close proximity, the timber that was necessary to bind the house together should be taken from the brig.

Dr. Syn's assurance that there would be no further trouble from Merry, went so far to dispel Meg's terror of the rogue that within a few days she was willing to venture out, escorted by Charlotte and the parson, to view the work of restoration being carried on under Josiah Wraight's direction in her old home, the "Sea-Wall Tavern".

It was Josiah Wraight's boast to the committee that every piece of wood left on the brig had been utilized for the tavern. Even the little hut erected as the office of works, and in which Josiah kept the plans, was knocked up out of the bulkhead of the fo'c'sle.

When Josiah went to meet Meg Clouder, he exclaimed: "Aye, Meg, there's more *City of London* than 'Sea-Wall Tavern'."

"Ay, yes, replied the doctor, "You see, Mrs. Clouder, and since so many good folk have helped to rebuild the tavern and out of respect for your brave husband, the squire is of the opinion that the house should stand now, and in generations to come, as a memorial, and as he is giving you a new licence to run the tavern to more advantage, now would be the convenient time to change the title from 'Sea-Wall Tavern' to 'The City of London'."

"Aye, and I think Abel would like it," put in Josiah, "for in days to come, when strangers look at the sign and say 'What has London to do with Romney Marsh?' why, the story will be told of how Abel and Parson Bolden died, and how the wreck not only rebuilt your house but brought us our new vicar. And what inn upon the whole of the Marsh has a finer sign than that? Just imagine *him* sticking out from an iron bracket between the two big bedroom windows, Meg, eh?"

Meg shuddered as she saw the honest Josiah patting the wooden face of the brig's figure-head. "Oh no," she said, "just the words on the wall, but not that ghastly thing—please, Josiah."

"Ghastly?" repeated the astounded foreman. "I calls it handsome. Now what might this gentleman be meant to be? A city sheriff or what, sir?" He thought that if Dr. Syn would only make the figure-head sound interesting, Meg might be reconciled to it.

"Why, yes," said Dr. Syn, "I can tell you all about this curious fellow, for during the voyage I enjoyed the full confidence of our ill-fated captain, whom I nicknamed 'the Mayor' in that he ruled over us in the *City of London*. The owners of this brig formerly possessed two, built for the New England trade. One was called *Gog* and the other *Magog*, and they sailed from Boston to the Pool of London. This was the figure-head of *Gog* until her sister-ship was sunk in fighting the notorious pirate, Clegg. Instead of building another ship they re-christened this one *City of London*, though as the captain pointed out, he had never heard of any good coming to a ship with an altered name. Fearing lest this vessel should also fall a victim to Clegg, they armed her with a brass cannon, and painted up poor *Gog* into a fighting uniform, so that the brig might seem to be a man-o'-war. Certainly, such merchant ships as we passed fought shy of us and steered clear. But for all that, we met Clegg's frigate four days out of port, and it would have gone hard with us had not our captain run into a mist and made good our escape."

"Well, then," exclaimed Josiah, "if that don't make this 'ere Admiral Gog more valuable still. What a sign for a tavern! It'll draw the whole Marsh for years to come."

"I'd rather have it empty, Josiah," cried Meg, "than that I should see that ghastly face looking in at my bedroom window."

Now Dr. Syn, to whom she had confided the dreadful horror of first seeing the figure-head upon the sea-wall, began to argue on her side. "The ladies have likes and dislikes, Master Foreman," he said, "and it is well that they can generally tell us their wishes, and here is Miss Cobtree in full agreement with Mrs. Clouder that the figurehead is not a work of art that any woman would covet. Therefore, we must find some other use for it. Since the master foreman is so struck with it, I propose that he sets it up in his building yard as a sign of his trade. You build boats, I hear, in your timber-shed, Mister Wraight. Well, what more fitting than to set it high on the shed's prow?"

This suggestion quite made up for Josiah's disappointment at Meg's disapproval, and nobody objecting, he had the figure-head immediately removed to his timber yard and set up high on his great work barn, where to this day it is the honoured possession of Josiah's descendants. Indeed, Admiral Gog in his resplendent uniform, is still one of the popular sights of Dymchurch-under-the-Wall.

On the day of his installation, Dr. Syn, who had till then remained at the Hall, took up his quarters in the vicarage, upon which the women of the parish, headed by the Cobtree ladies, had lavished as much care as they had already bestowed upon Meg's tavern.

"It's a wrench leaving you, my good Tony," he said, "although it is but for a matter of a few yards, but I know you agree with me that since this is the principal village of the Marsh it is meet and right for the vicarage to be maintained with that dignity it deserves."

"Well, I make it a condition that you dine every Sunday at the Hall, and that whenever I brew a particularly good bowl of punch that you shall be there for the ladling."

"Which means that I shall be with you every night," laughed Dr. Syn.

"And all the better, say I," cried the squire heartily. "In the meantime, my Charlotte has found you a jewel of a woman to housekeep for you. A quick tongue, which you'll no doubt cure, but one that can cook, and well. She's an ugly enough old widow too, so there'll be no scandal. She's a daughter to help her, plain as a cod-fish, so there you are. Name of Fowey. Hails from Cornwall or some such foreign place. But, as Charlotte says—she can cook. By the way, you seem to have done wonders with that rascal Merry, but I don't like to think of him around here."

"Oh, he's all right," said Dr. Syn. "I've got my eye on him, never fear. He seems to find quite a pleasure in obeying me."

Aye, and so he did, and he hugged himself when he did. And yet he did not obey in all things. For one day he went all the way to Rye and purchased there a knife. A long, sharp, hefty knife. And every night when he returned to his own room at the end of the long white cottages over against the "Ocean Inn", he would take out the knife from its hiding place to assure himself that it was sharp, both point and edge. And every morning when he went back to work he watched Dr. Syn out of the corner of his eye and thought to cheer himself when he was being more than servile of the knife's sharpness.

Meanwhile, the greatest pessimist would have said that at least Dymchurch-under-the-Wall in the County of Kent was a village ideally happy, but neither optimist nor pessimist could smell the black hate that smouldered in the heart of Dr. Syn's queer servant, Merry. But Merry bided his time and knew that it would come.

And Dr. Syn went in and out amongst the cottages daily, respected and loved by all, while Merry, shunning and shunned by all, thought of his knife, and nightly tried the edge and point of it.

CHAPTER III

MR. MIPPS APPEARS

As the months went by, Sir Antony Cobtree realized with growing satisfaction that there was no fear of his ever regretting the bestowal of his vicarage upon Dr. Syn. His only fear in connection with his old friend was that by virtue of his learning and popularity he would be tempted to accept some high preferment, and to counteract any such calamity he used his influence and got his favourite the extra and honourable appointment of Dean of the Peculiars, which not only gave the doctor the status of a dignitary, but substantially increased his income, and merely putting him under the obligations to occupy the principal pulpits of the Marsh for the delivery of an annual sermon, which expeditions were undertaken with quite a show of pomp, as Sir Antony invariably accompanied him, and ordered out his state coach for the purpose, so that it was not long before the fame of Cobtree's cleric was established near and far, which pleased the squire a great deal more than the doctor, who seemed perfectly content to remain an obscure village parson.

Under such patronage most men would have felt secure against the past, but Dr. Syn always kept his watch against calamity, and his first care was to conquer his own restless spirit.

Perhaps his hardest task in the part he had set himself to play was forcing himself to an indifference where Charlotte Cobtree was concerned. To add to his difficulty in this matter, the squire would always prove himself unsympathetic to the many young suitors who begged to be allowed to pay their addresses to his eldest daughter, especially since Charlotte invariably asserted that the young man in question was not for her. Then in a rage the squire would carry the story to his friend, beginning with, "Of all the pieces of impertinence"—and ending with, "I cannot understand Charlotte. It's my belief that she'll never marry anyone but you." And Dr. Syn would exclaim again: "Why, Miss Charlotte is far too young and too good to waste herself on an old widower like me. It's impossible."

And all the time, there was Charlotte running in and out of the vicarage on this errand and that in the most natural manner, and at each visit Dr. Syn suffered more and more from the longing that she would stay with him for good.

And then on a bright spring morning Mr. Mipps came trundling along by the churchyard wall with his worldly possessions in a sea-chest which he pushed on a squeaky barrow that he had stolen in Hythe from the yard of the "Red Lion".

Although for many years a stranger to Dymchurch anyone could have told that this quizzical little man was a mariner. He smelt of tar. He was covered in it. Not only had he given his sea-chest a generous daubing but he had screwed his scanty hair into a sharp tarred queue, which stuck out beyond his broken three-cornered hat for all the world like a jigger-gaff. He wore a faded blue cloth coat with tails which hung too low behind his short, thin legs, and his dirty, striped cotton bell trousers were furled up to show an ancient pair of thick shoes with brass buckles.

Although presenting a sorry appearance, his perky bearing gave the impression that Mr. Mipps was in excellent spirits. His clay pipe, with stem broken off close to the blackened bowl, puffed a continual smoke-stream into the nostrils of the long thin nose that roofed it. An economical pipe-man, Mr. Mipps, for the smoke that escaped from the bowl was sucked up through his nose to join the rest of it in his lungs.

He set down his 'borrowed' barrow by the low wall of the churchyard and looked around. Having the most admirable opinion of himself, he was never above taking himself into his own confidence by the simple expedient of talking to himself aloud, which he then proceeded to do.

"Well, Mippsy, I never did see an anchorage so snug and trim as this 'ere village, all kept taut and Bristol fashion by that old sea-wall."

Mr. Mipps suddenly broke off his meditations, for he saw standing on the sea-wall, the black-garbed figure of Dr. Syn. "That's him," he muttered. "Trim and alert, peculiar and odd as when he faced the mutineers on the deck of the old *Imogene* off Anastasia, and spit the ringleader through the neck with his small-sword. And here he is, settled down to his old trade of preaching same as he told me he would."

Dr. Syn had been watching ships in the Fairway through his brass telescope. The sea-wall was his favourite walk, and up on it, behind Grove House, the squire had given him permission to re-erect Josiah Wraight's hut, that had been made from the bulkhead of the wreck's fo'c'sle. So upon the sea-wall behind Grove House it now stood, railed around to make it the more private, and one of the spars was erected as a flag-staff. Its windows faced the sea, so that the doctor's privacy was further assured. In this hut, fitted up inside as a cabin, the doctor would as often as not write his sermons, and after a time Charlotte went so far as to accuse him of liking it better than the vicarage. Certainly, it was a snug retreat. On the wildest day he could sit there with the little stove alight and laugh at the spray lashing against the window panes.

Dr. Syn thrust the telescope under his arm and climbed down the steep grass bank of the sea-wall, and as he watched him, Mr. Mipps, becoming strangely nervous of a sudden, vaulted into the churchyard and took cover behind a tombstone. He heard the footsteps of his master crunching briskly over the gravel. Then they stopped abruptly. Dr. Syn was eyeing the sea-chest.

"Mipps—his chest," he read quietly; then in sharp tones added: "Come out of that, and let's have a look at you."

"All aboard, sir," replied Mipps, jumping up and saluting.

"And what do you want with me?" The Doctor's long, thin face was inscrutable.

"Well, sir," faltered Mipps, "knowing as 'ow you wished to settle down at your first profession, which you give up through no fault of your own, and hearing as 'ow a gentleman answering your description was beneficed 'ere, in my birthplace, I thought, sir, with all respects to your 'oly cloth, that you might be glad of a grateful old ship's carpenter what wants to settle down too."

"And what if I prefer to forget the past, eh?" A fierceness had flashed into Dr. Syn's eyes. "Suppose I deny ever having seen you before. What then?"

"What then, sir?" repeated Mipps, swallowing his disappointment with an effort. "Why, no offence took, sir, and I'll steer for an anchorage elsewhere. But I'd like you to 'ave this before I goes, sir, as it weighs a bit heavy in my coat-tail pocket."

After executing a difficult contortion with the coat-tail in question, Mr. Mipps drew from the pocket something wrapped in a bandana kerchief.

"What's that?" demanded the doctor.

"Your Virgil, sir, what was stolen by that cross-eyed nigger at Panama, who thought it was a book o' magic. Remember? Well, I fetched up with him a year ago, and he won't steal no more Virgils, sir, he won't."

Dr. Syn took the book and opened it. "My notes. I made them at Oxford. A long time ago, Mr. Mipps. A long time. I am glad to get this back."

"Glad you're glad. Good morning, sir." And vaulting into

the road, he picked up the barrow-shafts, turned it round, and started back the way he had come.

As Dr. Syn watched the quaint back view of the little sea-dog thus setting off without a grumble, his eyes grew kind. "Come back, you rascal," he called.

Round came the barrow and back came Mipps.

"As I said, I am glad to get this volume once more. Steer your chest to the vicarage there and if we can come to a very definite understanding, I'll find you the means of settling down."

"A job?" inquired Mipps hopefully.

Dr. Syn nodded. "But, remember this—I have never seen you before in my life. Got that?"

"Got it, sir."

Dr. Syn had taken the precaution of closing his study door behind the visitor.

"And what have you got in the chest, my good Mipps, that you hug it so tightly. The gold bar?"

Mipps shook his head. "No, Captain."

"Don't call me 'captain'—'vicar'," said Dr. Syn sharply.

"Yes, Vicar. No, Vicar," replied Mipps, putting the chest down onto the floor. "The gold bar got turned into guineas, and the guineas got turned into different things, what disappeared, such as drink, food and lodging. Then there come a sort of longing to be quit of travel, and I thought of home. I had no money for a passage, and merchantmen only employed men they knew, owing to fear of pirates, so I shanghaied a ship's carpenter in the Royal Navy and applied for his post for the voyage home. Had to get home, you see, Vicar, just as they had to have a carpenter. And what's more, Vicar, they got a better man than the one I detained, as the captain told me so."

"And how did you enjoy your time with the Royal Navy?" asked the doctor.

"A well-run ship it was, Vicar, and the discipline good. Put me in mind of your old *Imogene*. So long as everything was just so and spitted and polished, all was happy. I only had one unpleasantness the whole voyage, and that come of contradicting the captain before his lieutenant. They was arguing about Clegg, you see, and the captain said he'd seen him. Had him pointed out to him in a tavern in San Juan, and then, if you please, he starts describing him as tall, thin, handsome and elegant, till I come all over in a cold sweat and said: 'Well, that weren't Clegg, sir,' I say, 'and your informant didn't know what he was talking about.' Then I told 'ow I'd been captured by this Clegg and got treated quite well till I was put ashore. I described him as a great barrel of a man, thick-set, rough and ready, with great brass rings in his ears, arms and chest covered with obscene tattooin's, and a vocabulary unbeaten even in the British Navy. A real savage, I made him out, but on the whole a jolly savage. In plain words, sir, I described your enemy."

Dr. Syn nodded. "That was good. That was clever. You were always the man for me, and I believe still will be if you care to play a very different game."

"I'm game for anything, Cap—Vicar," replied Mipps.

"Aye, but you may be game for too much," warned the doctor. "In other words, you may be too game to settle down."

"But it's just what I want," replied Mipps. "I never relished dying violent like most of 'em. A quiet settle down and a good long solitary chuckle about old days. That's me."

"Suppose, then, that I give you a snug berth here as parish sexton, can you keep your mouth shut? Can you forget that we two went adventuring together? Can you forget that you ever saluted me as your captain on the poop deck of the *Imogene?* Can you forget that I was anything other than Parson Syn, Doctor of Divinity by degree of Oxford University?"

Mipps closed his eyes tight, and holding up his right hand, responded: "All them things I solemnly forgets."

Dr. Syn once more picked up his recovered copy of Virgil and began to turn the pages lovingly.

"Digging graves, now," he said casually. "I suppose you can manage that?"

"I've had to dig one or two in my time, sir, and quickly. Don't you remember that time when you and me——?"

Dr. Syn slammed the volume like the crack of a pistol. "No, Mr. Mipps, I do not remember," he said sharply. "I only remember to forget."

Mipps reproved himself by hitting his thigh with his clenched fist and biting his lip.

Dr. Syn opened the volume once more and continued in a casual voice. "You can pull the bell for service?"

"Ain't I handled ropes and rung watches all my life?"

Dr. Syn frowned.

"In the Royal Navy, sir," added Mipps with a wink.

"And since our village carpenter, dear old Josiah Wraight, has more than he can do as foreman to the Lords of the Level, he has lately refused to make coffins, a work he has never stomached, as he says, and our dead have to be accommodated by an undertaker from New Romney, which is not right, since I take it that Dymchurch is the centre of the Marsh."

"And should have its own undertaker, most certainly," nodded Mipps. "And in mentioning me with such a job, I think you show great wisdom. No one couldn't knock up a coffin quicker, solider, nor more reliable. A ship's carpenter of the Royal Navy is, I 'ope, qualified to measure up any corpse at the double as they say. I'll make inquiries this very day from the local doctor as to the names and addresses of his most likely patients, and when he thinks he'll finish 'em off. I could make tactful suggestions to the poor sufferers and find out in the course of conversation whether they can run to oak, and if they has any fancies as regards handles."

"You will not be jocular on such a subject," reproved the vicar.

"Not when addressing my ruler to the corpse, sir. Oh no. Solemn as an owl."

"And understand that in my parochial factotum there must be no strong language, and not much strong liquor. I shall expect you to set an example to the parish."

"And I'll set it," said Mipps with assurance. "You'll hear mothers telling their babies to do as Mr. Mipps does, and be good children."

"And remember—we have not been colleagues in America."

"No, sir."

"Very well," said Dr. Syn.

"No mention of it," replied Mipps solemnly.

"I'll bespeak a cottage for you. There's one available called 'Old Tree' at the other end of the village, and next door there is a small barn that will do for your workshop. Your position as sexton and verger will entitle you to sit at the lowest desk of the pulpit, and since you can both read and write, you can not only lead the Responses and Amens during service, but will earn a little more helping me to keep the parochial books and registers."

"That makes me sexton, undertaker, verger, bell-pull and clerk."

"A great responsibility, Mr. Mipps. You see then that your conduct must be exemplary."

"The blessed Archbishop himself won't look no 'olier then me, I gives you my word, sir."

"And one thing more," said Dr. Syn, "and perhaps the most important."

"Something else for me to do?"

"No. Something else you must never do. Wait here a minute and I'll tell you."

Dr. Syn went into the hall and opened the livery cupboard in the far corner. He returned with two glasses and a bottle.

"French brandy, Mr. Mipps. I drink to our better acquaintance and to our settling down."

"And I drinks my respecks, sir."

"Thank you. And talking of French brandy, Mr. Sexton—I hope you find it to your taste?"

"Very nice and mellow, thankee, sir," said Mipps, passing his glass for more.

"The Frenchmen are up to other tricks than fighting," went on Dr. Syn, "and I warn you, Mr. Sexton, not to traffic in any way with their brandy-runners, for that smuggling goes on, I have no doubt. This part of the country being independent and lying so handy to the French coast, there is a good deal of illegal money to be made with comparative safety. But it will not be so for long. Romney Marsh holds its independence only on its good behaviour. She is pledged against smuggling. She has promised and vowed to maintain the excise laws of England, and periodically suspicious Government officers show themselves inquisitive. That is the danger always. That is why I am ever exhorting my flock, for whom I feel responsible, not to traffic in any way with those devils across the water."

"But surely, Vicar, no Frenchman dares to venture over the Channel these days?"

"I have every reason to believe that they do occasionally," replied Dr. Syn. "But first of all, just for the sake of old times, which we'll remember to forget, we'll finish the bottle, eh, old friend?"

"To our settling down, Vicar," toasted Mipps.

"To our remembering to forget," toasted Dr. Syn.

CHAPTER IV

THE DEATH OF THE RIDING-OFFICER

THUS Mr. Mipps became sexton and undertaker of Dymchurch, as well as general factotum to the vicar.

In addition to making coffins, he opened a little store, where, amongst the coffin planks, you could buy anything from fishing nets to pickled onions.

Mipps became generally admired, and in the process learned many things that were so profitable that his conscience was quietened.

Although at first intending only to disobey the vicar for just a little flutter now and again, the excitement got hold of him, and before he knew where he was, he found himself a leader, and involved in the smuggling business up to the neck, which was usually the way with people who came to live on the Marsh.

On one point Mipps was adamant. No firearms were to be carried by his smugglers, only bats or stout poles which, in the hands of well-mounted men, were formidable enough. But with all his caution, disaster came, and from an outside source.

A riding officer from Sandgate was brutally murdered on the hills above the Marsh.

The news burst like a bombshell amongst the secret community of Dymchurch, and the barbarous act not only spread indignation, but also a haunting dread as to what the murderer might say when he was brought to trial, for the man was brutal physically and mean-spirited, so that the general hope was that he would not allow himself to be taken alive. Once in court, there was no doubt but that he would do his utmost to make many others share his fate.

His name was Grinsley and he ran a farm up at Aldington, but his chief source of income for many years had been derived from 'receiving' smuggled goods from the Marsh and passing them along towards London.

Apparently resenting some harsh treatment at his hands one of his labourers sought revenge by reporting him as a 'receiver' to the Excise Office at Sandgate, and the riding-officer on duty had been sent out armed with a warrant to search the premises.

Grinsley, knowing that his lofts and cellars would betray him, refused the officer admittance and threatened to blow off his head if he tried force.

The officer rode off to get an armed guard, which threw Grins-ley into an uncontrollable rage. Rushing to his stables, he mounted his fierce black horse and galloped after the officer, who, according to the testimony of an eye-witness, drew rein and waited for him to come up. "Thought better of it, eh, Mr. Grinsley?" he asked, smiling. "Well, it will save me the long ride to Sandgate."

"But not the short ride to hell," cried Grinsley, discharging a blunderbuss full in his face.

To the horror of the eye-witness, an old woman, who was gathering sticks and who in self-preservation had hidden from Grinsley behind a bush, the officer fell dead from his horse, and the murderer rode off.

When the news was carried to Hythe, a troop of Dragoons was ordered to arrest the murderer. But although they searched his farm at Aldington, watched the high road, and beat up the adjacent woods, Grinsley could not be found. Murderer and horse had disappeared.

It did not take long for the hue and cry to reach Dymchurch. Neither did it take certain 'gentlemen' long to realize that Grinsley's death was the best thing that could happen for their own safety, and in an effort to prevent him being taken alive for trial, they seized weapons, and with a show of great indignation hurried to the hill behind the Marsh. They carried firearms, in self-defence they said, as Grinsley was the sort to sell his life dearly. It was a rational excuse. Dr. Syn watched the angry mob rush off upon the trail, and thinking it to be as well that someone in authority should be on the spot to restrain them, he followed the hue and cry, riding up towards Aldington on his white pony.

On the way he met Charlotte Cobtree riding towards him.

"I rode out with my father behind the Dragoons," she said, drawing rein. "But when I saw all the people looking so grim, I had to come away. The man Grinsley is a scoundrel, but there are so many against him."

"They have not caught him?" asked the doctor.

"No, but in time they must," she answered. "I heard them planning to burn him out—why, one wouldn't do that to a fox."

"I'm afraid this man has little reason to earn your sympathy, my dear Charlotte," said Dr. Syn. "A fight is a fight, but what chance did he give that unfortunate riding-officer, who was but fulfilling his unpleasant duty?"

"I know, I know," nodded Charlotte. "But he's a fugitive—and—oh, I know it's all wrong—it must be, but I always want to shield a fugitive.'

"That is your beautiful nature, Charlotte." Dr. Syn smiled sadly. "I sometimes believe that whatever I had done or were to do, that you would still treat me with the same sweet kindness."

"Will you remember that you have said that, please?" she asked.

"Why do you say that?" asked the doctor.

"Because I want you to remember it, of course, just as I shall. Do you know that when I think of that Mr. Bone, the highwayman, who is sometimes as hard-pressed as this Grinsley, I rather envy the many women and girls who take a hand in watching over his safety. Can't you take to the high road to please me, Doctor?"

"If I did," chuckled the doctor, "I verily believe I should lead the authorities a dance."

"I am quite sure you would," she laughed. "Well, you may lead me a dance now. I will ride with you to the hills. I think your presence there will make all different."

So they rode together.

As they talked they had allowed their horses to walk gently on, but this conversation was interrupted by the captain of the Dragoons, who trotted away from his troop to meet them.

"So you have not yet unearthed the fox," said Dr. Syn, as the captain drew rein and saluted.

"Not yet, sir," replied the officer.

"But are you sure he has run to earth?" asked the doctor.

"We are sure of nothing at all, sir," answered the captain. "The rascal may be heading for London Town this minute."

Dr. Syn shook his head. "Now, I should first read the signs along that hedge. You see, it runs from Grinsley's farm right down to the high road."

Mechanically, he touched up his pony and trotted off towards the hedge. Mechanically, Charlotte and the captain followed.

"Our good parson has found something," said the Dragoon, checking his charger. Charlotte drew rein beside him. "He's dismounting."

Dr. Syn, with the rein over his arm, peered down at the roots of the thick-grown hedge. He then dropped the rein and walked on slowly, looking up and down the hedge. The pony, left to his own resources nibbled at the grass and stepped into the circle of the hanging reins, which after a little became a dangerous entanglement. Charlotte slipped from her horse, handed the reins to the captain and ran towards the pony. She soothed the fat little white beast, and lifted his forelegs in turn. Dr. Syn turned and looked at her as she freed the pony.

"Thank you, my dear," he said. "It was careless of me to leave the reins dangling. But I have found what I was looking for."

"And what is that?" asked the Dragoon who had ridden slowly towards them, leading Charlotte's horse.

"Just a bundle of clothes—that's all," replied the doctor.

"The clothes that Grinsley was wearing when he committed the crime!" ejaculated the Dragoon.

"Exactly," replied the doctor.

"But why did you expect to find them hidden in the hedge?" asked the captain.

"I thought it most probable that Grinsley would get rid of such tell-tale garments, when I read your posted description," said Dr. Syn. "But I did not expect to find them here till I rode along this hedge and looked into Grinsley's turnip patch. You can see over the hedge yourself, Captain, from your exalted position. Take a look, and you'll own that I should have been dense indeed had I not picked up the clue."

The Dragoon rose in his stirrups and looked across the turnip field in question, but instead of showing any enlightenment from what he saw, he merely shook his head.

"Well, then, sir, unless your clue has moved away, I confess to my denseness," he said.

"It certainly could not have moved away," replied the vicar, "and it is certainly conspicuous enough. But what would be denseness in me, is not so with you, for you are not of these parts, and therefore the landmarks are not so familiar."

"Let me see if I can guess it," said Charlotte, going to her horse to mount. Dr. Syn helped her to the saddle and she looked across the turnip field.

"Why someone has taken the scarecrow's clothes," she said. "Look, Captain, those sticks in the centre of the field with the black gloves hanging."

"Exactly," laughed Dr. Syn. "There was an old, long black coat and waistcoat and a black three-cornered hat. That was all Grinsley required. He hides his conspicuous clothes in the nearest spot, which is obviously the hedge, and puts on the scarecrow's over his own riding breeches and boots. Isn't that convincing, Captain?"

"Convincing enough to alter his description on the murder posters," replied the captain. "I'll ride over with this news to the Custom's officer. He's on the other side of the common. Thank you, sir. Thank you, Miss Cobtree," and he galloped away across the rough ground behind the beaters.

CHAPTER V

THE SECRET OF THE FIGURE-HEAD

ON the same evening Dr. Syn dined at the Court House in company with several gentlemen of influence upon the Marsh.

When the company broke up, Dr. Syn remained in the library, as the squire had something to say to him in private.

"The mail brought down a letter tonight from Lloyds about the wreck of the *City of London*," he said. "At last they are in touch with the cargo owners in America and ask me for the ship's papers which you had from the captain. If you will let me have them tomorrow, I will see that they are posted by the Hythe mail."

On his return to the vicarage, Dr. Syn found Mipps awaiting him for orders.

Syn smiled. "You had better seek out Merry and send him here before he goes to bed. I am not altogether satisfied with one or two things I have heard about him."

So the sexton departed in search of Merry, and Dr. Syn unlocked a cabinet and took from it the ship's papers which the squire had asked for. He filled a pipe of tobacco, poured himself out a generous allowance of brandy and seated in his high-backed chair, began to read through the log-book of the ill-fated ship.

On the last page Dr. Syn read with astonishment:

This is the last will and Testament of me, Mervin Ransom, Master and Owner of the brig, City of London, *trading between New England and Port of London, who having no kith and kin to my knowledge, bequeath what I possess to be divided equally amongst all and sundry persons, with no respect of rank or class, who may be voyaging upon the said brig at the time of my decease. The brig shall be broken up be it that she survive me, and her materials sold, the money divided as stated. I will not risk my brig having another master. She has known only one, the man Mervin Ransom who built her. The figure alone shall not be broken up, but let it be taken to some worthy shipyard or boat-builder's and be left there for a memorial. But before carrying this into effect let my beneficiaries take care for themselves to remove the let-in block between the shoulder-blades. It is caulked in securely and hidden by the folds of the cloak worn by old Gog the London Giant. In the cavity thus revealed will be found a string of pearls.*

As a young man I collected them myself, matching them carefully. They were plentiful enough in those days if a man cared to fare far and adventure a little. These I would not sell, but collected them for her who I hoped would marry me on my return. My return was postponed a long time, but when at last I made home she was dead. I kept my gift in the body of the figure-head—a gift to my ship. Perhaps in years to come these stones will adorn the neck of a beautiful woman. I pray God that her mind be beautiful too, for she for whom they were meant was perfect in beauty. But let the brig be broken up. That is the solemn adjuration of Mervin Ransom. Signed in the presence of my 1st and 2nd Mates, who herewith affix their marks.

Dr. Syn read the names and date. He was the sole survivor of the brig. The captain and crew were all dead. The pearls were his. The first thing to do was to discover if they were still there.

As he read the extraordinary document through again there came a knocking at the door. He got up, went across the hall and opened the door, admitting Mr. Merry.

"Mipps said you wanted me," he growled sullenly.

"You will accompany me to Wraight's yard with a dark lantern. Where is Mipps?"

"He left the 'Ship' on his way to Meg Clouder's tavern."

"Go and fetch him. Was Josiah Wraight with Mipps?"

"He left the 'Ship' before Mipps. He was going home to bed."

"All the better. Very much more convenient for what we have to do. We will give him half an hour to get to bed. You may go to 'The City of London' and call Mr. Mipps from the door. When he joins you, you will tell him that I want him to bring his bag of tools."

"It is raining. It is blowing half a gale," grumbled Merry.

"It was blowing a full gale when you murdered the captain of the brig," replied Syn.

Merry slouched off into the night.

In less than half an hour he was back again with Mr. Mipps. They found Dr. Syn waiting for them in his heavy black riding-coat, his face muffled in a scarf and his three-cornered hat pulled low on to his forehead.

"I brought the bag o' tools, sir," said Mipps, "but what's the game, sir?"

"We are going to pay our respects to old Gog, the figure-head of the *City of London.*"

So the three adventurers braved the weather towards the

avenue of trees outside Wraight's yard. There was little fear of disturbing old Josiah, who slept on the other side of the house adjoining his yard, but Dr. Syn took the precaution of placing Merry on that side, while he and Mipps took one of the many ladders from the shed and mounted it alongside the figure-head which had been fixed upon the corner of the roof.

When they stood behind it, Syn took the dark lantern and opened the shutter.

"There you are now, Master Carpenter," whispered Dr. Syn with a grim smile. "You see that line? It is as neat a piece of caulking as ever I saw, and it seems a pity to unpick it. It's got to be done, though, and quickly. The trees are creaking loud enough to drown any sound, but do it as quietly as possible. Get busy, Master Carpenter."

"Right, Vicar," grinned the mystified Mipps.

Syn held the light while Mipps, selecting a sharp tool suitable for the purpose, began uncaulking the tight seam of oakum.

"Drive in a gimlet and pull," said Syn.

Mipps found a gimlet, screwed it into the loosened block, and then pulled it out. Syn put his hand into the cavity and drew out a string of pearls.

"Listen," cautioned Mipps. "I heard a man gasp for breath. It's Merry watching. He knows what you have found."

"I intended he should." Dr. Syn dropped the string of pearls into his side pocket and descended the ladder, followed by Mipps who, after putting the ladder back in the shed, went in search of Merry, who had quickly hurried back to his post.

"You will accompany us to the vicarage, Mr. Merry," said Dr. Syn, as they turned from the builder's yard on to the high road and set their faces towards the village. "After your wait you will no doubt be glad of a drink."

"There is also the question of my having something to say which you will not relish," replied Merry, with a note of cunning triumph.

"Well, you shall say it over my brandy, Mr. Merry."

Dr. Syn led them round to the back of the vicarage. He always went to the stable to bid good night to his fat little pony.

"I have noticed, Mr. Mipps," he said, "that periodically my stable door is unlocked."

"Really?" asked Mipps. "Well, there's always a remedy to that, sir."

"You mean lock it up again?"

"Right, sir. First shot, sir," laughed Mipps.

"Unfortunately, the key seems to unlock the door and then disappear, and strangely enough, every time it has happened I see a chalked cross upon the lintel of the stable. Let us see if it is there now, shall we?"

He led the way in, approached the stall in which the fat pony was munching contentedly.

"There you are," he said, taking the lantern from Merry. "A white cross. And if it happens, as it has happened before on several occasions, tomorrow morning that chalk will have gone from the wood. What do you make of it?"

"Whatever could one make of it, sir?" asked Mipps.

"I make a good deal," growled Merry. "And so will a number of others before very long. You'll find every stable door open to-night, not only here, not only on the Marsh, but far and away over farms and manors as far away as Tenterden. And most of 'em ain't the luck of the chalky cross neither."

"Oh, it's lucky, then, is it, that cross?" asked Dr. Syn.

"Aye. It means that party what own that pony or that horse or that donkey or mule is favoured."

"You say that every stable door is open, eh?" asked the vicar. "It would be illuminating to verify that statement. Let us take a look at the squire's stables."

When they reached the long grey stone building in which the squire's magnificent horses lived, they found the door unfastened, and on going in they found every stall empty, except a loose box on which they saw a white chalked cross.

Dr. Syn held the lantern over the loose-box door, and recognized Sirius, Charlotte Cobtree's favourite, on which she had ridden to the hills that very day.

"Another favoured person—Miss Charlotte," sneered Merry. "You see all the other cattle have been taken."

"The squire must be informed of this!" exclaimed Dr. Syn.

"I think I'll go round and have a look at some other stables," said Mipps.

"Not yet," replied Dr. Syn. "I want you both in my study for a few minutes."

"Oh, well, certainly, sir; but I don't like to think all this is going on, any more than you do, sir. We don't want to see any of our parishioners feedin' the churchyard rooks."

"Don't worry on that score. It won't happen yet," replied Merry. "The Squire will look after the good name of his Marsh men."

"You said that you wished to make a statement," remarked Dr. Syn.

"Yes, over a drink which I can well do with," replied Merry.

"Come along, then, both of you." And the doctor led the way to the vicarage.

From a corner cupboard in his study the vicar produced glasses and a bottle.

"Draw up a chair, Mr. Merry, and dry yourself by the fire," he said cheerily. "Oh, and please take off your heavy coat."

"I'll keep it on," replied Merry.

"No. No. Indeed, you shall do nothing of the sort. It is wet."

Having poured out three glasses of neat brandy, Dr. Syn, who had thrown off his own top-coat, crossed to Merry and politely but firmly drew off his sullen guest's wrap-rascal.

"There, this can be drying while you drink," he said placing it over the back of a high chair close to the fire. "Pick up your glasses and drink."

Both men did not need a second invitation, for they were wet to the bone. Mipps, with a "best respects," swallowed his cheerfully at a draught, while Merry, with a grunt, drank his slowly.

His drink, however, was doomed to be interrupted, for suddenly seeing that Dr. Syn's hand was deep in the pocket of the drying coat, Merry slammed his glass down on the table and, with an oath took a step towards the vicar.

His threatening attitude was arrested by the vicar whipping from the pocket he was searching an ugly sharp knife.

"A very formidable weapon, Mr. Merry, as I live," remarked the vicar. "Mr. Mipps, I take it that a carpenter can always find service for a good blade. Put this amongst your tools."

"You leave it where it is," exploded Merry. "I bought it. What right have you to rob me of it?"

"The right of a good citizen in defending the next wreck on Dymchurch Wall, my friend," replied Dr. Syn. "You were told distinctly enough that you were not to provide yourself with a weapon when I robbed you of the knife that committed murder. Oh, you need not start like that. Mr. Mipps knows all about Captain Ransom's death.

"I thought it best that in case of any accident happening to me, that you should not be free to laugh at your deliverance from the murder charge. Now, what is it you have to say?"

"Why," replied Merry firmly, as the brandy gave him courage, "I have broken three of your high-handed orders. First, I have approached Meg Clouder—yes, and with an offer of marriage. What though she refuses, she won't always. Secondly, I have carried that knife for my own protection, and I tell you there's reasons enough for me being on my guard against a good number of these Dymchurch hypocrites, and lastly, I've disobeyed you again tonight. Do you guess how?"

"Of course I do," said Syn, with a tolerant smile. "You left your post at Josiah Wraight's, as I knew you would, and you saw me take these from the figure-head, and put them in my pocket. I wanted you to see me do it. That's why I took you along."

"Why did you want me to see you?" asked Merry. "I can bring an unpleasant charge against you if I have any more of your high-handed nonsense."

This threat the vicar ignored and contented himself with answering the question. "Do you know anything about pearls? I suppose not." He took the string of pearls from his coat pocket. "Well, let me assure you that these are so good that they could be sold in London for several thousands of pounds. I wanted you to realize that had you murdered me as well as the captain you would have got away with these as well as my sea-chest full of gold, not to mention the little matter of the captain's money-belt. You managed the business very badly that night."

"I wouldn't have known that there was pearls inside that figure-head," argued Merry.

"Oh yes you would, for their hiding-place was revealed in the captain's log-book which you threw aside as useless."

"Very well, then, I am no longer your slave to be ordered about just as it pleases you," returned Merry. "Accuse me of murder, if you like, and you'll not be a very creditable witness. They'll want to know why you kept your mouth shut so long about it, and when I tell them about the pearls, there will be your motive, especially when I say that I saw you kill the captain, and have kept my mouth shut out of charity. Mind you, I'm not above coming to terms. Every man for himself in this world. Give me the pearls and we'll say no more about it."

"Give *you* the captain's pearls?" repeated the doctor in amazement. "Now, why ever should I do that?"

"Because," replied Merry promptly, "I want Meg Clouder, and it seems to me that any woman would marry the devil himself if he dangled a gift like that in his wooing. So hand 'em over, Mister Parson Thief."

"I take it you can read, Mr. Merry?" asked the vicar pleasantly.

"Oh, I can read and write too, as you'll find if you force me to send a statement to the authorities," said Merry.

"Very well, then. Read this. No, I cannot allow you to touch it. The documentary evidence is too valuable to be destroyed, and I must show it to the squire before I present these pearls to his daughter. It is her twenty-first birthday tomorrow, Mr. Merry, and I am quite sure that the captain you murdered would approve of my bestowing his legacy to me in that direction. Perhaps I will read it for you."

And removing the book from the table on which he had placed it, Dr. Syn read to Merry and the delighted Mipps every word of Mervin Ransom's pathetic testament.

"And now, Mr. Merry, that you can see I am no thief except perhaps in the matter of robbing you of your knife, which I should advise you to keep to yourself, I further recommend one more glass of brandy and then home to bed." Saying which, he refilled all glasses and pronounced the toast: "To our mutual understanding in the future."

Whereupon Merry was handed his coat and dismissed, while the favoured sexton was detained to drink another glass.

"You have clipped a vulture's wings tonight, Vicar," chuckled Mipps.

"I believe so," replied Dr. Syn; "but there is one thing that worries me, and I venture to suspect that the unmitigated rogue who has just left us will do what he can to increase that worry."

"What is the worry, sir?"

"I am worried about many good people for whom I have a great affection," replied the vicar," and I worry because they are living in a neighbourhood in which stable doors are, upon occasion, left open at nights. Keep your eyes open, Mr. Mipps, and let me know what is going on. Perhaps you know something already. You hesitate, my good fellow. Is it possible that you have no wish to discuss the question of smuggling with your old friend?"

Mipps put on a quizzical look and scratched his head. "You see, sir, we can discuss it any of these nights and perhaps get no further. But tonight now, we have seen the stable doors open, and perhaps that means that something of the kind is actually afoot. Let me get out and about then without any more delay, and tomorrow, no doubt, I'll have a good deal of information to tell you."

Dr. Syn seemed to think this a happy notion, and dismissed his sexton with one more drink.

C

Mr. Mipps repaired as fast as his legs would carry him to the parlour of the "Ship Inn", where he was welcomed by Mrs. Waggetts and the company.

Since the Dragoons were known to be up in the hills scouring after Grinsley, the ingenious little sexton had seen a wonderful opportunity for a safe "run" upon the Marsh, and as the usual signals had been passed, a fully loaded lugger was already lying outside the bay waiting for the final signal to put in for a landing.

For some time after Mipps had left the vicarage, Dr. Syn found pleasure in thinking out how he would present the pearls to Charlotte. He went to his sea-chest and drew out the scarlet velvet coat that he had discarded for ever. With his scissors he cut off the two gold-embroidered pocket flaps, and these he sewed together with needle and thread from his old sea-days' housewife. He then removed enough gold braid from the coat to form the letters 'C.C.' and when he had dropped the pearls into their velvet pocket and locked them for the night in his sea-chest, he felt he had spent a good hour before going up to bed.

His labour of affection had banished all worry about the smugglers.

Worry was the last thing that entered Mr. Mipps's head as he saw the kegs being carried ashore from the lugger. He was safe. He had two men watching the Preventive man's lodgings, who would stop any informer reaching him, and if he were to issue forth on his own initiative, they were to play informers themselves and lead him in the other direction towards Hythe, while the landing was in reality taking place on Knockholt beach.

But one man did worry. Captain Faunce went from patrol to patrol up in the region of Aldington. Not a sign of Grinsley. Dismounting at Aldington Knole he climbed the hill with a sergeant attending him.

Beneath them was stretched out the whole map of the Marsh. It was difficult at first to see just where marsh joined beach and beach the sea, for clouds of mist drove along beneath them. For some minutes, they watched the white vapours rushing along over the flat surface. Mist clouds that seemed to rise from the white ribbons of dyke water and joining others in their mad and windy stampede. In the distance they could hear the grinding of the waves, and now and then the sea would show through a blown rift of these ground clouds.

It was during one of these wild whirlings of the mist that the sergeant broke silence with: "See that, sir?"

"What?" asked Captain Faunce.

"Why, a ship, a boat. There again, sir. See over there."

Faunce nodded. "No doubt it's the Sandgate Revenue cutter."

"Or a smuggling lugger from France," suggested the sergeant.

"From France, eh? And near in shore. See, there's a boat putting off. Sergeant, what if our man is in hiding on the Marsh after all, in spite of the Dymchurch squire's incredulity? He's no doubt got many friends across the water with whom he has traded."

"Come along and let's get to horse."

And thus it was that the full regiment of Dragoons rode hell for leather across the Marsh upon this misty, windy night.

In the meantime, Mr. Mipps, now knee-deep in the waves, encouraging the unloading of the kegs, now up on the windswept beach superintending the loading of the horses, saw his dreams of yet another run being successfully terminated.

And back in the vicarage Dr. Syn slept peacefully, dreaming of Charlotte Cobtree and pearls.

CHAPTER VI

DOCTOR SYN'S MIDNIGHT VISITOR

Now Dr. Syn always slept with his four-poster curtains drawn back and the lead-rimmed casement set wide open, for he liked to hear the sea grinding up the beach and slapping against the sea-wall. He was a light sleeper, though, when it came to other sounds than the waves to which he was so used.

On this particular night he awoke, hearing a noise of someone clambering up the old ivy roots beneath his window.

He raised himself on one elbow and from beneath the bolster drew out a loaded pistol.

Mr. Mipps climbed the ivy easily and leaned across the window-sill into the bedroom. From this point of vantage he intended to awake and arrest the vicar's attention without alarm. But the vicar was awake, and perceiving only a shadow silhouetted against the driving white clouds, was determined to keep his visitor at that point of disadvantage and to arrest either his escape or advance, for at the moment he afforded him a very sure target.

"If you move, I'll fire," whispered Dr. Syn. "I have you covered."

"Don't shoot, Captain," whispered the intruder in answer, " 'cos there'll be death enough on the Marsh this night without it."

"Ah, Mipps, is it?" said Dr. Syn. "Now what are you doing here? Why do you talk of death on the Marsh? And why do you call me 'captain'?"

"May I come in and tell you, for at the moment my back view is an excellent target for any fool's blunderbuss?"

"You may come in," replied Dr. Syn.

"Right, sir, then I'll tell you all about it. An 'orrible affair is takin' place."

"I can guess it, sir," hissed Syn, as Mipps clambered over the sill and slid into the room.

"You've disobeyed orders, eh? Is it smuggling you've been trafficking with?"

"Someone had to look after the fools," pleaded Mipps, "and you know, Captain, you likes a drop o' brandy yourself just as I likes a bit of excitement. Well, we was landing kegs on the beach as calm as you please, when down gallops them damned Dragoons looking for Grinsley and collars the lot of us."

"You too?" demanded the vicar angrily.

"Yes, but I had my face muffled, slipped my cables in no time, slithered off in a passing puff of mist and come 'ere for 'elp. Now, Vicar, I take it you ain't never goin' to stand by and see the pick o' the parish strung up like mutineers, I knows. Mind you, it wouldn't have happened if you'd been a-leadin' of us. If there's one man what can still save the parish necks, it's you, Captain Clegg."

"How could I save 'em?"

Mipps realized that Dr. Syn was already searching his mind for a possible way out.

"Blest if I knows," he answered honestly, "but you knows or will if you thinks. God be praised you're the head of the parish. The captured men belongs to your flock, and the sheep are bleating for the shepherd and you ain't the one to fail 'em, I knows that."

There was a long pause, during which the vicar, still grasping the pistol, drew his knees up to his chin and clasped them with both hands. As he cudgelled his brain, he allowed the weapon to slide down the tented coverlet beyond his drawn-up toes. He then drew off his nightcap and twisted it convulsively in his fingers.

Dr. Syn was marshalling all his faculties to think of a way out for his unfortunate parishioners.

Then it happened.

Mipps received the vicar's screwed-up nightcap full in his face. The bedclothes were hurled up and away in an enveloping wave, and with an emphatic "Damn you", Dr. Syn leapt across the room, upset a row of calf-bound volumes from their shelf to the floor, and from behind this ambush grasped a bottle of French brandy.

After taking a long pull, the well-remembered and oft-dreaded voice of Clegg spoke sharply:

"From now on, Mister Sexton, your damned-fool sheep shall have a shepherd who will keep his crook about their silly necks, and the exciseman shall dance to the scarecrow's tune."

"The scarecrow?" echoed Mipps.

"That's what I said, you little fool—the scarecrow. He stands in the Tythe field. Saddle my white pony, which you and your smugglers can thank God you left behind. And put the panniers aboard. In the larboard basket pack me up eggs, butter, and any other nourishment for the sick you can lay hands on in the larder, and in the starboard you will put the scarecrow's rags—ay, hat and all and tarred tow wig, and lash 'em down under a white napkin. Where are those fools captured?"

"Knockholt Beach. Tied hand and foot. Sitting on our kegs and guarded by half of those damned Dragoons."

"Where's the captain?"

"Waiting for the other half of his men, who've ridden to Sandgate for the Revenue cutter."

"Take this key and unlock a bag of guineas that you'll find in the top right-hand corner of my sea-chest."

The sexton, with the key in his hand, hesitated. "You can't never bribe that captain of Dragoons. He's a gentleman."

"Don't argue—obey," ordered the vicar. "Has Mother Handaway rented her stables to anyone yet?"

The sexton shook his head. "There's no farmer what would take it. It's devilishly lonely and they say she's a witch. The devil has queer taste in women if he visits her, which they all say he does."

"Saddle my pony, and get me the guineas."

Dr. Syn dressed hurriedly without lighting a candle, took another tilt of the brandy which seemed to empty the bottle, slipped his pistol into his side pocket, and went down the stairs.

The pony was saddled, and with guineas in his pocket, and the pony's baskets packed as he had directed, the doctor mounted.

Then turning to the sexton, he whispered. "Now I'm in this against my will, but I would sooner help the parish than the outside authorities. You must get as near to the prisoners as you can with safety, and then if I can draw off the Dragoons, you must free them and get those tell-tale kegs into safety. But, remember, if I get through alive, I have had no share in this night's adventure. I am now going to visit old Mother Handaway. She is sick. Remember that, will you? She is sick and has sent for the vicar."

Saying which, he started off the fat white pony along the coast road.

Mipps followed leisurely, and called in at his cottage. When he came out, he had a pair of loaded horse-pistols in his great-coat pocket, a brass-barrelled blunderbuss under his arm, and the sharp knife which Dr. Syn had taken from Merry in his belt.

CHAPTER VII

THE SCARECROW RIDER

A QUARTER of an hour later Dr. Syn was challenged by two Dragoons who were watching the road that led to Jesson Farm. He checked his pony.

"But I am Dr. Syn, vicar of Dymchurch," he protested, "and am but on my way to visit a dying old woman on the Marsh."

"Sorry, sir," replied one of the soldiers respectfully, "but we've orders to let no one pass. You'll have to ride with us to the beach and report to the captain."

There seemed nothing for it but to obey, so Dr. Syn trotted alongside the Dragoon, rode up the sea-wall slope and down a sandslide to the beach.

Here, around a fire of driftwood, the Dragoons mounted guard over their prisoners.

"I'm sorry this has happened, sir," explained Captain Faunce; "we were hunting for Grinsley when we surprised these wretched men unloading a French lugger. I'd rather by far have captured Grinsley, whom we suspected of being the cause of the lugger in the Bay; but I must do my duty."

"And where is this lugger?"

The Dragoon smiled. "We could not ride our horses across the Channel, and the Revenue cutter is some miles away."

"And do you think that Grinsley was on board?" asked Dr. Syn.

"Oh, good gracious, no," exclaimed the officer. "These poor fellows have all taken oath against such a thing and I know they are honest, except in this unfortunate business of the kegs."

"You, too, are an honest man, Captain Faunce," replied Syn. "You show your sympathy and your sentiment without shame, and I thank you. Therefore, on the strength of your generosity, if I pledge you my word that this shall never happen again, will you free these unfortunate fellows?"

The Dragoon shook his head sadly. "I'm sorry, sir. It is too late. I have sent half my men for the Sandgate cutter to arrest them. But if you are, as I understand, sir, visiting a sick woman upon the Marsh, let me not be further blamed for having detained you."

71

Dr. Syn looked at the prisoners. Needless to say, he recognized them all and was astonished to find so many respectable parishioners amongst them.

"My poor friends," he said sadly, "you have brought this calamity upon yourselves. I can do nothing for you, it seems."

Turning his pony, he rode up the beach with his Dragoon escort, who passed him by the sentry and watched him jogging across the Marsh until he disappeared into the mist.

Now not far from Mother Handaway's isolated cottage was a gipsy encampment. It was towards this that Dr. Syn directed his pony.

Dr. Syn had a shrewd idea that some of the gipsies would be awake on the night of the run, as it was the cheapest means of obtaining liquor, so he was not surprised at being challenged as he rode into the circle of caravans.

It was a gipsy lad of about eighteen who demanded what he wanted.

"I must see your leader, Silas Pettigrand," he replied.

"The chief is asleep and must not be disturbed. You must see him in the morning," said the gipsy lad, with his hand turning the pony's bridle.

Dr. Syn leant from the saddle and whispered a Romany password.

In three minutes, Silas of the Pettigrands stood before him.

"You know my people, it seems," said the gipsy, by way of greeting.

"In Spanish America—yes," replied the doctor. "I wish to purchase the black horse you have tethered behind your caravan. I noticed it yesterday, as I rode up to the hills, and it is a horse after my heart, and I have need of him."

"He would be difficult for you to manage after that pony. He is a wild fellow. My own sons can hardly sit him."

"I prefer an animal of my own breaking," replied the parson. "How much?"

"It is an animal of mettle," went on the gipsy. "But since you come here with such a message on your lips as you gave my youngest son, I will not ask more than twenty guineas. I confess, though, I took him for ten from a hunting squire in Sussex who was afraid of him and glad to see him go."

"The labourer is worthy of his hire," quoted the parson, "and you are honest with me since your tribe are horse dealers. I will give you thirty guineas. That is twenty for the horse and ten for your Romany oath of silence concerning the transaction."

"You have him, then," answered the old man, "and I will include saddle and bridle."

"I shall not need a saddle—but a bridle—yes, and a pair of spurs until the animal and I are better acquainted."

"You are a horseman, evidently," said the gipsy in admiration.

"You will hide my pony till I call for it in the dawn, and I will come to your caravan now and pay you the gold. I must also change my clothes there."

The gipsy led him to his caravan, took the money and the oath of silence, and then left him to change his clothes while he went out to cover the pony with a cloth.

Accustomed as he was to strange transactions with queer customers, old Silas could scarce believe his own eyes when his visitor reappeared.

The neat parson had given place to the devil in rags.

It was not only the blacked tow-curls which streamed from the battered three-cornered hat that gave such a fiendish look to the face, but rather a cruel, reckless deviltry that flashed from the eyes and smiled through the tight-set lips. This had obliterated a good face with the stamp of hell.

Striding towards the coal-black horse and leaping on to his back with the accustomed ease of a circus rider, the weird figure spoke to the gipsy in an altered—croaking, raucous voice. "I shall visit you before the dawn, and we will breakfast together. You will find my contribution to the feast in the near-side pannier upon the pony. And, by the way, look after my pony, for I shall return to you on foot and must ride it back to Dymchurch, after I have bestowed this magnificent creature in hiding. All very mysterious, eh, friend Silas of the Pettigrands? But believe me, it is not for myself, but for many others for whom I go adventuring. I am secure in your silence?"

"To you I can speak when to others I must keep silent," replied the gipsy solemnly. "For many years the safety of James Bone the highwayman, has been in my care. Let that satisfy you that I trust you as you may trust me. It is a life bargain."

"Then till the dawn—good tenting," cried Dr. Syn.

As though objecting to the bargain of these weird men, and certainly disapproving of yet another human being thinking he could master him, the black horse reared and plunged furiously.

"You see?" said the gipsy, not displeased that the animal was behaving as he had prophesied.

"And you will see," retorted the rider with a laugh, as he dug in the spurs deliberately.

Off went the beast with a scream of rage across the field, leapt the broad dyke on to the road, and the gipsy listened to the ring of the hoofs as he galloped along it.

Meanwhile, he saw the weird figure chased, encircled, and again uncovered by the sinuous, ghostly ribbons of mist.

Fifty yards ahead the road curved to avoid the dyke, but Syn kept his wild steed straight at it, took off from the road, cleared the water easily and thundered on; took the next dyke and the next in full career, and so across four fields till he reared up at the door of Mother Handaway's hovel.

Whatever the old woman's creed was, she not only looked like a witch, but thought herself one. Her features were pinched, her sharp, curved nose and pointed chin guarded her one-toothed mumbling mouth like a pair of nutcrackers. Her eyes were beady and bright and protected by thick grey eyebrows that matched the straggly beard upon her chin. Her hair hung loose in long rats' tails. Her fingers were long and bony, and for ever clawing something invisible as she mumbled. She was hump-backed and in the worst weather she would not wear shoes or stockings, but would hobble along in a quick running glide upon bare feet.

Mother Handaway had heard the thud of the horse's hoofs getting nearer and nearer, and instead of being surprised she seemed to expect that the wild animal was bringing her a visitor, for she flung open the door, covered her face with her skinny claws, and prostrating herself, whimpered: "Hail, Master."

"Aye," replied Syn, in a truly terrible voice, "I am your Master. Your Master the Devil. But see to it that you tell no one that I favour you by appearing to you in the flesh, for if you do they will seize you for the witch that you are. Take this bag of guineas"—and he flung down the half-filled sack upon the threshold. "Each coin is stamped with King George's head and spade, though it was minted in the furnaces of hell. With it I buy your stable, in which you will hide and keep my horse. You will feed it as you are directed. But have a great care that no one sees it, for if they should, it will mean death. So long as you keep it truly well and hidden you shall never lack for gold. Is it a bargain?"

"Yes, Master," answered the old woman. "But are you in truth Satan himself that I have raised by my incantations?"

"Aye," replied Syn in a deep voice. "But you must call me 'the Scarecrow', for as such I come to rule the Marsh. I shall bring my horse to you before the dawn. After that, I shall send my chief messenger to fetch the horse when I have need of him."

"How shall I know him, Master?" asked the old woman.

"I will send him in the guise of a man who can be seen travel· ling the Marsh without exciting suspicion. Do you know the sexton of Dymchurch?"

"Yes, Master. He is one of the few men who is not afraid to talk to me," replied the witch. "I know him well. He and his master, Dr. Syn, have often come to cheer me."

"The holy vicar of Dymchurch?" asked Syn scornfully.

"Aye, but he's a good man, for all his sancity," argued the witch. "I mean, he is a man of wide sympathies. Both he and Miss Charlotte are not ashamed of bringing me nourishing foods. We must take people as we find them, Master."

"Bah!" exclaimed Syn scornfully. "Good people are my enemies. Are they your only visitors?"

"There is another man who is good to me. I forgot," added the old woman. "I speak of Jimmie Bone, the highwayman. When the chase is hot I harbour him."

"Well, that, too, is good," continued Syn, "for he is a fellow that I may yet have use for. See to it, though, that none of these visitors sets eyes on my horse."

"What must I call the horse, Master? Does he answer to a name?"

"He is called Gehenna, and he is wild and fierce. If you so much as lay hands on him, he'll send you to hell before your time."

Dr. Syn swung him round and gave him both spurs. The horse leapt forward and feeling the spurs drive into him relentlessly, galloped away into the rushing mists.

The storm now took a curious turn. The wind increased till it became a gale and before its fury the mist shrouds leapt as though the Marsh were invaded by sheeted giants. Then a stinging sleet shattered down in a torrential burst. The frozen shafts of rain stung the horse into madness and Dr. Syn used the cruel elements to subdue the vice in the horse. He kept the animal facing the storm till he had mastered his spirit and then at last, when he turned his back to the storm, he knew that the animal was his. The spirit was still there, the high, fierce mettle, but the viciousness had gone as far as he was concerned. Then Syn drove the spurs in again and rode like the wind and with the wind towards the distant sea-wall. The pursuing sleet gave the horse pace, and in company with the whirling shapes of flying mist, the black animal galloped with the weird black figure of the Scarecrow on his back.

And the thrill of it went to Syn's head like wine, and he laughed aloud. "Even the elements are on the devil's side tonight. On, Gehenna! On! Faster, you great brute! Faster! The devil in scarecrow's rags rules the Marsh and he rides to Hell on Gehenna. On! On! Faster!"

On the beach the soldiers tried valiantly to keep their fire alight, for it was to serve as a beacon to the cutter. But the wind had arisen, and already the waves in the Bay were dashing up against the shingle. It was doubtful whether the cutter would brave such a storm. Blinded with smoke, the Dragoons kept piling on driftwood, while the rain ran from their brass helmets. Suddenly one of them cried out: "Look!"

At the same moment a piercing laugh echoed from the sand-hill behind them. Even the officer, Captain Faunce, was transfixed with horror at the spectral horseman that had appeared upon the sky-line. It seemed that the storm had opened hell gates to let the devil ride out.

But their superstitious dread was given the lie by the horse-man himself, for after his maniacal laugh, which made his black mount rear and scream, in a derisive voice he cried out: "Leave these poor fools alone. I'm the man you want. Grinsley, the murderer. But you won't catch me this side of hell."

Captain Faunce sprang into the saddle, drew his pistols from the holsters, and pulled both triggers. The right one, damped with the rain, misfired, and the left went wide, though Dr. Syn heard the bullet whizz by.

"Mount and after him, boys," cried the captain. "Granger and Metcalf, stay here mounted, and guard the prisoners. Any treachery, use your sabres without mercy."

The other troopers scrambled for their horses, and led by their officer, galloped towards the sand-hill.

Waving his hand in farewell, Syn turned his horse and slid down the bank on to the road, jumped the dyke on the farther side of it, and led the hunt madly across country for the distant hills.

In the meantime, Mipps had taken advantage of the confusion and profiting by the smoke of the fire which kept blinding the Dragoons, he managed to crawl behind the prisoners and sever their cords with his knife, going from one to the other with a whispered word of caution and concealing himself behind the captured kegs.

By the time Dr. Syn had led away the chase, he had freed all the men and had only the two Dragoons to deal with.

When he considered that the chase had gone clear away, he sprang up, and covering the chests of both troop horses with his pistols, he sang out: "About turn, you two, and follow the hunt. You may take a murderer, but you don't take us."

"What the hell——?" cried one of the troopers, but Mipps interrupted.

"You've no chance, the prisoners are all free. Twenty of us against you two. If you move forward or put your hands to your sabres, I fire, and my pistols ain't damp. Have respect for your horses. About turn."

By this time the smugglers were all on their feet, and were grabbing such weapons as they had been deprived of. These were mostly stout cudgels and poles. Some of them ran to where their horses had been tethered and mounted.

The Dragoons saw that their only chance of re-capturing the men was by getting more help, so as if bowing to the inevitable they turned their chargers and galloped away after their colleagues.

"Quick, lads!" cried Mipps. "Stamp out the fire. Load them kegs on the pack ponies, and away with them as arranged before the soldiers get back."

The smugglers, overjoyed at their deliverance, worked feverishly to get away before the possible arrival of the cutter which they could now see tacking from Sandgate in the teeth of the driving storm.

"Seems to me," laughed one, "that we owe our freedom to this Grinsley."

"That wasn't Grinsley," replied Mipps. "That's our new leader, if we behave ourselves. If we get clear away this blessed night, he'll lead us, I'll take my oath. And, what's more, we'll never get laid by the heels if we obeys him. And if we gets him, why, he gives the orders and not me."

"Who is it?" they asked

"Never you mind. No proper names is best, as we've found out, but amongst us he's the Scarecrow, that's what he is."

"I know," cried one of them. "I can tell who he is by the way he rides. It's Jimmie Bone, the highwayman. Now isn't it?"

"Maybe," allowed Mipps; "but he's to be called The Scarecrow from now on, and if he takes on the job and don't lead them Revenue men a dance—well, you wait."

. . . . .

As the dawn broke, Dr. Syn, looking remarkably clean and fresh in his clerical clothes, jogged along the curving Marshland road towards Dymchurch. He presented a marked contrast to the Dragoon officer whom he met at the cross-roads, leading a lamed charger.

Captain Faunce's red coat was mud-stained, and he had lost his helmet.

"My faith, Captain," cried the vicar, drawing his pony's rein, "the storm has wrought havoc with you. I just reached the cottage I was bound for when it broke. I was fortunate. My clothes are dry."

"I've been chasing Grinsley all night," explained the captain. "And all to no purpose. They say that the devil looks after his own. Anyway he taught that recruit of his how to ride, for I'll swear Grinsley learned his horsemanship in hell. The rascal played with me. Would wait for me to draw level with them, then off he'd go again like lightning. And so it has been all night, for it's but an hour ago that I lost him for good in the woods behind Lympne. With my horse lamed I gave him best."

"And where are your men?" asked the vicar.

"I outrode the rascals early in the chase. Not seen them for hours."

"And your prisoners?"

"Safe under lock and key at Sandgate, I hope," replied the captain.

At that moment a trumpet call rang out, and along the sea-wall they saw the Dragoons riding.

"They make a brave picture in the morning light," said Dr. Syn. "The red coats and the helmets."

"Hope they feel better than I do," grumbled the officer. He blew a shrill blast on a whistle. Up went the leaders' hand and the troop halted. Then seeing their officer signalling to them, the troop sergeant slid his horse down the steep embankment and galloped towards them.

"We couldn't keep pace with you, sir," he explained; "but we got Grinsley."

"You've got him?" repeated the officer, smiling.

"Yes, sir. As you disappeared into that first wood, he broke cover, on his black horse to your left, and we chased him inland till finally we ran him down in Tenterden."

"How long ago?"

"Must be over two hours, sir. The church clock struck four as his horse fell dead."

"And where is Grinsley?"

"Dead too, sir. Metcalf ran him through the neck as he tried to break past him."

"But I heard a clock strike four when I sighted him again the other side of the wood. In God's name—was he then dead?"

"Makes one believe in the supernatural, that sort of experience, said Dr. Syn quietly.

"And Metcalf killed him, you say?" questioned the astounded officer. "But I left Metcalf to guard the prisoners."

The sergeant then broke the news of the smugglers' escape and how the cutter had arrived to find a deserted beach.

"Ah, well, we can get 'em again," laughed the officer. "I dare swear you can identify your own flock, Vicar?"

"I purposely did not look at them," answered Dr. Syn. "Though you could hardly expect me to hand over my own parishioners if I had. I am a man of peace. I can promise you, though, Captain, that you will never take them again in the act of cheating the Revenue."

The captain turned to the troop sergeant. "Are you sure it was four o'clock by Tenterden church?" he asked.

"As sure as I saw Grinsley killed, sir."

"Good God!" muttered the captain—and whether it was from cold or fright, Dr. Syn saw the gallant Dragoon shiver

CHAPTER VIII

DR. SYN IN DANGER

DR. SYN stepped out into his garden and surveyed with every mark of pleasure the bright spring morning. Not a sign of his night's exertions could be traced as he briskly walked amongst the flowers, picking the best blooms for a birthday bouquet.

He passed on into the squire's garden, and stepped to the open french window greeted the family at breakfast.

"My dear Charlotte, I have picked a few flowers from my garden," he said, "with an old man's blessing on this important birthday."

"Oh, I am entirely spoilt!" laughed Charlotte, who ran round the table, took the flowers, pressed them to her face, and curtsyed. "I accept the lovely gift, but not the description you give with it. An old man's blessing. Why, my dear godfather, I never saw anyone look more sprightly. No, don't go hunching your shoulder up and trying to look old."

"But I want to look old in order to claim an old man's privilege, my dear," he said, smiling. "I should like to be the first outside the family to salute you, and also I claim the privilege of a godfather to give you a gift that will be more to your liking than a few Marsh flowers."

"Nothing could be more to my liking, believe me, and please let me kiss you for them," she answered.

So, much to the amusement of her sisters and mother, Charlotte kissed Dr. Syn and then asked him to kiss her.

"Well, here is the gift," he said, laughing, and handed her the red sachet.

"Oh, and my initials on it!" cried Charlotte. "Oh, Doctor, did you work this? No. It is too neat for a man's sewing."

"Bless you, I'm an old traveller. I had to learn to sew after a fashion. But open it, please." Dr. Syn watched her face as she bent down towards the sachet.

The beauty and obvious value of the pearls set everyone gasping, including the delighted Charlotte.

Cicely chuckled. "You are not going to tell us that you value the Marsh flowers as much now, I hope."

"Flowers and jewels are both beautiful," answered Charlotte, "and I value them both for themselves and for the kind heart that gives them."

When Dr. Syn had confided the history of the pearls and had hung them round Charlotte's neck with his blessing, he handed the log-book to the squire.

"Well, there's no doubt," exclaimed Sir Antony, "that Charlotte lives up to your dead captain's hopes. Let us quote what he says: 'Perhaps in years to come, these stones will once more adorn the neck of a beautiful woman. I pray God that her mind be beautiful too.' Well, I think we agree that, despite her looks, Charlotte's mind is at least beautiful.

"But she can be dashed obstinate at times," added the squire. "But since you are her advocate, we'll allow then that she deserves the pearls. Secondly, there is no doubt that you, Doctor, by virtue of being the sole survivor of the captain's brig, become his lawful heir, and have therefore every right to give them to Charlotte if you so wish."

Now although the whole village from the squire down seethed with excitement that day, an exception must be made of Dr. Syn. The events of the night before seemed to interest him not at all. He spent the day largely in the pleasant company of Charlotte Cobtree, for, as he put it, 'a twenty-first birthday is a very great occasion'. The dinner hour having been postponed till a late hour that day, the early evening found the doctor on his white pony riding beside Charlotte, and although many times upon the ride he had entreated her not to bother about his slow jogging but to enjoy a gallop, she refused to ride from him.

"Well, you are twenty-one, Charlotte," replied Dr. Syn. "You have every right to please yourself. Thank you very much."

For some time they rode forward at a gentle walk, and Dr. Syn's thoughts began to concentrate upon the new life of adventure that seemed to have been thrust upon him.

It was she who interrupted his train of thought with: "Oh, Doctor, whatever makes you scowl like that? Have you forgotten it is my birthday?"

"No, Charlotte," he answered, smiling, but without looking at her. "But when you get to middle age the past has a way of obtruding itself, and to men who have lived an adventurous life it is generally the unpleasantnesses of the past that thrust themselves to the front. A young girl like you could not be expected to understand the depressions that come with middle age."

"No?" she queried. "Perhaps I understand these depressions —in you—better than you imagine. Perhaps I understand more than anyone else where you are concerned, and the reason is that I am certain no one loves you more than I do."

"That is very kind of you, my dear," replied the doctor. He did not dare to look back at her, but kept his pony just a little ahead. But she watched him closely.

"You see," she went on, "my father is your oldest friend and I am, in many ways his confidante. Do you suppose then that, both loving you as we do, we have not been guilty of discussing you? We have, and I know as well as he does of the tragedy that drove you to America.

"That is all finished. It is a closed book," said Syn simply.

"Not quite, is it?" went on Charlotte. "Now that I am grown up, may I claim the privilege of telling you what I think? From what my father has told me, you were influenced to go abroad in a spirit of revenge. It was natural that when your wife betrayed you, all your love for her should be killed. You never blamed her, so my father tells me, but on the man, who had been your friend, you were determined to heap pŭnishment. Unsuccessful in this, at last even that passion died in you, and you return to start life again with us. Why do you not accept that fact that your wife is dead, Doctor?"

"Because it is not right to accept a fact that is only told by a liar and a cheat," he answered. "If I were to marry again and there was a child, and then my wife was found to be alive after all, what of my child then? What of the woman that had given it to me?"

"It would be but a legal quibble to make it wrong," replied Charlotte. "For my part, I would break any law for the sake of the man I loved."

The tone of her voice was so compelling that Dr. Syn checked his pony and looked at her. She, too, drew rein involuntarily and met his gaze, leaning slightly towards him from the saddle. Her face was above him, for she rode a man's horse and he was crouched on his pony.

For a few long seconds their eyes met, and with a grave glowing hers took hold and clung to his, binding him to her as the hands do in matrimony. Instinctively the doctor was disarmed. He felt the warm blood of youth once more in his veins. Was it possible that this beautiful girl loved him?

As he asked himself the question, she answered it with a slow nod and added: "I would take the risk. I love you."

He felt his back straighten, he knew his eyes glowed as hers did. Subconsciously, he cursed the secrets that compelled him to ape an older man. He longed to change his pony for the fierce black horse he had conquered in the night. He wanted to appear to her the man of adventure that he was. And that very want betrayed him, for he dismounted like a young man and stood beneath her, drinking her in as, leaning forward, she let her curl brush his face.

"Why don't you say what is in your heart?" she urged.

"I can say that," he whispered. "Yes, at least I can say that with all honesty. I love you. But in all honour I can never ask you to marry me. I would to God I could."

"Because your wife may be alive?" she asked.

"There are other things," he went on. "Aye, things black and damnable. Did you know the half of them, you would turn from me."

"Let me be the judge of that," she said quietly. "For now in all fairness, I have the right."

"Aye, were the secrets mine, you should share them. But I put others on their oath never to tell those secrets, even to their wives."

"They were men, then—these sharers of your secrets? I am glad of that, for I began to be jealous. And do they live—these men? Could you not ask them to release you?"

"I believe the most of them are dead. But an oath is an oath from which even death could not release us."

She bowed her head slowly, dismissing all desire to know, since he had sworn to keep silence. Then she laid one hand upon his shoulder and added: "Even though you say these things were black and damnable, I do not blame you, for my heart tells me that in all your life you could never have done anything except your honour forced you."

"Thank God, I can say aye to that," he answered. "In the worst moments of my poor life, when my hands were stained with blood, my honour drove me to it. A rough-hewn honour it may have been, for I was then amongst savage men. In the Last Day I shall have no fear in answering the Judge's charge on that score, but to tie you to such a man—who cannot share his memories with you—my honour forbids that, my dear."

"But suppose my honour is rough-hewn, too?" Her fingers gripped his shoulders tightly. "Suppose I confess that were you the worst of criminals standing with a noose about your neck upon the open scaffold, I should still be proud to say 'I love you'."

"Good evening, Vicar. Good evening, Miss Cobtree."

Out of the flatness of the Marsh a third party had appeared.

Hidden by the height of Charlotte's horse, and having taken advantage of the cover of a deep dyke that ran all the way from the high road to Mother Handaway's field-bound cottage, Merry had approached unseen, and quietly walked round the head of Charlotte's horse upon them.

"Good evening, Mr. Merry," she said, in a voice clear of any embarrassment. The love that had shown from her eyes during her confession still danced in them. She had not troubled to alter her expression. Mr. Merry might have been her dearest confidant for all the trouble she took to disguise her feelings.

With the doctor it was different. Automatically, imperceptibly and yet rapidly he changed. When he turned towards Merry he was the kindly, elderly person with something of a stoop that was so familiar a figure to all on Romney Marsh. He looked at Merry's sea-boots, wet with dyke water, and his kindly eyes took on an expression of reproof.

"You ought to know better, my man, than to spring out of a hiding-place without warning when a sensitive animal like Miss Charlotte's horse is standing near. It was foolish. I thought you had horse sense."

Without waiting for his reply, he turned to Charlotte's horse and ran his hand beneath the girth. "No, it is not too tight, my dear, though perhaps the saddle needs adjusting."

"Help me to dismount, then," she said, "and while you fix it, I will just run over the field to speak to poor Mother Handaway. Lift me, please," she pleaded, "for if I jump I may trip in my skirt and roll into Mr. Merry's dyke." She laid her hand on Dr. Syn's shoulder and turned to Merry. "By the way, what were you doing in the dyke? Catching something?"

"Avoiding someone," answered Merry, turning his head towards Mother Handaway's cottage. Then he pointed. "Him, to be exact."

"That man on the horse coming towards us? Why?"

"Ah! You don't know who he is. Neither of you know. But I know. I keeps an eye open on Romney Marsh, and there ain't much I don't know. And I knows that I ain't stopping around to be shot at by no jocular highwayman."

"Highwayman?" repeated Charlotte, with no hint of the usual shudder which was customary amongst women as well as many men at the very sound of the word.

"Ay, and it's the famous Jimmie Bone, if you wants to know," whispered Merry. "For a long while I've wished to see him unmasked, and up by the cottage I did. He was arguing with the old witch. Something about a stable that he could no longer use, and he seemed very put out. There's a hundred pound on his head from the authorities, but I ain't waiting to tell him so." And leaving the horse's head, Merry slithered down the dyke bank and plunged into the cover of the rushes.

Jimmie Bone saw the manœuvre, and checked his horse, while he tucked his three-cornered hat under his arm for the few seconds required in which to adjust a black mask that covered him to the mouth. Then clapping his spurs he put his horse at the intervening dyke, cleared it and galloped to the next, taking it with an ease that showed consummate horsemanship. In a few seconds he was alongside the dyke in which Merry was plunging, and had pulled from his holster a long pistol. Dr. Syn noted that Mr. Bone rode a black horse, not unlike Gehenna, who had apparently forestalled his stable, and remembering Grinsley's black mount, he told himself that black horses were evidently in fashion amongst the local rogues.

"Now then, what's the game? Come out of it, you water rat," cried the highwayman to Merry. "Trying to cheat an honest gentleman of the road from his lawful dies, is it? Come on, it's your money or your life, so fork out and sharp's the word."

"Come now, Mr. Bone, is it likely as hough I had money?" whined the terrified Merry.

"Likely? I should say it's certain," replied the highwayman, "considering as how you ain't the cove to do something for nothing and you was give a gold spade for carryin' a message from certain gents I knows in Rye—aye, a message to yonder old Mother at the cottage, and considering you showed her that same guinea and there ain't no inn between there and here where you could spend it, considerin' all that, I says stump up sharp."

"But look here, Mr. Bone——"

"And not so free with your Mr. Bone," cut in the highwayman. "We've never been interdooced to my knowledge, and I've no wish to know yer better, although I'll be obliged to be better acquainted with that there guinea. Toss her up."

"I'm a poor man——" began Merry, reluctantly holding out the guinea piece.

"And I'll be the richer by a guinea," laughed the highwayman stretching his hand down and taking the coin reluctantly held out to him. "And now, you stop over this side of the dyke while I deals with these others. Why, sakes alive, if it ain't a parson! Now why the devil couldn't you have been anything but that, and an old 'un, too." For while the highwayman had been attending to

Merry, Dr. Syn had taken the opportunity of putting on his reading spectacles. "Oh sakes, had you been a justice of the peace, a well-fed lawyer, or even some portly merchant from London city, why then I'd have robbed you willingly. Why, I never yet have robbed a parson. A selfish virtue, sir, but if I did it 'ud be the ruin of all good luck that seems to stand as faithful by me as the horse I ride. Now, the lady is different. I'll relieve you, miss, of the pretty pearl string about your neck, which I see you have taken pains to hide as far as possible beneath your kerchief. I'll come over for it."

Jimmie Bone turned his horse and rode in a circle back towards the dyke, which he leapt in style. He was now separated from Merry by the water, but upon the same meadow as the others.

He now rode towards them with his horse-pistol presented.

Now although the last thing Charlotte wanted was to lose her precious pearls, it was not fear for their safety that now clutched at her heart, but for the danger towards which Dr. Syn was walking. He certainly looked old and very forlorn, as he limped slowly across the rough grass to meet the highwayman, who reined in his horse and waited.

"No nearer, reverend sir," warned Mr. Bone.

Dr. Syn stopped and blinked through his glasses at the black mask. "I have always heard it said of you, Mr. Bone," he replied in a quavering voice, "that as robbers go, you have at least something honourable about you. I do not exactly agree with your mode of life. Naturally, my profession forbids me to go so far, but I have always been pleased to hear you praised for a certain dare-devilry which every Englishman admires. And just as you have an aversion to rob or illtreat me because of my black cloth, so have I an aversion to killing you sitting there so magnificently on that fine animal. Whether you will get Miss Cobtree's pearls remains to be seen, but it is quite certain that you will have to fight me first."

Mr. Bone laughed. "Do you mean a duel, reverend sir? Is it possible that you carry a piece of artillery in one of those long pockets?"

Dr. Syn shook his head, blinked through his spectacles, and continued nervously. "No, no. I do not carry a pistol. Though, strange as it may seem to you, I know a good deal about them, and was at one time accounted a reasonable performer. I take it now, Mr. Bone, that the pistol you are presenting at my head at the moment is made more to intimidate than to give an exhibition of accurate shooting."

"It shoots straight enough, though," replied Mr. Bone, "as you might find to your cost did you attempt to cross me too far."

"Might find, eh?" repeated Dr. Syn. "So you allow that there is room for doubt. I take it that you would not feel too secure in using such a weapon for a duel?"

"Since you are so insistent—well, no. I should use one of these in that case." And Mr. Bone drew from his sash a very fine duelling-pistol.

"Ah, that's a weapon," exclaimed Dr. Syn. "That only demands a sense of direction and a steady squeeze on the trigger. Are you an infallible shot, Mr. Bone?"

"What do you mean?" he demanded. "I can hit a mark nine times out of ten."

"A mark may be large or small," replied the vicar, shaking his head in disbelief.

"Make it large enough to see and I'll hit it," said the highwayman.

"I will," answered Dr. Syn. "Now, it is a virtue of mine, and of my capacious coat pockets, that I never stir abroad without a good piece of chalk, a length of pack thread, and a good sharp knife. Whenever I see a good stick or a pliable twig, I think of my young rascals in the parish who are for ever crying out for whips, cudgels, or fishing-rods. My knife"—he fumbled in his side pocket and produced it—"is, as you see, a good one. It is strong, it is sharp, and what is so important, it is admirably balanced. It is a knife to throw, Mr. Bone, and, like your pistol, I shall boast of it that nine times out of ten it hits the mark. I am beholden to a dreadful rascal for the instruction—a Chinaman, Mr. Bone—and it has amused me to keep in practice a hobby that has on several occasions saved my life. Now, before we begin to settle this business concerning Miss Cobtree's pearls, I will lay you a guinea against the one you have appropriated from poor Merry there, that I will throw more accurately than you can shoot. Don't be alarmed, I beg. The crack of a pistol will excite no comment on Romney Marsh. A rabbit, or a water-rat—why, the boys will shoot at them, you know. Besides, look around you. As far as the eye can see, there is not a human being stirring but ourselves. You would have ample time on that delightful horse to make good your escape. Here's the chalk. I make a mark on this old gate-post. So! Now, Mr. Bone, make good your boast."

Mr. Bone chuckled beneath his mask. "You're a queer cove, ain't you? Well, I'll win your guinea and then take the lady's pearls."

He thrust the cumbersome horse-pistol into the holster and leapt to the ground. "And what distance must we set for this stake, Mr. Parson?"

"You see the chalk mark. It is not large, I admit. Make it whatever you please and take the first shot."

The highwayman looked at the parson suspiciously. But the sight of so much blinking senility disarmed suspicion. Mr. Bone was a big man, tall, broad, and athletic. One blow from his great fist would catapult the frail parson across the dyke. He walked back some yards from the post, followed by his black horse, who in turn was followed by the black-garbed parson.

"I think that far would be accounted a good shot, eh?" asked the highwayman.

"Just as you like," replied the parson. "The light is good, with the sun behind us."

The highwayman muttered something to his horse, who obediently knelt down. Mr. Bone also crouched on one knee and steadied his pistol upon the saddle.

"Here, you," he called to Merry. "Get on that mound there and keep a sharp look out. I have no mind to be taken through this folly."

Merry walked to the mound in question, but he was more interested in the fate of his guinea, and he looked for danger behind the highwayman's back, so that he could watch the shooting.

After a considerable time taken in shuffling himself into a position of comfort, Jimmie Bone took long and deliberate aim, the crack of the shot rang out and he got up from his knees.

"I think I have driven in the very centre of your chalk-mark," he chuckled.

"I think you have gone so wide that you have missed the mark entirely," chuckled the parson. "Aye, post and all."

"I tell you I can see a mark in the centre of the cross," exclaimed the marksman.

"I think you'll find that is just a mark in the wood. I fear you've gone wide. You shall have nine more shots to hit, if you wish to make good your word. Nine out of ten, you said."

"I'll find the bullet in the post first, before I waste more powder," snapped Mr. Bone, stepping over the prostrate horse and walking to the post.

However, he found that the parson was right in that the centre of the cross was a piece of faulty wood that had not taken the chalk. He began to run his hand slowly down the post, stopping his finger upon every mark in the hope of discovering the passage of his bullet. It annoyed him to fail in front of this parson and the pretty girl.

Charlotte, meanwhile, was watching Dr. Syn and saw what the highwayman had got his back to. Syn's left hand drew the horse-pistol from the holster and with a sudden jerking swing flung the knife with full force.

With an oath the highwayman sprang aside, only to find his movement arrested by his coat, for as his hand had lingered on the thick post, the flying knife was driven right through the stiff buckrammed slack of his broad laced cuff.

"I found your sleeve a more tempting mark, Mr. Bone," said Dr. Syn, advancing to the impaled highwayman with the horse-pistol levelled.

"Here's your guinea," cried the baffled highwayman, "or do you mean to try for the hundred guineas the authorities have put upon my capture?" He tossed the guinea towards the parson who caught it and threw it to Merry.

"Oh dear, no, Mr. Bone. I only wished to point out that when you levelled this piece of inaccurate artillery at my head, I was not taken at such a disadvantage as you thought. Indeed, I should very much dislike you to flatter yourself upon that point."

"That pistol's accurate enough, with luck," grumbled Jimmie Bone, "so unless you're out to kill me, keep your finger off the trigger."

"Have no fear, Mr. Bone," replied Dr. Syn. "I am well used to pistols, and really could not have missed that post after such preparations. I congratulate you, though, upon the admirable way you have trained your horse. However, we must now deal with Miss Cobtree's pearls, which, as I said, you will have to fight to get. Keep your hand away from that knife, Mr. Bone, for a moment. Come across the water, Mr. Merry. You will act for Mr. Bone, no doubt, while Miss Cobtree will act for me. This shall be all in order, Mr. Bone. A fair fight. And I assure you the pearls are worth the fighting for. Several thousands of pounds they would fetch in the London market. But when I tell you that they were given to Miss Cobtree for her birthday today, perhaps your sense of fairness will make you withdraw your threat and ride away in peace."

"Miss Cobtree, eh?" repeated Mr. Bone. "She'd be the daughter of Cobtree the magistrate, and ain't he the cove what has put a hundred guineas round my neck? It seems to me, then, not unfair for me to take several thousand guineas from his daughter's neck."

"As you please, Mr. Bone, and always supposing you can make good your boast, which I am at liberty to doubt after the failure of your former boast. Mr. Merry, you will pluck out my knife there, while I help Miss Cobtree to dismount."

He backed towards the horses, still keeping the highwayman covered with the pistol, while Merry splashed his way across the dyke to get the knife.

Charlotte leaned from her horse with one arm round the vicar's shoulder, and as he lifted her to the ground she whispered: "Why not send him packing? You have the pistol and I the pearls."

"Because I have the wish to show you that you have not given your love to a weakling, my dear."

She was about to speak in answer when Merry, who had pulled out the knife from the post and thereby released Mr. Bone's cuff, suddenly sprang at the highwayman with the knife raised.

With a savage curse, Mr. Bone ducked, caught Merry with one arm around the waist, and with the other hand twisted the wrist till the knife dropped. He then drew back, and with a sledge-hammer blow knocked Merry backwards into the water.

"That was just, Mr. Bone. He deserved it for treachery," said Dr. Syn.

"Aye, he was tempted by that hundred pounds alive or dead that old Cobtree has put up. Well, he ain't earned it yet, I think. And now what, Master Parson?"

"You have a good punch, I see, which I shall do well to avoid," chuckled Dr. Syn. "I remember now that you were something of a heavyweight before you took to the road. You knocked out the Camberwell Smasher at Tunbridge Fair, if I recollect."

"That's it, and my advice to you is not to tempt me to deal with you as I dealt with him," laughed Mr. Bone. "I'd rather have them pearls without a fight and ride off peaceful."

"Possibly, but oh no," laughed the doctor. "At least, I shall be very surprised if you do ride off with the pearls. But I'll take off my glasses and my coat. I should suggest you take off your riding-coat."

"I'll keep it on," replied the highwayman. "When I have finished with you, and let us hope the damage done will not affect your preaching, I shall take the pearls and ride away before you raise the alarm."

"Oh, but there is to be no alarm, I assure you," corrected the parson. "This is but a friendly bout, I hope, and I wish you would not boast so of the pearls." Dr. Syn folded his coat and laid it tidily on the grass. "Well, if you will not remove your coat, at least take off your mask. It gives me so much to aim at."

"Do you really mean that we are to fight with fists?" asked the amazed highwayman, seeing that the parson was calmly rolling up his shirt-sleeves, and opening and shutting his hands as he blinked at them.

"But, my dear Mr. Bone, you see I have got ready. We will fight to a finish. A knock-out and with fists. The usual ten to be counted. Slowly, my dear Charlotte."

"Well, it is not my habit to linger too long in one spot," said the highwayman. "True, there's no one visible at the moment likely to cause me trouble, but away yonder towards Dymchurch, there's a clump of trees behind which one cannot see, and I've been warned that the Dragoons are out. So come along, my gallant game-cock, and let us hope your preaching will be better than your fighting."

"Oh, I hope it is," replied Dr. Syn devoutly, taking a few steps forward and then awaiting attack in a somewhat awkward attitude of defence.

"It will be no disgrace to say you've been worsted by Gentleman James," laughed Bone, advancing.

"You are sure you would not prefer to remove your mask?" asked the waiting parson timidly.

"I only removes it amongst relations, and they are all dead. I have no wish to give away a description of my beauty."

"Oh, but your heavy boots and spurs," pleaded Dr. Syn.

"Used to 'em. I notice you keep on your buckled shoes. I likes fighting shod, like you."

Mr. Bone suddenly rushed. Dr. Syn stood his ground, and though Charlotte was terrified at the tornado attack of the great highwayman, she was surprised to see him stagger back with his hand on his jaw. Dr. Syn had apparently parried the sledge-hammer blows, and struck once, but the stroke got home. It enraged the highwayman, for he leapt forward again and clinched. Dr. Syn seemed mildly surprised at this form of attack. His arms were tied by the great bulk of his antagonist. He seemed to have no space in which to hit. For the moment it seemed that Mr. Bone had got it all his own way, and wishing to finish the comedy and pay the parson back with interest for the lucky blow on his chin, he tried to hold the parson with his left arm while withdrawing his right for a smash-out blow.

What followed was too quick for Charlotte to understand. But the highwayman missed his blow and Syn was clear of that crushing left arm. His knuckles had managed to inflict a murderous jab into Bone's ribs, and as the highwayman's fist whistled past his side-jerked head, up came the parson's left and reached the same spot on the jaw. Mr. Bone cried out in surprise and pain, and, recovering his balance, followed up Dr. Syn, who had leapt clear. But unwilling to submit to another of those grim clinches, the parson played for defence, parrying the mighty blows with apparent coolness, but retreating steadily round and round before the infuriated rushes.

At every attack it seemed that the slim figure of the parson must be overwhelmed, and yet his face remained untouched, and even his wig, which he had not removed, was still sitting tidy and tight upon his head, and as blow after blow was rained at him, the parson's face was ever guarded and the blows turned aside.

From a distance it would have seemed that the highwayman was getting it all his own way, because of the other's persistent retreats. After each attack, he leaped back to avoid another clinch.

Mr. Bone felt the blood trickling down his neck, and this infuriated him. He now attacked with lower blows, and at last landed a murderous stroke into the parson's ribs. Dr. Syn leapt back, pressing his hand against the spot and drawing in his breath with an audible hiss. It may have been a sporting instinct on the part of Mr. Bone to let the parson recover himself, or it may have been that he took a few seconds to recover himself for a further effort to drive home that advantage, but it is certain that the big man held back for a few definite seconds, breathing hard. Dr. Syn used the pause first by calmly lifting his wig from his head and throwing it clear away upon the grass. He then appeared to Charlotte and Merry to be using his brain and taking the measure of Bone's fighting qualities. He knew, therefore, that his best policy was to fight as he had been doing on the defensive and at all costs to keep clear till he had worn down his antagonists patience and strength.

It so happened, however, that the pause had placed Dr. Syn facing the distant clump of Dymchurch trees, and since the highwayman had his back to them, he did not see what the parson did—for between the trees the setting sun was flashing upon the brass helmets and breastplates of the Dragoons.

Now Dr. Syn had only to mention the fact to Mr. Bone to terminate the fight. What was more to the point, he could finish the fight as victor and by picking up the pistol which had laid beneath his coat, he could order Mr. Bone to mount without the pearls and to ride for his life.

Against this was his desire to finish the fight under Charlotte's eyes, and it was this that made him risk Mr. Bone's safety.

Once more he threw himself into an attitude of self-defence. Once more Mr. Bone advanced, preparing to launch himself in a tornado attack. But, instead, he was met in full career by a second tornado. Dr. Syn had sprung into the attack like a mad hurricane, and Mr. Bone got a taste of his own smashing method before he was aware that such a thing existed. Back he was driven with well-landed blows, steadily back towards the dyke.

"Mind the water, man!" cried Dr. Syn, after sending him reeling to the very bank.

But the highwayman was game. He rushed again, only to be met by the parson's counter-rush. Down went Mr. Bone, blinded with blood that soaked down through his silk mask.

Charlotte forgot to count. Dr. Syn had to do it slowly, with one eye on the giant upon the turf and the other towards the Dragoons.

On the ninth count, however, Mr. Bone once more showed fight. Leaping to his feet, he rushed the parson. A quick sidestep and a lightning left hook to the jaw followed almost instantaneously by a punishing jab to the ribs with his right, left Dr. Syn standing the victor, for Mr. Bone uttered a sigh of pain, sank on his knees, and then collapsed.

CHAPTER IX

CHARLOTTE NAMES HER THREE HEROES

"OUR highwayman is a game fighter, my dear," said the doctor to Charlotte, who had left the horses to Merry and had come closer, "but he has learned in too easy a school. Strength he has, but no knowledge. Get some water from the dyke in my hat while I raise his head." He sank his voice to a whisper so that Merry could not hear, and added: "We must get him away before that party of Dragoons catch sight of him."

Charlotte took the doctor's hat and kneeling beside the dyke, filled it with water, while the doctor gently removed the blood-stained mask from the unconscious man.

It was then that Merry saw the distant Dragoons and determined to gain the hundred guineas for the taking of Mr. Bone. He leapt on to Charlotte's horse and galloped to the dyke, plunged down into the water and climbed the opposite bank, and before the others had realized his purpose he was away at full speed.

"Quick, Charlotte," ordered the doctor, "the man is none so badly hurt, but that rogue is for putting his neck in a halter. Ah, he's coming round."

Indeed, as soon as the water was splashed on to his face, the highwayman opened his eyes.

"Well, it's hands up, Mr. Parson, and I own when I'm beat." He twisted his lips into a smile. "You saved the lady her pearls, and it serves me right for having threatened to take 'em. But had you got to take off my mask?"

"Your face is safe as far as we are concerned," replied the doctor. "We shall only remember you as a masked man who refused to uncover. And the sooner you get on to your horse the better, for the gentleman you deprived of the guinea has ridden off to put the Dragoons on your trail. He was off before we could stop him."

The highwayman struggled to a sitting position and looked at the distant rider.

"Aye, and the curse of it is, that the old witch who lives yonder will no longer give me stable room," he muttered. "I'll confess that for more than a year I have found her place handy.

94

Well, it will have to be riding then, I reckon, and before those soldiers come out from the trees."

"Wait till that scoundrel disappears, and I will see to it that the old woman gives you safe hiding." Dr. Syn recovered his wig and adjusted it.

"She's mad, sir," answered the highwayman. "Said she could no longer see to me or my horse. Nor could she take my money, because she'd seen the devil himself who had forbidden her any other service."

"If the parson cannot over-ride the devil, he is no use at his job," laughed the doctor. "Look, Merry is already behind the trees. Let me mount your horse, and do you get up behind me, and I will undertake your safety. Charlotte, do you mount the pony and trot over by the bridge, and when the Dragoons ride up, let me do the talking."

He sprang into the saddle, but the highwayman's horse, trained only to obey his master, plunged and reared in indignation, till Mr. Bone quietened him.

"You ride as well, Master Parson, as you fight, and you deserve a better mount than yonder fat pony," he said. "As to your fighting power, my faith, but my head is still spinning. I have never been so punished in my life."

He mounted with difficulty.

"Hold on to me," urged Dr. Syn. "And there's need of haste. Can you stand a gallop?"

"I have ridden so full of Bow Street runners' lead that my horse was lamed with the weight of it," laughed Mr. Bone.

"Then hang on," replied Dr. Syn, and he urged the horse down into the dyke, not caring to risk his legs with such a jump. "We can leap the others, but not this," he said, as they plunged through the water up to their thighs, and climbed the further bank. Then he set the horse to the gallop.

Charlotte watched them as she led the pony along the dyke to the nearest brick bridge, and she realized that Syn was the best rider on the Marsh, and the discovery made her understand many things that had long puzzled her. However, she was to be puzzled a good deal more before she reached home, but once more her love gave her the solving of the riddle, which she found only seemed to make her love him the more.

When she reached Mother Handaway's cottage she was met by the old witch, and was most astonished at her words.

"Oh, Miss Cobtree," whispered the old lady, "never come and visit me more. I say this to repay you for all the kindness you have shown to an old witch whom everybody shuns. But never come here again, and oh, above all, never have dealings with the vicar of Dymchurch. You do not understand, but I tell you he is the devil. What has happened to the real vicar I cannot tell, but the devil is going up and down the Marsh in the likeness of him. He'll know I've told you, dearie, but I'll endure his wrath out of love of you."

"You are talking nonsense, Mother," replied Charlotte, who was amused at the old woman's wild fancy. "Why, I love Dr. Syn. He is my godfather, but for all that I am going to marry him, when he asks me."

"Aye, he'll ask you. The devil will use any wile to get a soul in his clutch. But shun him, my dear. Keep clear of church when he is there, for the foul fiend can be honey-tongued to a pretty girl. I know, who am his servant. I practised the black devilry from a child and I have seen manifestations, and he even promised to visit me in a flesh form, and now I am his stable-woman, I feed his great black beast of a horse and I must call him the Scarecrow, he tells me. But he has provided for me. I may have guineas by the bag that are minted in hell for all that they bear the royal spade and head."

"And where is this fierce black horse of his?" asked Charlotte, resolved to humour her.

"In the hidden stable. It is a pit built of stone behind the cow barn. It was made by the smugglers years ago, and my grand-mother showed me the secret. Its roof is covered with growing grass. I once saved Jim Bone, the highwayman, by giving him shelter there, and ever since he has used it when the chase was hot. I told him that now he could not use it again, when suddenly the devil appears as he said he would, in the likeness of Dr. Syn. He has stowed him away there. Oh, there's room enough for ten horses. And there's no one could find the door. Ah, those smugg-lers, they knew things in those days."

"They still do, so they say," laughed Charlotte.

Dr. Syn agreed that they had been cunning fellows who built the door which he had just fastened behind him. It stood in the steep side of a deep dry dyke and when closed looked nothing else but a great heap of dried bulrush reeds.

Satisfied that all was well, and that in Jimmie Bone he had now a faithful and useful colleague, he walked along the dyke and climbed up it at the side of the cottage.

"You see, my dear Charlotte," he said, with a smile, "a parson must do what he can for all his flock. Now, these gallant Dragoons that are cantering towards us are not my parishioners, and as to the rascal Merry—why, our masked friend is worth a score of such, and he happens to be in the greater need at the moment. Therefore he has my help. It is the lost sheep that the shepherd seeks."

The Dragoons drew up on the high road, while Captain Faunce, led by Merry still mounted on Charlotte's horse, and followed by two troopers, came galloping across the fields, jumping the dykes, till they reached the three figures grouped around the white pony.

"You've never let him go, sir?" cried Merry, as he looked in vain for the sight of his capture. "You'll have lost me a hundred guineas."

Dr. Syn smiled. "And what are a hundred guineas compared to the safe keeping of Miss Cobtree's pearls? I confess I was mightily glad to see the last of him. And let me add that if you have lamed Miss Cobtree's horse, there will be trouble for you. Good evening, Captain Faunce. If you wish to reach the Sussex border before this masked gentleman of the road, who may or may not be the famous James Bone, I should recommend a cross-country gallop as quick as possible."

"This man tells me that you gave him a leathering," he replied.

"I learned in a scientific school, that is all, sir," laughed Dr. Syn. "Besides, he had the double disadvantage of not wishing to remove his mask, and of not fighting for what was honest. Miss Cobtree's pearls were in danger, so what else could I do, God forgive me, but fight?"

"I take it then that you can only identify his clothes and figure. You did not see his face?"

"I told you he would not remove his mask, but I should imagine that he will be marked where I drew the blood through it. True, my knuckles are torn, but not seriously."

"Might as well chase highwaymen as smugglers," laughed the captain. "It's all in the day's work, and a gallop will do the horses no harm. Hand over Miss Cobtree's horse—you, and get up behind Trooper Harker. We'll need you to identify his clothes and horse."

The wretched Merry was only too glad to obey. The chances of his hundred guinea reward were not quite spoiled, and he was none too eager to be left with Dr. Syn.

"I'll lay you a guinea you will not catch him this side of the border," said Dr. Syn, shaking his head.

D

"Perhaps not, since he's well mounted and knows the country," answered the Dragoon. "But I'll lay *you* a guinea that we do catch him over the border—aye, and bring him back, too, in spite of the Sussex magistrates. At all events, his horse will be commandeered for our regiment, and from what I hear, he rides a noble animal."

"Is that him over there?" said Dr. Syn, shading his eyes. "Surely there is a black speck riding straight into the setting sun."

The others looked in the direction.

"Your eyes are stronger than mine, then. The sun blinds mine."

"Oh, but surely—surely" went on the doctor. "It seems impossible, though, that he could have ridden such a distance in the time."

"We'll show him that the Army can ride too," laughed the captain. "Come along, men. If I lose that horse, I lose a guinea too, for the doctor's offertory."

Rising in his stirrups, he signalled his distant troopers with his arm, who after some sharp, incomprehensible orders from a junior officer, started off into a canter along the high road, while Captain Faunce, followed by the two troopers, one of whom carried Merry as a passenger, galloped across country in the direction supposed to have been taken by the redoubtable Bone.

"Did I not tell you he was the devil in disguise?" whispered Mother Handaway to Charlotte. "Avoid him, my dear, if you value your soul. Oh, don't look at me like that with laughter in your eyes, as though you thought me mad. I tell you, he said so himself when he rode to me in the storm on his wild black horse. 'I am the devil,' he said, 'but you may call me Scarecrow. I come to rule the Marsh,' he says, 'and you will keep my horse.' It is an animal from hell, my dear. 'I shall send you a messenger from time to time. He will appear as the sexton of Dymchurch, for I shall be going up and down myself as Dr. Syn, the preacher.' Tell no one, dear, lest he strike us dead, but you are young and pretty and have been good to me. But I cannot have you visit me any more. Avoid me for your own safety, but, above all, avoid him, the devil."

But Charlotte, looking at Dr. Syn as he jumped on to the pony's back in order to get a better view of the pursuit, thought that if this amazing parson were indeed the devil, she would be very well contented to serve him.

On the ride back she put some of her thoughts into words.

"I am glad our friend, Mr. Bone, is safe. I am glad, too, that you saved him. You had certainly punished him enough."

"For wanting to rob you of your pearls?" he laughed. "Oh no, not half enough. He deserved a good hanging."

"But you forgave him," she answered, "and I think I know the reason, for you and I have much in common. We both respect adventurers."

"Well, there is always something attractive about a man who takes great risks, even though they may be taken against law and order."

"Do you believe that our highwayman played the Scarecrow last night in order to help Grinsley?"

"Oh, where did you get *that* idea?"

"From your henchman, Mipps, of course. I get all my gossip from him."

"I am very fond of that old fellow, as you know, but I find that he can invent a piece of gossip with as great an ease as he can afterwards believe in it. For instance, he most firmly believes that poor old Mother Handaway, who is quite mad, has dealings with the devil."

"Then you think I should not take Mipps and his wild yarns too seriously?" she laughed.

"Certainly not. He is an old sea-dog. Very superstitious. As for his yarns—well, he loves spinning them. Now why should Mr. Jimmie Bone concern himself with trying to save Grinsley at the risk of his own neck?"

"Because he was the better adventurer," she answered promptly. "Just as you, being a greater adventurer than Mr. Bone, have risked a lot to save his life. I have a feeling that we are to hear more of this Scarecrow whoever he may be. Take it from me that his black horse will ride the Marsh just as the highwayman's will be seen again upon the roads."

"You will be adding another adventurous rascal to your romantic list soon," he laughed.

"You mean Clegg the pirate?"

Dr. Syn smiled and laughed. "He at least seems to have disappeared. My correspondents in America have now ceased to mention him."

"And it is a long time since you have spoken of him, too," she pouted. "You know how his adventures thrilled me when you first spoke of them to my father. Now when I want to talk of him I have to put my head close with Mr. Mipps."

"And what has Mipps to say of Clegg these days, my dear, for you may take it from me that the rascal is dead?"

Charlotte shook her head. "Only to the authorities. And I am glad he is dead to them."

"You are a strange, romantic girl, Charlotte," said Dr. Syn. "I wonder now why I was stupid enough to put Clegg into your birthday thoughts. The fellow is not worthy of such a place, I assure you."

"You know he is," replied Charlotte hotly. "Besides, it was not your remark of him that put him in my thoughts. It was this."

With her gloved hand she drew from the bosom of her riding-coat the red velvet sachet.

"Why that?" asked Dr. Syn.

"When you first gave it to me this morning, I wondered where I had seen it before," she replied steadily. "I knew that its colour was familiar. That it reminded me of something—and then I remembered. It was the colour worn by my romantic ghost."

"Ghost?" he repeated.

"On the night of your return, as I went to call Mrs. Lovell to Meg's bedside, I saw the vision of a romantic figure reflected in the pier glass of your room. The door of the powder closet was open, you see."

"That was nothing. It was my farewell to vanity. You see, I was not always a practising parson in America. I went there to seek revenge, God forgive me, and not to carry on God's work. That came later."

"You cut this, then, from that gay coat?"

"I did. Perhaps, Charlotte, I had better destroy the coat. It is in my sea-chest."

"It would be better," she answered simply. "I know now why you do not talk any more of the pirate Clegg."

Dr. Syn said nothing. She went on: "It was Mipps who talked to me about Clegg the other day. He most loyally described him as a thick-set man, but when I said that did not sound as romantic as one could wish, he cried out: 'Ah, but you should have seen him in battle, calmly stalking the poop deck in his red velvet, and the cannon balls flying round him as thick as the tattooings on his own arms and chest'."

Dr. Syn recognized the description as fitting his old enemy, Nick Tappitt, but he only sighed and said, "Ah, so the red velvet reminded you of Clegg, eh?"

"Doctor, when you are ready to tell me all your secrets, then

I shall be ready to marry you. I could protect you if I knew everything. And remember, I have added to my heroes the Scarecrow who saved the villagers last night."

"Your heroes?" he repeated.

"There are three of them now—Clegg the pirate, the Scarecrow smuggler, and Dr. Syn, the fighting preacher."

"Perhaps some day, Charlotte, I may be weak enough to tell you all."

"I shall wait till you do," she answered.

After that they rode in silence to the village.

CHAPTER X

THE GRIEVANCE OF MR. JIMMIE BONE

CAPTAIN FAUNCE was piqued. The fact that he had failed to arrest the highwayman was annoying, especially when he became convinced that the notorious Bone was also the mysterious Scarecrow by whose daring his prisoners had escaped from his guards.

Amongst others who believed in it was the Preventive Officer. For some time past he had had his suspicions that he could put his hand upon the highwayman, but he did not think it his duty to arrest him, since a gentleman of the road had nothing to do with the Customs. Moreover, he was not the man to earn a hundred guineas on a man's head. The man had a popular reputation amongst the poor, and were Jimmie Bone to be arrested on information received, it would be short shift for the informer.

This knowledge frightened Merry, and he told as much to Dr. Syn, who took such a serious view of it that he persuaded Merry to slip over into Sussex till Romney Marsh became safer. This plan suited Dr. Syn, for as he mentioned to Mipps: "There is enough to do regarding a certain business without that rascal hanging about the vicarage with his eyes open."

So Merry departed for Rye, and through a kindly recommendation from the vicar of Dymchurch, he was given odd jobs in the Mermaid Tavern.

It was after a particularly long day of parochial work that Dr. Syn insisted that Mipps should join him in his study for a drink, and it was while they were sitting in the dim candlelight that Mipps suddenly cocked his head towards the ceiling and began to sniff like a terrier.

"What's wrong?" whispered the doctor.

"Someone upstairs," replied Mipps. "I can smell a horsey sort of odour about the place. There's a creak going on now above deck."

"Very well, then, Mipps," whispered Syn, "we will satisfy ourselves. Pistols and upstairs."

They left the room quietly, Dr. Syn going first with a pistol in his hand. Through the hall and up the stairs he went, to his bedroom door, which he pushed open, stepping aside into the dark passage as he did so. Mipps waited on the other side of the door, also with his pistol ready.

"Whoever you are," said Dr. Syn quietly, "will you be good enough to show yourself? I may add there are two of us here, both armed, but purely in self-defence. We have no quarrel with anyone who is in trouble."

Dr. Syn saw the curtains of his four-poster stir by the open window.

"Who is with you?" demanded a voice.

"My sexton, Mr. Mipps," replied the doctor. "He's a man you may trust as myself. But he shoots as well as I do."

"Very well, then, there need be no shooting," the voice answered. "I have come to you for help. Where can we talk?"

"You will follow me downstairs to my study, and Mr. Mipps will follow you. Please come out, and consider yourself quite safe."

The shadow of a big man in a long overcoat crossed the window and came out of the door.

Dr. Syn took a quick look at him and smiled. "Ah, it is my old friend of the boxing ring, Mr. Bone. I trust you will honour us by having some of my excellent brandy." He put his pistol in his pocket, and walked down into the hall, followed by the highwayman. Mr. Mipps followed, but taking no chances, kept the stranger's back covered with his pistol.

In the candle-lighted study, Dr. Syn poured out three glasses of brandy. "You may remove your mask, Mr. Bone. I should like to see whether or no your jaw is recovered."

"And that's the devil of it, sir," replied Mr. Bone. "There's a scar upon it which bides well to keep me a close prisoner for some time, unless you come forward to release me. Work's work and play's play, you see. I work at night in a mask, but how can I pick up information by day, when I am not able to take it off? A man can hardly walk into a tavern and drink in this thing." And Mr. Bone removed his black mask and flung it down on the table in disgust.

Dr. Syn handed his guest a glass of brandy.

"You mean that certain parties are now looking for a gentleman who carries a scar on his jaw bone?"

"Aye, you have hit it, reverend sir, as surely as you hit my jaw," replied the highwayman ruefully. "Mind you, there's not the poorest man on this Marsh who'd betray me for a hundred guineas, except that rascal who rode off for the Dragoons, and he's disappeared to Rye, they tell me."

"Then what is it you fear, Mr. Bone?" asked Dr. Syn.

"The fact is, I have got that Preventive Officer on my track. He's after me because he says I'm the Scarecrow."

"And are you?" asked Mipps, looking very interested.

Mr. Bone favoured the sexton with a withering scowl.

"Yes, *are* you?" repeated Dr. Syn, as seriously.

"No, I am *not*," replied the highwayman, banging his fist on the table.

"Keep your voice down, sir," warned Mipps. "There's mice in the panelling here, and it's no use fidgeting 'em."

Mr. Bone scowled again at the facetious sexton and went on: "Why should I be hounded down for something I am not doing? The smugglers are keeping quiet at present, but it's common enough knowledge that this new leader is making great preparations. There's whisperings in many a tankard that goes echoing all over the Marsh, and inland, too, up in the hills. Now, I've come here for help. Maybe I know who this Scarecrow is, and, maybe I don't. If I do, as one adventurer salutes another, neither wild horses nor you two gentlemen could drag that information out of James Bone. I hope I know how to behave like a gentleman."

"A gentleman of the road, eh?" smiled Dr. Syn. "Well, Mr. Bone?"

"Well, Mr. Parson, it comes to this," went on the highwayman tersely. "I take it that there's no one who knows more about the Marsh folk than you. Doctor Syn, vicar of Dymchurch, has got the reputation of keeping folks' business to himself."

"My dear sir, that is merely one of the duties of a parson."

"Exactly. They tell me so," replied Bone. "Well now, if I can give a guess as to who this Scarecrow is, no doubt you can give a better, and that being so, what about getting this mysterious gentleman to free me from taking over his responsibilities?"

"I see your point, sir," replied Dr. Syn. "Whether I can help you or no remains to be seen. Have you any proposition to make?"

"I have. That evening when you set this mark on my face, you also saved my life. In so doing, you showed me a horse, a fierce black beast that I take to belong to my brother outlaw—this Scarecrow. Well, I likes the sound of this Scarecrow. He risked his neck to save them smugglers and he saved 'em just as surely as you saved me. That shows him to be a gentleman of spirit. He is the one man who could free me from this absurd rumour that I am the Scarecrow."

"And what could he do to free you?" asked Dr. Syn.

"Listen," continued the highwayman, "there's a rumour whispered that in ten days' time, which is the night of the full moon, there's to be a 'run'. Now, sir, I have a little job of my own upon that night. There's a coach journeying from the City of Westminster to this part of the coast, and it's going to be full of golden guineas for shipment to certain agents in France. It's bad enough to know that there's traitors in and around Whitehall who'll smuggle British gold to our old enemies, but what about Englishmen who are willing to arrange this matter and then turn traitors to their other traitors and rob both England and France of the lot?"

"And how do you figure in this transaction, Mr. Bone, may I ask?"

"Why, reverend sir, they gets me to do their dirty work, which they're afraid to do themselves. Mr. Bone, gentleman of the road, is to hold up the coach, and then he's to hand over the bulk of the money to these double traitors."

"And you do intend to carry this out?" asked Dr. Syn.

"All but the last clause, reverend sir. Possession being nine points of the outlaw's law, they can whistle for their money, just as the waiting French lugger can whistle for a wind to get 'em clear of our ships of war in the Channel."

"And how does the Scarecrow come into this shuffled counter-plot?"

"Why, reverend sir, like this," went on Mr. Bone. "I holds up the coach. I gets 'em to unload her. I gives the coach her marching orders, when just then up gallops the Scarecrow himself and on behalf of the Dymchurch smugglers he robs Mr. Bone and in sight of the others gives Mr. Bone his marching orders. Some of the Scarecrow's men remove the guineas to a place agreed, and we two then goes shares."

"And the story gets around that poor Mr. Bone has been robbed by the Scarecrow of his lawful, or rather unlawful, dues, eh? I see." Dr. Syn chuckled as he filled up the three glasses.

He then filled a churchwarden and lit it at one of the candles. As he stood watching the two men he drew briskly at the pipe, surrounding his head with clouds of tobacco smoke.

At length he broke silence.

"Mr. Bone, I will see what can be done for you. You will return to your 'hide' at Mother Handaway's, and there I will communicate with you as soon as I can make the necessary connection with this Scarecrow."

Dr. Syn paused, put down his pipe and slowly filled his own glass to the brim from the brandy bottle. He then raised it with the steadiest hand, passed it backwards and forwards beneath his nose with obvious appreciation of its aroma, and then looking first at Mipps and then at Mr. Bone, added:

"And if so be that this Scarecrow refuses to free you from your embarrassment—why, damme man, if I don't dress as the Scarecrow myself and rob you of those guineas." And he tossed off the brandy at a gulp.

"Good God," muttered Mipps, following his vicar's example and draining his own glass.

Mr. Bone held up his glass and said: "That is what I expected from the gallant gentleman who knocked me about and then saved me. But you can take this message to the Scarecrow, reverend sir. You can say that the authorities will never get information out of Mr. James Bone regarding any of his secrets; and you can add that should he ever be in need of a brave lieutenant to serve under him, Mr. Bone would not be found wanting."

He then drained his glass. Mr. Mipps took the liberty of filling them again—all three.

CHAPTER XI

THE RED-BEARDED BRIDEGROOM

IN spite of the dryness of his erudite sermons, Dr. Syn, in his capacity of Dean of the Peculiars, which gave him the privilege of periodically preaching in the magnificent parish church of Rye in the adjacent county of Sussex, had gained a considerable popularity in that town. Whenever he took the short journey across the Kentish ditch into Sussex, he would put up at the "Mermaid", and amidst the bustle of that great old inn he was ever a welcome guest, taking a lively interest in all, from the very exalted "mine host" down to the humblest kitchen wench. It was therefore not surprising that Merry, in spite of his forbidding personality, found himself readily enough employed upon presenting his credentials from Dr. Syn.

Amidst the fleeting population of the busy "Mermaid", he did well, but it was towards two permanent guests that he chiefly focused his attention and willingly gave a thousand little services.

These two men were something of a mystery to the townsfolk of Rye. Magnificently dressed in the modish fashion of London, with a deal of foreign swagger, and a prodigal disregard for money, with which they appeared to be possessed in plenty, they cut a brave figure.

Although adorned with much lace and finery, their faces and figures gave the lie to any accusation of foppery which in other men their dress would have proclaimed. They were both sufficiently independent from the prevalent fashion of exquisites to wear bearded chins. The shorter of the two, who called himself Colonel Delacourt, was obviously the leader. Stockily built, and tattooed like a South Sea islander, which showed towards evening when, merry with dice and drink, he would cast aside his gay velvet coat, undo his cravat, flowered waistcoat and silk shirt so that he showed his hairy, be-pictured chest, and he would call on his companion to cry the stakes. And the play was high. The two men presented a marked contrast, for Captain Vicosa, whom the colonel addressed as "Captain Vic", was a red-bearded giant—a great leonine-looking fellow with perhaps even more swagger than his black-bearded companion and patron.

To the tactful inquiries of mine host of the "Mermaid",

Colonel Delacourt gave out that he had made a fortune in the Indies, where he maintained he owned much home property in the plantations, and he introduced the red-bearded and handsome "Captain Vic" as his partner and manager, who had come to England with him to transact certain businesses connected with the Crown colonies.

Despite their fineries, the two men were excused from anything appertaining to the coxcomb. Men and women recognized and respected their obvious masculinity.

The reason of their enforced stay at the "Mermaid" was the fact that Madame Delacourt had given birth to a daughter upon the very night of their arrival, and although the child was doing well enough, the mother was rapidly sinking. The Rye doctor who attended her, although a married man, was not above saying that "Madame" at the "Mermaid", was the most beautiful woman he had ever seen. He described her to his friends as a Spanish Madonna, but he owned that he was going to be hard put to it to save her life. She was listless. She showed no affection for the baby girl, and the doctor suspected that she not only feared her husband but hated him.

His manner to her was loud and rude, and her enforced convalescence filled him with ungovernable irritation. And yet, strange to say, he showed great affection to the wee mite that lay smiling in the big drawer beside her bed. He would swing into the room when far advanced in drink, swear that the child was his, and catch it up against the protests of the woman whom the doctor had recommended to attend the baby, and carry it into the adjoining room, where he diced and drank with the red-bearded Captain Vic. He would twine the little fingers around the dice-box and help her to throw the dice against his companion, and cry out with joy at her cleverness when the score was thrown high.

One service only Merry resolutely refused to perform for them. They told him to ride to the Romney Marsh and find out and order to attend on them one Jimmie Bone, a highwayman, for whom they had employment.

Merry excused himself saying that it was more than his life was worth to undergo such a duty. He told them the story of his attempted betrayal of Mr. Bone, making himself out a most worthy citizen in that he wanted the high roads rid of such an outlaw.

The answer he got from Colonel Delacourt surprised him.

"Well, I am rejoiced that you failed, Mr. Merry. Your good citizenship, as you call it, may have lost you a hundred guineas, but I tell you we have need of Mr. Bone that is more valuable than such a paltry sum. So you refuse to be our go-between, eh?"

"I tell you, sir," whined Merry, "that if Mr. Bone meets me he'll pistol me without a tremor."

"That means you'll have to do it, Vic my lad," said the colonel, striding in a rage to the window which looked down upon the cobbled street. "You know enough of my history to be sure that I am not in the mood to ride Dymchurch way. The very sight of the Romney Marsh would drive me into the doldrums with my lady's everlasting regrets dinning in my ears."

All of which, at the moment, was Greek to Mr. Merry.

"I'll go if I must," growled Captain Vic, "but be damned to Merry for a cowardly knave, say I."

"No, no, Merry's a good servant to us, you must admit," went on the colonel, "and we'd never get our drinks so easy without him, seeing that all the chambermaids avoid us like the plague since you started kissin' 'em. Merry can't go—that's flat. Merry, give the captain a glass of brandy, and fill one for me."

Merry did as he was told, and at that moment they heard the rumble of wheels over the cobbles, the crack of postboys' whips and the stirring notes of a coach horn.

"More visitors, by God. Let's hope it's someone to dice with," cried the colonel, taking the glass of brandy from Merry's hand. "Fill a glass for yourself, Merry, and never mind what the captain says—he's drunk. There'll be no need for you to meet this Mr. Bone. We want no murder done any more than you."

As Merry proceeded to fill a glass for himself, the colonel gave a cry, which was followed by the noise of a smashed glass.

"What the devil's wrong with you?" growled Captain Vic, looking up at his patron with bleared eyes.

Colonel Delacourt had staggered back into the folds of the window curtain, and his glass of brandy lay shattered and unheeded at his feet.

"Good God," he muttered, and all the drink went out of his face, leaving him stark staring sober. In answer to the captain's repeated question, he but mumbled something unintelligible which brought the red-bearded one to his feet with an oath. He lurched across to the casement and peered out at the bustle of inn servants round the coach.

"There's only two passengers alighting," he said, "and I fail to see why they should upset a man of spirit. A doddering old parson and his shabby servant, I presume. A little cove with a ridiculous brass blunderbuss under his arm."

"Doddering parson be damned," gasped the colonel. "And the little cove too. Well I know them."

"*You're* drunk, or you'd have jumped to it by now."

"Who are they?" said Captain Vic to Merry. "Do you know 'em or don't you, since the colonel's daft?"

Merry had looked down at the little man in black who stood awaiting his master, who was collecting a paper case and some books from the inside of the old vehicle.

"I knows 'em too well," replied Merry. "And I wishes 'em both more ill-luck than I fear will come to 'em. That's Parson Syn of Dymchurch and his sexton, Mipps."

"Here, you don't mean——" began Captain Vic, swinging round on the colonel.

"I do," snapped the colonel. "Parson Syn be damned. It's Clegg, I tell you. Aye, and the little rat with the blunderbuss is his ship's carpenter—two of the bloodiest pirates that ever terrorized the sea, and my most mortal enemies."

"What did you say, sir?" asked Merry, hardly able to believe what had been said, and yet hoping there might be truth in it.

Whereupon, Colonel Delacourt, after bolting the door, recounted something of the terrors of Clegg, and how Clegg had followed him from sea to sea in order to get his revenge.

"And revenge for what?" exploded the colonel. "Why, for robbing him of the burden next door. He's welcome to her now, if he cares to relieve me of her. I mean my wife, Mr. Merry."

"Your wife? But was this parson sweet on her, sir?" he asked.

"Sweet?" repeated Delacourt. "He was married to her, you fool, and I, like a fool, carried her off. She's his wife now in the eyes of the law, not mine. But the child's mine. Illegitimate, but mine."

This news was getting better and better. Here was Dr. Syn's wife, in the possession of another man, true, but still Dr. Syn's wife.

"I told him she was dead, but even then he followed me," went on Colonel Delacourt.

So Dr. Syn did not know that his wife was living, and so near. Here was at least a means to strike shame to Charlotte Cobtree, and this pirate talk of Clegg—that would be sufficient weapon against the doctor. There was a bigger price on Clegg's head than on a hundred Jimmie Bones'. Clegg had fought the world. All manner of ships he had sunk, ships of all nations. Yes, Clegg was wanted internationally. Here indeed was the most glorious and unexpected revenge on a man he hated. Meg would be his yet, and he would strip those pearls from Charlotte Cobtree's neck to give to her.

"And how long will this damned fellow stay here?" asked the colonel. "I've a mind to slip my cable and leave a letter for him to call for his dying wife."

"You'll do nothing of the sort," growled Captain Vic. "Have you forgotten why we are employing this Mr. Bone?"

"I know I'll do nothing of the sort," replied Delacourt. "But not for that reason. I stay here because the child ain't fit to be taken from its mother yet—that's all."

"Well, praise to God you're crazy about the kid," said Captain Vic. "Otherwise, there's no telling but you'd be off if I gave you the chance."

"How long does he stay—this parson, and what's he here for?" asked the colonel of Merry.

Merry told him that he usually came by this—the Saturday—coach and stayed in the "Mermaid" till Monday. "He will preach a sermon tomorrow morning and will dine with the rector afterwards. He'll no doubt be supping out tonight as well, but he'll take a drink in the common bar and stand treat to all the fishermen. That's his way to popularity."

"Then we must lie low up here. We'll admit no one but the saw-bones, and that only to avoid him talking of us to Dr. Syn. Merry shall watch and fetch and carry for us. We're prisoners here till the fellow takes coach for Dymchurch on Monday."

Merry told them a good deal. The good brandy made him talkative. Besides, it was good to relieve his spleen against Dr. Syn to two men who shared a common hatred. Both colonel and captain dropped their attitude of masters to a servant. They clapped Merry down at the table, plied him with drink, and vowed they were all friends together, and as gentlemen they would take oath to hound Dr. Syn to his death. Merry, who gave them full details of the doctor's miraculous preservation from the wreck, was in favour of a public accusation against him as Clegg, but to this the colonel would not consent.

"We'll kill him first," he declared, "and accuse him after, so that his tongue cannot wag against me. As Colonel Delacourt I am safe enough, but as Nick Tappitt—well, there are things I have no wish to be made public. A gentleman does not care to do his washing in the High Courts. But we'll kill him, by God, and then see him hung in chains. And you, friend Merry, shall be in it with us."

Flattered by their friendliness, Merry went on to tell them of his passion for Meg Clouder, whom he described in such glowing terms, that although the colonel damned all women but his baby girl as plagues and nuisances, Captain Vic became so enthusiastic on Merry's behalf that he avowed he would win Meg for him.

"You're a morose sort of a devil," he declared, filling up Merry's glass, "and for all that I love you as a sworn brother in arms, I'd take my oath you'd never win a cow-girl, much less this beautiful young hostess you speak of. Now, I have a way with women of all classes and ages, as the colonel will bear me out. Many's the kicking filly, aye, and demure young miss, too, who has rued the day she let Captain Vic get away with her; and I'll tell you what I'll do. I'll marry the wench myself and then abandon her. You can then take her on the rebound if you've the manhood in you that I imagine. How's that?"

After a good deal of argument, for at first Colonel Delacourt did not relish staying in the same inn as his arch-enemy without his henchman, it was decided that Captain Vic should have a post-chaise and set off that very afternoon to Dymchurch. Meanwhile, Merry was to watch Dr. Syn as he came in and out, and the colonel was to lie low in his sitting-room, with as much drink as he needed supplied by the dutiful Merry.

"And you'll not take it unkindly of me, friend Merry," asked Captain Vic, when the post-chaise was at the door, "if I make love to this Meg of yours in good earnest?"

"You can do what you like with her," replied Merry. "There's no soft love about me I doubt whether there's love at all, for at times I hate her for upsetting me. Break her spirit, my captain, then throw her to me. So that I possess her at last—aye, and her inn, too—you can do your worst to her."

"The worst will be well for you," answered the captain. "For if she comes to hate me, why, she'll love you all the more for giving her protection."

"I wonder," growled Merry. "She hates me like hell, but that's all one, so that I get her."

"You shall have her, Mr. Merry; you can take Captain Vic's word for that."

So the red-bearded one departed, full of glee that he was escaping from the gloom of Madame Delacourt's sick-bed, and with the prospects of a diverting adventure at the end of his journey.

Just as the colonel was figuring that the post-chaise carrying Captain Vic would be nearly to Dymchurch, Merry announced the local physician. After an examination of his patient, he returned to the sitting-room, closing the bedroom door behind him. He looked more serious than usual, which was quite enough to enrage the colonel without the following pronouncement:

"Colonel Delacourt," he said, "your wife is sinking, and as far as I am concerned, her decline is unnecessary. Her body is well enough, allowing for her condition, but it is her mind that is wrong. She has not the will to exert her strength, and without that will, I am useless. Now, it happens, by the best of good fortune, that there is alighted at this inn a man of such high spirituality, and possessed of such charm of manner that where my poor eloquence has failed, he is one who might succeed. He is beloved by all who know him, and it is his mission in life to attend to the comforts of afflicted souls. I propose to bring this gentleman up to see your wife."

"Oh, you do, do you?" growled the colonel. "And who might the gentleman be that he can claim admittance to my lady's sick-room? A doctor?"

"Yes, a doctor," replied the physician gravely. "A learned doctor of divinity, but the broadest-minded man of his cloth that I have ever encountered. In short, it is Doctor Syn, vicar of a place called Dymchurch across the Kent border. He is below stairs now and will be delighted to take a glass of wine with you, so that you may be the better acquainted before he visits your poor wife. I will bring him up, with your permission."

"Which you will not get, my interfering doctor," growled the colonel. "My wife is a foreigner, and her religion has nothing to do with the Church of England, and the last person she would wish to see is this parson friend of yours."

"There, Colonel Dealcourt, I must contradict you," said the physician. "I spoke of this good man to your good lady, and as I spoke, I could see that her spirit seemed to burn with a new life. Let us go together to her now and ask if it is not her wish to see this Dr. Syn, since you will not take my word for it."

Colonel Delacourt staggered to his feet with his fists clenched.

"You may be a good physician, sir," he said, "but you must own that I have paid for your services up to date in good money. I trust that you will consider it your duty to continue your professional visits to my wife and daughter, just as I shall consider it my duty to pay your fees handsomely. But I do not desire spiritual advice from you or your friends, and I take it as an impertinence that you should propose introducing a stranger to my wife in her present state. Call tomorrow, sir, with your physics as usual, but let me have no more of this parson nonsense."

"She is your wife," returned the physician, "and on this point I must not go against your authority."

"I can promise you that," interrupted the colonel.

"But I must tell you that I like you the less for your decision," continued the doctor. "And one word more, and here I speak within my province, and if it offends you—blame yourself. Your friend has ridden off in a post-chaise. For long or short, I do not know and care less. But since you are alone, I command you to abstain from further liquor, and I presume you will not now consider it your duty to keep the night-owl awake with your cursed songs. Good afternoon."

"Oh, go to hell, and come tomorrow for your money," retorted the colonel.

Below stairs, in the handsomely appointed sitting-room which was always set aside for Dr. Syn, the physician found the Dymchurch parson receiving some of his many friends in Rye. Leading him aside, he told him of the colonel's objection to parsons, adding his opinion of husbands who can drink, gamble and sing ribald songs at the very threshold of their wives' sick-rooms.

"Add to that, sir, the fact that the wife wished to see you, and said your visit would be a great comfort to her, and yet this bully refused point-blank. I wish he had gone away with his companion, who, they tell me, has taken chaise for your Dymchurch."

"I wonder, now, why he has gone there? I must speak to Merry on the subject, and if necessary we will keep an eye upon this other offensive man."

"You'll not have difficulty in recognizing him," replied the physician. "I have never seen so conspicuous a man. His red beard flames like a furnace, and he carries two golden balls from his ear-lobes that put one in mind of a pawnbroker's sign. A flashy, handsome, swaggering braggart if ever there was one."

And in the meantime, the gentleman under discussion had arrived at Dymchurch and entered the cosy bar of The City of London Inn. To say that such a magnificent specimen of a man lifted poor Meg off her feet is but to state a literal truth, for, after treating the usual following in the bar with as much drink as they could carry and presenting each villager with a guinea when Meg was not looking, to leave him a clear coast for his wooing, he lifted Meg right over the drinking counter and carried her out like a baby on to the sea-wall. crying in one breath to the pot-boy to mind the custom, and in the next declaring his undying passion for the girl in his arms.

The tide was far out and the setting sun reflecting the golden light of the sands caused the beard of Captain Vic to sparkle red. Meg thought she had never seen such a glorious man, never encountered such colossal strength.

With a cry of joy, Captain Vic raced along the deserted beach laughing at the bewildered face against his shoulder. When he had run far from the village, he sat himself down against a breakwater, with Meg still in his arms who, woman-like, protested that he would soil his fine velvet coat if he leaned against the tarred and seaweed-covered wood.

Captain Vic assured her that he had a score of coats every bit as fine hanging up in his wardrobe at the "Mermaid" in Rye, and that failing those there were a score of fashionable London tailors who were pestering him to order more. He kept vowing that he loved her, that he had never loved before, and that when he had heard of her beauty that very day, he had known she was the right wife for him and had set off immediately to claim her.

When she heard that it was Merry who had raved about her, she trembled with fear and told her impetuous lover of her dread. He assured her that she need have no fear of any man while he lived to protect her, and he went on in the most gentlemanly fashion to tell her the arrangements he was about to make for their immediate wedding.

"Whether we live on for a time at your inn or take ship to my vast plantations in the Indies, is for you to decide, my Meg," he added. "Naturally, I will not sleep at your inn, but will take rooms at the 'Ship', for everything must be above board for the sake of your sweet reputation. But on Monday I will ride into Hythe, take out a special licence from the magistrate and then we will be married quietly and return in the evening as man and wife and confront this village with our happiness.

Meg protested against such a hurry, but she owned that the sudden romance of it appealed to her. Whereupon, Captain Vic kissed her heartily and told her the affair was settled.

On the whole, Meg was not averse to being married quietly at Hythe, for she was afraid of the opinion of the Dymchurch folk who had loved her husband. She was not at all easy in her mind, however, in taking such a serious step without consultation with Dr. Syn, but this was impossible since the reverend gentleman had taken the opportunity of his journey to Rye to pay a number of visits to certain of the clergy in that district, keeping with him the redoubtable Mipps as his body-servant, who also took opportunity at each place to pass word from the Scarecrow concerning the arrangements for the mightiest "run" ever undertaken by the smugglers.

Meg was anxious to take Charlotte Cobtree into her confidence, but Captain Vic, after some argument, persuaded her against this, saying that since Meg was so young a widow it was more seemly not to announce her second marriage till it was an established fact.

"Besides," he added, "it will only seem that you are telling her in order to conjure rich presents out of the squire's family, and since I can give you money to play ducks and drakes with, we will buy all you want ourselves and make you feel the more independent."

Thus it was that Meg and Captain Vic departed one morning by special coach to Hythe without a word to anyone as to their purpose, and returned to "The City of London" as man and wife.

CHAPTER XII

THE BEACON ON ALDINGTON KNOLL

THE evening that Dr. Syn returned from his profitable little tour over the Sussex border, he dined with the Cobtrees, in order, as he put it, to learn all the gossip of Dymchurch since he had been absent.

"Well, Doctor, the most extraordinary news is this," said the squire. "This daughter of mine here, this Charlotte, has at last, and in your absence, chosen her twenty-first birthday present from me, and you'll never guess what it is. You see, Doctor, like all the other romantic misses of the neighbourhood, she has thought fit to admire this mysterious Scarecrow, because he saved the necks of a number of Dymchurch lads. Now, although her Sirius is accounted one of the best hunters on the Marsh, she must now have a black horse too. Why? Oh, because the Scarecrow rode a black horse, if you please. Well, I tell her, so did the murderer Grinsley."

"And so did Mr. Bone the highwayman," added Dr. Syn, laughing across the table at Charlotte.

"Oh, and another thing concerning which I have not yet arrived at the truth. Our Meg Clouder has gone off to Hythe only yesterday and returned married, if you please—married to some captain who lays claim to be a gentleman, but who has returned to take up his married quarters in "The City of London". It infuriates me to think of it, and I shall most certainly have something to say to our Meg."

"She must have been very lonely there, you know, Squire ——" began Dr. Syn.

But the squire cut him short with: "Oh, you will always find excuse for everyone, Doctor, but why couldn't the jade let us into the secret? Our Charlotte called in yester evening to take her a shawl she had worked for her, and it was: 'Oh, Miss Charlotte, what do you think I have been and done? You will not be cross with me? You will not let squire be angry?' Squire angry, if you please, as though I was a bad-tempered curmudgeon. 'But I've been and got married,' she says, 'and oh, Miss Charlotte, he's a gentleman in fine clothes and rolling in guineas'."

"Whereupon," added Charlotte, "out there steps the bravest looking gentleman, tall, well dressed and handsome, with the largest red beard you ever saw. I should not have been surprised had he announced that he was Clegg the pirate."

"Instead of Captain Vicosa, known as Captain Vic, eh?" added Dr. Syn. "For I take it that in these clean-shaven days there are not two handsome adventurers with red beards in the neighbourhood, and I heard tell of such a man at the Mermaid Inn last week. I wondered why the rascal set off so briskly for Dymchurch in a hired chaise."

"You say 'adventurer' and 'rascal'," said the squire. "Do you know anything about him, then?"

"Nothing at all," replied Dr. Syn, "except that his companion, who appears to be a most undesirable colonel, has adopted that rogue Merry as his particular satellite. No doubt this Captain Vic, as they call him, heard of Meg through that very rogue."

"Well, we will keep an eye on him, whoever he may be," said the squire. "Let us hope for Meg's sake, that he is not so bad after all."

After telling the squire all he had heard from the Rye physician concerning the visitors at the "Mermaid", Dr. Syn took it upon himself to visit "The City of London", where he discovered Meg's husband already far gone in liquor, and brow-beating not only his pretty wife but everyone else in the bar-parlour.

Upon Dr. Syn refusing to accept a drink with such a bully, Captain Vic flew into a rage and damned all parsons in good round terms, which brought tears of shame into poor Meg's eyes. The vicar, however, stood a round of drinks to the men in the bar and proposed Meg's health and happiness; and when Captain Vic with an oath told him not to be high-handed in his bar, the doctor turned on him, saying calmly but sternly:

"I must point out to you, Captain Vic, if that is what you are pleased to call yourself, that this girl whom you have married so hurriedly, is well beloved by every one of us here in Dymchurch, and for her sake you will do well to behave with the civility which we have been accustomed to receive in this inn—an inn, let me add, that has been re-built by loving hands who wished to show their appreciation of Meg and her gallant husband, who gave his life that others might live."

"Gave his life for *you*, you mean," retorted Captain Vic. "I heard that you were the sole survivor."

"Perfectly true," replied Dr. Syn, "but had Abel Clouder had his way, he would have saved the whole ship's company. Being the sole survivor, however, makes it all the more my duty to see that Abel's young widow is happy, and to that end I expect you to help me, or you may find that we can force you to this duty."

And to a chorus of approval from the other men in the bar, Dr. Syn walked briskly back to the vicarage.

Here, to a late hour, he sat with Mipps, a large surveying map of Romney Marsh spread out before them, over which they pored, for all the world like two commanders planning a mighty battle. When the various dispositions of men, horses and pack ponies had been settled, Dr. Syn produced the brandy bottle, and pledged success to the greatest "run" ever planned in the history of the Marsh smugglers.

"And if your leaders carry out these orders to the letter, I can see no flaw in the campaign, my good Master Carpenter. And now for the greatest surprise of all. We have, as you know, allowed Captain Faunce and his Dragoons to know that these preparations are being made for the night of the full moon."

"Aye, sir," interrupted Mipps, "and I still fail to see why we had to let 'em know. No doubt you have some good reason."

"The very best of reasons, my good Mipps," went on the vicar. "It is essential that the Dragoons, or at least a few of them, should be witnesses of the robbing of that coach. In order to establish the fact that Jimmie Bone is not the Scarecrow, they must see the Scarecrow rob the highwayman."

Mipps nodded and scratched his impertinent-looking nose. "We seem to be doing a good deal for this fellow, Bone, don't we, sir?"

"He will have his uses later, believe me," replied Syn. "Your rumours about the Scarecrow put him into an awkward fix, and it pleases me to extricate him, so upon that night nothing must go wrong, and nothing left to chance. That is why, like a wise stage manager of a playhouse, I have called out the men three nights before the 'run' to rehearse in full detail. We shall accomplish two 'runs' instead of one, that is all, and the Marsh men's profits will be doubled."

Mipps grinned. "And both nights is to go forward on the same plan, eh, sir?"

"There is only one difference," replied Syn. "On the first night it will be necessary for you and me to command the beach, and when the pack ponies leave the hills, the Upton brothers will fire the great beacon from Aldington Knoll, which will bring the luggers in shore. But on the second night, I shall leave you in command of the beach, and no one but the Scarecrow himself must fire the beacon."

Mr. Mipps pulled a long face. "I must say, sir, that in a big affair like this 'ere, I prefers to ride at your side. Is this alteration absolutely necessary?"

"Of course it is," replied Syn. "However careful these guinea runners may be with their preparations, as Mr. Bone has wisely pointed out, one must allow for delays with post horses, and until that coach arrives and puts on its skids at the top of Quarry Hill, Mr. Bone cannot hold it up, and until Mr. Bone holds it up and gets the sacks of guineas out on to the high bank on the right side of the hill going down, the Scarecrow will be powerless to rob him. Just as soon as this happens and the guineas are safely removed by the Scarecrow's men, why then the Scarecrow will gallop to Aldington hell for leather and fire the beacon. See?"

"I see, sir—but——"

"No 'buts', Master Carpenter. Orders are orders," snapped Syn.

"Yessir. Orders is orders, and 'ere's my best respec's," replied Mipps, draining his glass.

"And don't forget to keep that red-headed bridegroom of poor Meg's under your spy-glass. Remember, he is one of these double-dealing guinea runners that are employing our friend Bone."

"By the way, Mipps, I notice that you are wearing your Sunday suit these days. I am glad to know that you have discarded your old coat, and I shall be glad to provide you with a new suit if you will order it. We must have you smart and ship-shape for your Sunday duty."

"The new suit is ordered and paid for, sir," replied Mipps. "I gets two guineas for that torn old suit of mine. We knows that women has strange notions sometimes, but Miss Charlotte wanting my old black suit what was going green, and being willin' to give two guineas for it fair give me a shock. Told me not to tell no one, but I tells my commander, of course."

"So she wanted your old suit, did she?" asked Syn, thinking seriously.

"And what do you think she wanted it for?" went on the sexton. "Why, to put it in the copper and give it a baking, just as we did aboard the *Imogene* when we run into that plague of lice. Remember?"

"So she put your old suit into the boiler, did she? That's very interesting."

"I thought it was rather silly," replied Mipps. "It wasn't as dirty as all that. And what she wanted my old suit for and give two guineas for it beats me."

But Dr. Syn was thinking of her new black horse, and the two purchases began to find connection in his mind. For many minutes Mipps watched his master closely, not daring to move in case he interrupted the train of thought.

At last Dr. Syn jerked himself out of his reverie.

"I was thinking, Mipps, I was thinking."

"Never seen you look so serious since the time you marooned that 'orrible mulatto on the coral reef," said Mipps.

"Ay," exclaimed the doctor. "We have seen things. We have seen things."

"That we has," returned Mipps. "The glimpse I got of that red-bearded scoundrel of Meg's put me in mind of something. Remember a night a few years back in Jamaica when you was dining with a rich planter?"

Syn nodded. "We sold him a cargo of goods, and I went to collect the money. He told the authorities who I was, and if you and the lads hadn't fired the house, I might not be here today."

"Oh, he hadn't caught you. You've got out of worse traps than that without help."

"Maybe, but you saved me nevertheless," returned Syn. "But what put that in your mind? Meg's husband, did you say?"

"Aye, sir. That there planter had red hair, and I never sailed yet with a red-haired man that I've took to. Something unnatural about red hair in a man, I says."

"He was a tall handsome fellow, too, was that planter," added Syn.

It was Mipps' turn to nod. "Bit queer if it was the same, only growed a beard, for I tell you, I don't like the sound of this Captain Vic."

"It would be very queer, Mipps," replied Syn thoughtfully.

CHAPTER XIII

"DEATH TO THE SCARECROW"

NEITHER Captain Faunce nor the Dymchurch Preventive Officer were the men to ignore the information they had gleaned about the Scarecrows' proposed "run" on the night of the full moon, and three days before, the village looked on with secret misgivings at the arrival of Colonel Troubridge, who had personally led a full squadron of Dragoons from Dover Castle, to augment the little force already commanded by Captain Faunce.

They commandeered the big field that lay between the sea-wall and the Ship Inn, and here they set up camp, while Dr. Syn was inspecting Charlotte Cobtree's new black hunter in the squire's stables.

"And will you tell me, Charlotte, why you have not only bought this glorious animal when I know you were more than satisfied with Sirius, but also why you purchased for two guineas that old suit of poor Mipps? For I believe I see the semblance of a connection between the two purchases."

"And that semblance is?" she asked.

"Why, the Scarecrow," he replied. "The ragged black suit, and the magnificent black horse."

"How clever you are, Doctor," she answered. "Yes, you are quite right, but I trust you will keep my confession and your guess to yourself. If this Scarecrow will not tell me who he is, I am curious enough to take the pains of finding him out. You remember he is one of my heroes. He, and Clegg and yourself. Perhaps I may even have the privilege of helping the smugglers as the Scarecrow did. At all events, I'll satisfy my woman's curiosity. There is, at least, one who can ride safely on the Marsh at night—the Scarecrow. Well, I have the horse and I have the clothes, too. If the Scarecrow cannot trust me and say 'I am the Scarecrow', why, I can ride out as he does until I can say: 'Ah, so you are the Scarecrow'."

"I beg of you, Charlotte, not to undertake any such mad adventure," said Dr. Syn sternly. "You don't realize your danger."

"My dear Doctor, when you ask me to marry you, why, then I promise you I will mend my ways, but till then I must do as I think best."

"If I could ask you, you know that I would," he answered. "But for you and your future, I can still be unselfish, I pray God."

"Honourable men are so often most selfish in their very unselfishness," she answered.

He might then and there have demanded an explanation. He might even have made the confession that had been in his heart to make to her for some time, but the squire joined them, full of indignation that the Dragoons had been so greatly increased in numbers.

"I'll not brook this interference from the Dover military while I am magistrate upon the Marsh," he cried. "Captain Faunce is a nice enough fellow, I admit. His behaviour has always been most respectful towards me as Lord of the Level, but this colonel is as red in his temper as his face. I could find it in my heart to wish that this Scarecrow fellow would give him a good fooling."

"I shouldn't be at all surprised if he does, Father," said Charlotte, with a mischievous glance at Dr. Syn.

"I shouldn't be at all surprised either, my dear," replied the doctor solemnly.

The worthy squire would have been very much surprised had he read what was passing in his vicar's brain. And sure enough, the "fooling" that the squire wished for took place that very night.

Since there were three nights before the full moon, and the proposed "run", Colonel Troubridge thought it highly strategic on his part to allow most of the men village leave till eleven o'clock, and they were all instructed to keep their ears open for any information that might be dropped from garrulous villagers in the bars. But Mr. Mipps was equally strategic, and he trotted from bar to bar and back again, the picture of injured innocence in the eyes of the troopers, but seeing to it very ably that the villagers kept their mouths shut.

Certain hints about the full moon "run" he allowed to get about, but no one gave away the important fact that thousands of barrels were only awaiting the signal from Aldington to be landed on Jesson Beach and carried to the hills for hiding.

The Upton brothers had been instructed to stand by their beacon after "lanterns out" had been sounded by the Dragoon trumpeters. Then they were to wait two hours by Monty Upton's great turnip watch, which could be relied upon, and then the beacon was to be fired.

An hour and a half of this allotted time had gone. The Marsh lay black and ominous; a vast stretch of mystery and dark horror to the Dragoon sentry who stood guard upon the sea-wall·

And then suddenly the Marsh changed. With a suddenness he had not expected, the moon came up over the Channel. It flooded the Marsh in its eerie light. He could see the black shadows of the dyke hollows. Were there corpses there? It was easy to imagine so in that still silence. He did not know that those dykes were filled with crouching, waiting men. It spoke well for the Scarecrow's preparation that the sentry thought he had never seen a vast track of land so desolate. So destitute of life. If only he could just see one living man. He did not know that his eyes were travelling over hundreds of hidden heads.

He turned to the sea for comfort. He looked first in the direction of Folkestone and the increasing moonlight showed him a sight that made him gasp. A lugger had been run ashore some two hundred yards away. There were men sitting upon barrels. They had their backs to him, for they were facing the lugger and a man who leaned against the mast with one hand steadying himself in the rigging.

What were the orders for the Regiment? "And any rank meeting with a man dressed as a scarecrow may shoot to kill. Death to the Scarecrow."

The sentry forgot this terror of the sexton's yarn as he dropped down behind the sand-hill that crowned the sea-wall. He was shaking with excitement. The man standing on the lugger was obviously dressed as a scarecrow. He sighted his carbine upon the Scarecrow's chest. He must wait till he could keep his sight steadier. Damn that sexton whose story had made him jumpy.

As he dropped, the sexton whom he had already damned, slithered upon his stomach immediately behind him and wriggled down the slope of the sea-wall. With the silence and skill of a Red Indian from whom he had learned much, Mr. Mipps, a sharp knife in his teeth, crawled towards the horse lines guarded by the two drunken and sleepy Dragoons.

Along the lines he crawled, noiselessly severing the picketing ropes.

The sentry took his time, steadying his aim. "Death to the Scarecrow". Well, he must not, would not miss; and behind him crouched two fantastically dressed men with their faces smeared with tar, waiting for him to shoot. But the sentry took his time. It was not pleasant to kill a man in cold blood. And yet orders protected him. The blame would not be his. He wished to kill and yet he wavered, and in the interim he slowly steadied his aim.

Behind him, under the shadow of the sea-wall, Mipps crawled

silently and went on with his cutting. To two horses out of every three he gave unconscious freedom.

Suddenly one horse stampeded down the lines.

" 'Ware horse," cried an awakened guard.

The noise acted upon the nerves of the sentry's slowly squeezing finger. With a sharp crack his carbine fired.

Immediately there arose pandemonium from the sleeping camp. The sentry heard it for a few seconds only, for a heavy weight seemed to drop upon him from the sky. He was bound round the legs and arms with cord. He was lifted by two strong and dreadful-looking men. They swung him backwards and forwards and then he was flung out from the sea-wall down upon the sand beneath. As he went through the air he remembered that the man who had been his target had fallen forward over the bulwarks of the lugger. He had fired and hit. Had he killed the Scarecrow, and would the smugglers now seek full retribution? Heavy in cuirass and helmet, he fell hard, and for a time remembered no more.

In the awakened camp everything was in wild disorder. The majority of the horses which had been freed by Mipps stampeded past the Ship Inn and out upon the high road, where they were goaded into a full stretch gallop by a dozen or so of wildly caparisoned horsemen, who, in fantastic costume and waving lighted jack-o'-lanterns above their heads, encouraged the frightened horses to make their escape, with wild yells and howlings.

The remaining horses added even more to the camp's discomfiture, for dragging the damaged lines and pegs behind them they galloped this way and that, became entangled in tent ropes, and upset the piled stacks of carbines. Men awoke into a cursing confusion. The colonel, in night attire, shrieked and swore and shouted for Captain Faunce to turn out the guard.

"Stand to your horses, you fools," he roared.

But there were no horses that his men could stand to. They were a struggling mass of entangled rage—those that were left, and already two-thirds of the fine animals were heading in wild stampede towards Hythe.

Swearing as became a colonel of Dragoons, he pulled on breeches and boots, jammed his brass helmet on the top of his tassled nightcap and buckled on his sabre over his white flapping shirt.

In this incongruous costume he dashed out of his tent.

The sight which now met his infuriated gaze would have been

enough to irritate a saint, much less a roaring Dragoon. Tents were collapsing on all sides, smothering men in a writhing mass. The canvas of his own tent was being ripped by the lashing hoofs of an entangled charger, while such of his men who were in the open were rushing this way and that, some to save their own skins, and others more dutifully trying to catch the maddened animals.

It was then that a strange apparition galloped at full speed through the camp. A snorting black horse on whose back sat the fearsome figure of a man dressed as a scarecrow.

With dreadful cries of "Over, Gehenna", which seemed to lift the great animal over such embarrassments as piled saddlery and accoutrements, the figure passed within a few yards of the colonel's swaying tent. Turning in his bare-backed seat as he passed, he laughed derisively in the colonel's face, and in bravado fired off a pistol above his head.

"Catch him. Kill him," shouted the colonel, drawing his sabre and rushing after the galloping horse. "Death to the Scarecrow. A hundred guineas to the man who brings him down."

But the Scarecrow had gone through the camp like a great black thunderbolt, and with a piece of incredible riding dashed straight up the steep bank of the sea-wall.

A few stray shots were fired, but they were wild and went whistling out to sea. "Get me a horse. Get me any horse, and I'll ride him down myself," yelled the colonel, running at top speed for the sea-wall.

High above him sat the laughing Scarecrow, checking his horse to enjoy the confusion, but when the sweating colonel was half-way up the bank, he turned his horse towards the stone groyne, rode down it and galloped away over the hard sand towards Jesson.

"Bring me a horse and I'll catch him yet," shouted the colonel. "Where's the sentry? What the hell was he doing?"

The sentry in question was by now sufficiently recovered from his fall to move. The sound of his colonel's voice brought him back to his wits. He cried out from the sands: "I've shot the Scarecrow And the others are too scared to move. There, sir. There."

The colonel peered down at the huddled sentry who was struggling to free himself of his cords, and then he saw the group a hundred yards away.

"There they are, some of 'em. Come on, men. We'll capture them, and the lugger. Look, smuggled goods, too! Forward, my men. Come on."

Followed by some half-dozen half-dressed Dragoons, the gallant colonel climbed down the steps cut in the sea-wall and with drawn sabre ran towards the group of smugglers.

"Surrender, damn you," he shouted. "You're under arrest. You'll all swing. Hands up."

Exasperated that not one of the sitting men deigned to move, he delivered a resounding smack with the flat of his sabre against the back of the nearest smuggler, who just lopped forward and fell face downwards on the moon-bathed beach.

"Hi—you," he shouted—and then added in a hoarse whisper: "What the hell?"

Hell indeed—for so gallant a colonel to hear the laughter of six of his troopers when the laugh had been raised against the said colonel.

The six smugglers and their leader who was lolling over the bulwarks of the lugger by reason of the good shooting of the sentry, were but effigies. Dummies of straw-filled clothes. And the barrels on which they sat were not dummies. Six barrels of excellent liquor. Smuggled liquor from France, and chalked around their hoops, the following messages: "To our gallant Dragoons from the Scarecrow. Drink, tomorrow we die. Drink, boys, to the Scarecrow and his Nightriders". And then on two brandy kegs inside the lugger: "With respexs to Colonel Troubridge" on one, and "For our gallant Captain Faunce" on the other.

"Take this stuff to camp," said the colonel. "And in it we'll drink damnation to this impertinent fellow. Then mount what men we can and ride with me. We'll drink to him as he swings on a local gallows."

"Look, sir," whispered one of the troopers.

The colonel looked and swore a mighty oath.

A huge beacon burned on Aldington Knoll. From its base and right across the Marsh were "flashers" signalling. The flying black horse of the Scarecrow was approaching Jesson Beach, which, in place of its desertion a minute before, now literally swarmed with men. The colonel estimated that there would be at least two hundred on the beach alone, but more irritating still was the object of their watch. Under full sail and driving in with perfect formation was a fleet of some twenty boats, luggers and smacks. The organization was perfect. The men on the beach divided into groups and waded out into the sea, waist high, to meet the grounding fleet.

The colonel shouted for horses (for he had every intention of attacking this superior force, though he guessed they would be armed to the teeth). He compared the confusion of his own camp with the strict precision and organized methods of the Scarecrow, and his shame only drove him into a greater fury. Waving his sabre, they set off hell-for-leather through the straggling village street and out on to the winding Marsh road, hoping to cut in inland and arrest the procession of pack ponies making for the cover of the hills.

To make matters more difficult, the yokel who had been pressed for the services of guide was either a knave or a fool, for the troop began to realize that they were riding in circles; so on the advice of the colour sergeant, the officers agreed to tie the yokel to a five-barred gate, and with the promise of a sound thrashing on their return, the colonel left the roads to their exasperating windings and led his men across country in the direction of the knoll.

The yokel, who was no fool, watched them blundering into the wreaths of mist that arose along the many intersecting dykes, and listening to their splashes and curses, he grinned for his own satisfaction. When he considered that the soldiers were too far off to bother further about him, he let out at the top of his voice three piercing screams like a screech-owl, which, had the Dragoons only known, had been the sexton's instructions to him, when he could no longer delay the Dragoons' attack.

But there was nothing to attack. By the time they reached the hills and climbed up the ridge that swept along to the Knoll, they could see nothing moving on the Marsh beneath, but the fleet were already far out in the Bay and tacking for Dungeness.

When they scoured the Knoll for hidden men, they found nothing but one keg of brandy, standing beside the dying beacon. The message in chalk around its sides did not improve the colonel's temper. "A noggin for all ranks prevents Marsh colds. Scarecrow."

They took his advice. They broached the keg upon the spot and served the noggins round, and then dejectedly rode back to give the yokel his hiding.

But they never found him. There were too many five-barred gates upon the Marsh, and too many twists to the Marsh road, and at every gate encountered, opinion was divided as to whether it was the gate in question or whether it would have been possible for the yokel to have slipped his cords and vanished.

It never occurred to them that the Scarecrow's watchers had covered the whole Marsh and that within a few minutes of those cries from the screech owl, a smuggler had crawled out of a handy dyke and set his colleague, the yokel, free.

The success of this "run", with the enormous profits which it entailed, added to the discomfiture of the military, and the heroic reputation of the mysterious Scarecrow.

For the next two days Colonel Troubridge raved and swore; blustered and quarrelled with the squire, and was eventually only calmed down by the tact and persuasiveness of Dr. Syn, who came forward with the only practical suggestion of dealing with the Scarecrow.

"Since the good name of Romney Marsh is at stake," he declared, "I intend to preach from my pulpit this very Sunday upon Law and Order, and I am going to make an appeal for volunteers who will help your good fellows to rout out this Scarecrow and discover the 'hides' into which the contraband must have been placed."

Sunday was the eve of the full moon, and the morning service was packed to the doors. With great eloquence the doctor appealed to all good men and true to stand by the Law, and as the congregation filed out after the service, names were taken by the sexton of all those who would help either in supplying horses, arms, or other support.

To each man who was enrolled in this band of volunteers was presented a white armlet to be worn on the sword arm, and on that very Sunday evening Dr. Syn rode out upon his white pony to review a hundred and fifty Dymchurch men who had answered to the call. This astonishing response was due to the fact that Mipps passed the word from the Scarecrow himself that every smuggler was to wear the armlet of Dr. Syn. In short, they were to run with the hare and hunt with the hounds.

Colonel Troubridge was impressed. He admired the quiet way in which the vicar handled the difficult situation. It was an honest effort to regain the good name of the district.

This ill-assorted regiment of civilians was divided into three parties of fifty strong and by a general vote each party was commanded by one of the three Upton brothers respectively.

They were a good and obvious choice, for each brother possessed the necessary swagger to carry things off, and their popularity with the women and girls of the neighbourhood added to the general enthusiasm for recruiting.

This voting had also been assured by special orders of the Scarecrow, and although many of those grim-faced farmers felt a meanness in thus working against their good vicar, the profits which they had already received from the Scarecrow easily

E

bought their disloyalty to Dr. Syn and their loyalty to their capable and mysterious leader.

Not so the Uptons. They were better informed than most, and they realized that what Dr. Syn did, his cloth compelled him to, and they more than suspected that the reverend gentleman would be very grieved did his measures help to bring "Death to the Scarecrow". Besides this, they always took the side which promised adventure, and there was no doubt about adventuring when serving the Scarecrow. So they obeyed his orders, pretending to obey the vicar's, but well aware that if the Scarecrow escaped capture no one would be more relieved than the sympathetic Dr. Syn.

But the doctor was in full agreement with the squire for causing broadsheets to be printed with "Death to the Scarecrow" set out in bold type. The belief that the wanted man was none other than James Bone, the notorious highwayman, was printed beneath this heading and called upon any who possessed information which would lead to his capture to lay it at the Court House.

"Death to the Scarecrow." The rhythm ran in Mipps' head that Sunday night and communicated itself to his hammer as he hit in the nails which formed the name on the lid of a fastened coffin.

"Death to the Scarecrow," said Mrs. Waggetts, as she watched him perform this sad operation, for the coffin contained the landlord of the Ship Inn. Slowly sinking, he had passed away during the stampede of the Dragoons, and Mrs. Waggetts blamed the Scarecrow in her grief.

"Death to the Scarecrow." Captain Vic kept reading it from the broadsheet stuck on the wall in Meg's bar-parlour, and he set out on horse-back to see his colleague, Colonel Delacourt, at Rye. He had a good deal to discuss with the colonel, for not always having been as drunk as he looked, he had listened to whisperings that had gone on in the bar, and he knew very well that Jimmie Bone was not the Scarecrow. Indeed, he had hit upon a theory which he was anxious to convey to his colleague. Dr. Syn was Clegg. There was no doubt about that. He knew it, and so did the colonel. But what if Clegg were the Scarecrow? A man of brains and a man of courage and quick invention, safely hidden under the parson's cloth. The more he thought of it, the more certain he believed it to be true.

He found the colonel sober enough, but irritable. His wife, while sinking slowly, had kept asking her husband to allow her a visit from Dr. Syn. She was desirous of making her peace before dying.

"She don't seem to see my danger," scowled the colonel. "Should this scoundrelly parson set eyes on me—well, it's one or both of us."

"Get me a bottle of wine and I'll set your heart at ease on that score," laughed Captain Vic.

Merry was sent for, and wine was brought.

"Come, Merry," he laughed, clapping him on the back, "you shall sit down with us, for I owe you a good drink. I have married your Meg, and I ain't giving her up to you yet a bit. All depends on how friend Bone succeeds tomorrow. If he's caught and splits, we may well have to run for it, and if so I ain't showing my face for any woman in a run like that. In which case, she's yours. If Bone succeeds though, well, she's yours when I tire of her."

"Oh, so you'll run, will you?" scowled the colonel. "And what about me?"

"Why, you'll run too, my buck," replied Captain Vic. "If your wife won't mend and won't die, you must leave the obstinate baggage."

"But the child! I'll not leave the child."

Captain Vic tilted himself back in his chair and laughed at the ceiling. "A couple of bearded bucks running round the country with a baby. That would be a fine sight! No, you'll leave it with the woman here. She'll be glad of the good pay you'll give her. As to your dying madame, why not return the property you stole from Dr. Syn, eh? From what Merry tells me, he's sweet on that pretty piece of baggage, the squire's daughter. He can hardly marry her with his wife alive."

"He could divorce her, fool. God knows he has cause," replied the colonel. "Besides, I've no wish to identify Colonel Delacourt with Nick Tappitt."

"Nor shall you, my buck, for I tell you we're talking round the mulberry bush, and things is going to happen very different from what you think. First, give me a sheet of paper, for I have need to send a letter to this baggage, Charlotte Cobtree."

"What about?" asked the colonel. "We've got to go carefully, my friend, or we'll have Clegg on our track."

"Say rather, he'll have us on his," replied Captain Vic.

"You know something," said the colonel.

"I do," nodded Captain Vic.

"What is it? Lay your cards on the table, for God's sake."

"There you are, then." Captain Vic produced a paper from his side pocket and slammed it down upon the table.

The colonel grabbed it, while Merry stood up, the better to see. They read it together.

"Death to the Scarecrow."

"Now don't imagine that I've done nothing but make love to Merry's Meg, or rather to my legal wife, as I should say. No, colonel. I've listened, and I've got Meg to listen, too. She's mad about me, and does whatever I tell her. Aye, no one can say that Captain Vic hasn't a way with the women. Tomorrow night this Scarecrow is going to 'run' again. Colonel Troubridge of the Dragoons maintains he will not dare. The squire agrees with him, so does Dr. Syn and the Preventive Officer. But knowing Clegg, I say he will. He's never wanted in daring."

"Clegg?" repeated Colonel Delacourt.

"Clegg," repeated Captain Vic. "For, believe me, Clegg, Dr. Syn and this Scarecrow are all one and the same. An unholy Trinity, if ever there was. On the way here, I rode by Aldington Knoll. There was the burned-out beacon that so fooled the Dragoons. There also was an idiotic yokel, piling up wood lumps in readiness. For what? A 'run' tomorrow night, and take it from me, it's to be the Scarecrow and the Scarecrow only that is to fire the beacon."

"Well? What then?" asked the now excited colonel.

"Why, we three will wait for him," whispered Captain Vic. "Merry is with us in that we all desire the death of Dr. Syn. If he's an unholy Trinity, why, so are we. There's plenty of cover there on the Knoll. We take it. We take firearms. Muskets or pistols as we shall elect. We get dead on our target before he comes along, and as he fires the beacon, why, we fire to kill at point-blank range. 'Death to the Scarecrow', says the Law. It will not be murder."

And at the same time, back in Romney Marsh, Colonel Troubridge and Captain Faunce rode together. They were exercising their chargers, and passing the "Shepherd and Crook" they halted for a drink. They remained in their saddles while the pot-boy ran to serve them, and the colonel pointed to the broadsheet on the door, "Death to the Scarecrow".

"Is the wager on, then, Faunce?" he asked. "Two hundred guineas to you if the Scarecrow 'runs' tomorrow night."

"Right," replied Faunce. "And I tell you, sir, you are throwing your money away. I have met the man twice. Twice he has scored off me by brave effrontery. Believe me, sir, he'll ride again tomorrow night, and I trust that your loss to me will be made up in the glory you will have in taking him."

"Death to the Scarecrow, then," whispered the colonel as he drank in his saddle.

"Aye, sir. We hope so, but I add to him my best respects," and Captain Faunce drank too.

"Death to the Scarecrow." It was read and spoken of all that Sunday night in bars and parlours, in kitchens and bedrooms.

"Death to the Scarecrow." The words went round and round in Charlotte Cobtree's brain.

It was Monday night, and she sat through dinner next to Dr. Syn and listened to Colonel Troubridge telling him and the squire exactly where he would be patrolling in a few hours' time for the Scarecrow.

The squire kept asserting that there would be no "run", and in this was supported by his wife, his younger daughters and Dr. Pepper. But Charlotte would offer no opinion, even though she was urged to do so by Dr. Syn, who agreed with the colonel that they had been wise to set their preparations against it.

"I should think so, indeed," said Colonel Troubridge. "I agree with Captain Faunce that the fellow is so flushed with success that he'll attempt to show his superiority once more. If he does, and I hope he will, well, it's my opinion he'll over-reach himself. Faunce has given those brave Upton lads their orders. In about an hour they'll ride off to their allotted posts. That means that when all is favourable for the Scarecrow to signal in his luggers the Marsh will be hiding one hundred and fifty resolute men with white bands upon their arms. Then I shall ride out with my men and keep patrol under the hills. Our signals are arranged, and at the first sight of the Scarecrow anywhere, we shall rally and charge."

"Poor Scarecrow," sighed Dr. Syn. "If he's arrogant enough to show himself he'll have a great run for his pains."

"Run?" repeated the colonel. He'll not run far, for I promise you he'll never get through the ring we are setting round him."

"You certainly have not left anything to chance," said Dr. Syn. "The only point on which I disagree with your methods is the way you are wasting your best man—Captain Faunce."

"Well, it's his idea and he's so set on it that I gave way," replied the colonel.

"I never like anything that is unjust," said Dr. Syn.

"Why, what is Captain Faunce doing?" asked the squire.

"As I told Dr. Syn," explained the colonel. "Faunce suspects that facetious little sexton Mipps, and he thinks he will do more to hinder the Scarecrow or even to find the Scarecrow by setting himself the task of watching him and his precious coffin shop. He is taking his galloper with him and another trooper. Although of course there is no thought of arresting Mipps——"

"I should think not, indeed," put in Dr. Syn.

"Yet," went on the colonel, "he will be guarded, and should he stir abroad, followed."

"How amused poor little Mipps must be," laughed Charlotte Cobtree.

"The rascal will now think more of his own importance than ever," chuckled the squire. "However, I agree with the vicar. Captain Faunce has got the wrong bee in his bonnet this time."

"By the way, Squire, have you guarded your stables tonight?" asked Dr. Syn.

"Now, if that hadn't completely slipped my memory," he replied." But there's time to rectify that, for it is not dark yet. I recommend a stroll before we take to our port. Let us walk as far as the stables. The air will do us good."

The squire led the way out into the garden to the stables, with the colonel and Lady Cobtree, Charlotte and Dr. Syn following. The two younger girls stayed behind to tease Dr. Pepper, who declared that he preferred looking at good wine to empty stables.

Sure enough, the stables were empty again. The ostler in charge maintained that he had only left them once in order to prepare a poultice in the loft for a lame horse. True, he had heard a stamping beneath him, but never dreamed anyone would be so bold as to "borrow" the squire's horses in broad daylight. Some of them had already gone with the volunteers, but the squire had lent those willingly, and now wished he had lent the best animals instead of having them commandeered by the Scarecrow's men.

"Which shows that the rascal means to run his cargo," cried the colonel triumphantly.

The only animals left were the horse that needed poulticing and Charlotte's two hunters. There were the chalk crosses marked upon their stalls.

"Whoever the Scarecrow may be, it is evident he is fond of me," she said to Dr. Syn.

"And who could help being fond of anyone so beautiful?" asked Dr. Syn.

·   ·   ·   ·   ·

"Death to the Scarecrow." The cry went out from a hundred and fifty throats as Dr. Syn's volunteers rode out with white armlets and such weapons as they could assemble.

After them rode Dr. Syn upon his fat white pony.

"Bring back Charlotte's admirer—this Scarecrow, Doctor," laughed the squire, "and we'll place him in the Court House lock-up to await his trial."

"Death to the Scarecrow." Charlotte Cobtree wondered how many of those volunteers really wished those words to come true.

On condition that they retired to bed by ten, the squire promised to arouse his daughters when he received news of the Scarecrow's riding.

"I still maintain, however, that he is not the fool to try."

"Death to the Scarecrow." Charlotte Cobtree, realizing the dangers against him, hoped to be for once disappointed in her hero, for if he rode, it seemed he must be caught. She went to her room and sat down before her dressing-table. Then she saw the sealed package, bearing her name and leaning against the mirror. It had not lain there when she had dressed for dinner. Who had put it there? She would ask the housekeeper to find out, but first she would see what it was all about. She broke the seal, and Fear with his icy fingers clutched at her heart.

"Death to the Scarecrow". It was one of the broadsheets, but there was writing upon the back. The handwriting was that of an educated man. She glanced at the signature—Vicosa—some-time captain of the *Santa Maria* of the Port of Spain. So Meg's husband had been a sailor.

Honoured Madame,

A gentleman now residing at Rye, and for whom I am acting as agent, has given me certain information with instructions to act upon it in his interests. We are in a position to vouch for the most important truth of what I am now about to tell you, and for the rest it is based on supposition. For instance, since no gentleman can with any certitude vouch for what is in a lady's heart, however glaring the circumstances (as in your case), we presume to suppose that you are in love with Dr. Syn, vicar of Dymchurch. If this is so, then you will do well to do what this letter instructs you, or you will see your reverend lover upon a common scaffold. He is wanted by many Governments in order to answer his crimes with his life, and by England not the least, as you will fully appreciate when I tell you that he is none other than the notorious pirate, Clegg.

Furthermore knowing that the man called the "Scarecrow" is not Mr. James Bone, the highwayman, as everyone foolishly supposes, it occurs to us that the one person of genius in this neighbourhood who is capable of carrying out these daring "runs" of contraband might very easily prove to be Clegg, or shall we say, Dr. Syn?

Certain it is that the gentleman instructing me to approach you has made up his mind to get the reward for denouncing Clegg, and if he also earns the extra reward for securing the Scarecrow too, he will be all the more compensated. Then why do we hesitate, you may ask? Say it is that we admire a pretty girl who we feel sure will help us to help her lover. You have only to bring to us this afternoon the string of pearls which Dr. Syn took from the figure-head of the City of London *wreck and gave to you, and the gentleman for whom I am agent will undertake on his word of honour to keep his knowledge to himself. Bring them to me before your dinner without fail at "The City of London", and make no mention of it to my wife, Meg, for women chatter most abominably, and that you would not wish.*

Failing the delivery of the pearls, Dr. Syn will be denounced as Clegg to His Majesty's officers here in Dymchurch this very night, where no doubt he will be riding on his Scarecrow business.

> *I am, Madame,*
> *Your obedient servant,*
> *Captain Vicosa.*

P.S. Understand, madame, your pearls or Death to the Scarecrow, Death to Captain Clegg, and Death to Dr. Syn.

CHAPTER XIV

"DEATH TO THE SCARECROW" (CONTINUED)

CHARLOTTE read this infamous letter twice, then rang the bell for the housekeeper.

"When did this letter get here?" she asked. "And do you know who brought it?"

"It was that odious man, Merry, Miss Charlotte," explained the housekeeper. "He brought it a few minutes ago from a friend, he says, and since he said it concerned your lover, Miss Charlotte, which I took to be a gross impertinence, I did not like to give it to you in front of the others downstairs."

"It *does* concern my lover," replied Charlotte. "And you must help me to help him."

"Your lover, Miss Charlotte?" repeated the housekeeper. "But I thought, in fact, below stairs we all hoped that the good Dr. Syn——"

"Yes, you are right, my dear," interrupted Charlotte. "It is Dr. Syn, and he is good as you say. But there are certain wicked men who are his enemies, and this very night he is in danger, and I must get to him and warn him. Give me a cloak. I'll go down your back staircase and you can tell me if the way is clear. But wait, there is a bundle of clothes I must get first."

From a drawer she produced a bundle of dirty-looking rags tied round with a cord. Passing her arm through this, she fastened it to her shoulder and then drew on a voluminous black cloak with a hood which she pulled over her face. The letter she put into her bodice.

The housekeeper advised her to take off her pearls, as they would only add to her danger if she wore them, but she shook her head and told the dear old lady not to be nervous on her account.

"I am going to ride my new horse, and I shall be safe enough on him," she said. "When I have gone, lock my door. Tell the others when they wake that I was very tired and did not want to be disturbed till breakfast time. I shall be back by then."

"Oh, my poor child, don't go," whispered the housekeeper. "It is not right for you to ride at such a time of night alone."

"But it is right for me to save my lover, isn't it?" she argued. "I must find him and warn him. And I shall be safe enough."

The ostler in charge of the stables was easier to deal with than

137

the housekeeper who let her out of the back door, for hearing footsteps, and thinking it must be one of the Scarecrow's men, he left the lantern burning in the harness room and made himself scarce up in the hay-loft.

Charlotte selected a riding switch and bridle, and with the lantern went into the stall to harness up Gehenna, for she had named him after the Scarecrow's horse. She then led the splendid animal out of the courtyard, through the side gate and so out upon the road.

The village was still as death, and yet as she walked along at the horse's head she knew that the ring of the hoofs brought prying eyes to darkened windows in the cottages. The women and old men, aye, and the children, too, of Dymchurch, were keeping vigil in the dark, for they were all anxious to know what was happening out on the eerie Marsh.

Charlotte walked on past "The City of London". It was all dark and the shutters close fastened. She wondered whether Captain Vic would be still there, or whether he was already out upon the trail of Dr. Syn. She never doubted the accuracy of this terrible information against the man she loved, for she had already half-guessed at the truth of it, and she was now on her way to the one man who could tell her the truth. She made straight for the coffin shop to see Mipps.

Her one fear in this was the remembrance that Captain Faunce was watching it. Sure enough, there he was on the high road in front of the shed where Mipps worked, and she caught the glint of another breastplate on guard at the bridge that led over a broad dyke to St. Mary's. The other trooper mentioned by Colonel Troubridge at dinner was no doubt watching up the fork of the road that led to the hills.

Charlotte thought quickly and decided on a bold action. With her hood well over her face, she passed Captain Faunce, and assuming a rustic voice said: "Dark night, mister. But the moon gets up later."

"Where are you going, my good woman?" asked the Captain. "The Marsh is not too healthy tonight. There will be trouble most likely, for the soldiers are out after smugglers."

"Aye, mister, I knows it well," replied Charlotte, "for ain't I the wife of the new riding officer from Sandgate? Bad luck to these scoundrels, I says, for this Scarecrow wouldn't think twice of making me a widder if my Tom rides on his tracks this night."

"Is that his horse?" asked Captain Faunce, bringing his

charger nearer. "A fine animal from what I can see in this darkness."

"Aye, the Government issues good cattle," she answered. "But what chance 'as one man got against so many?"

"There's plenty of volunteers to help him this night, not to mention my own regiment of Dragoons. But what are you doing here with your husband's horse? No saddle either."

"Don't use one. He can ride, can my husband. He stopped at the 'Ship Inn' for a bit of information," she explained. "I works there myself in the kitchens. His horse has a loose shoe, and since the farrier there has gone with them volunteers and Mr. Mipps here has a forge, I come along to ask him to see to it. I hope he's awake."

"I 'eard you," replied a voice from the open bedroom window of the cottage.

"Not asleep, Mr. Mipps, yet?" asked Captain Faunce sarcastically.

"How can I sleep, I ask you, thinkin' of you three Dragoons 'anging about," replied the sexton irritably. "Funny thing, ever since I was a nipper the one thing I could never abide has been a Dragoon. Me uncle was the same. Any soldier or sailor would be welcome at his place—the 'Chequers' at Aylesford that was up Maidstone way, but he'd never serve no Dragoon, no more would the pot-boy nor the barmaid what squinted. Didn't trust 'em. However, riding officers are different. Bring your old man's nag round the back and I'll have a look at his treadables."

Charlotte led the horse away from Captain Faunce round to the forge which opened on to the little garden. Captain Faunce rode a yard or so from the coffin shop, so that he could keep his eye on the forge door, which after much noisy exertion, Mr. Mipps, carrying a lantern, unfastened. As soon as he had tied the horse to a ring, he closed the doors and picking up a hammer began to strike it on the anvil.

"Thought at first it was the Scarecrow's horse," he whispered. "Who are you, now?"

Charlotte put her fingers to her lips in warning and then pushed back her hood.

"Mipps, I have come to you for help."

"Miss Charlotte? Whatever's happened?" He banged once or twice on the anvil.

"We can trust one another, Mipps, I know," she whispered, "for we both love your master. We love him as Dr. Syn, just as we love him as Clegg or the Scarecrow. Oh yes, I know."

"So he blowed the gaff to a pretty girl and never told me. Oh my old commander. Well, if you loves him you'll not blab."

"I do love him, Mipps, and so do you."

"Amen," responded the sexton.

"And don't imagine he has told me anything. He has not," she went on, "for he would never betray another's secret. But love can solve most riddles——"

"Lovely love," sighed Mipps. "There was a girl I knew in Saratoga——"

But she cut him short. "What I guessed, I now know. Read this and then help me to save him."

"Give it to me, miss, and you take the hammer. Every time I kick give the anvil a good 'un. That'll keep Faunce quiet."

Mipps held the paper close to the lantern and then almost touching it with his long sharp nose his gimletty eyes devoured the words. Every now and then he would kick out sideways with a thin leg, particularly when the shameful letter most angered him, and Charlotte dutifully smote the anvil with the hammer.

"Did you give this rascal the pearls?" he demanded suddenly.

"I got the letter too late. Merry brought it, I hear."

"Yes," said Mipps, "and he was not letting Captain Vic get hold of 'em. That's why. Kept the letter back a-purpose. He thinks he'll get them pearls himself by further blackmail. Well, he's as good as dead already. So's that there Captain Vic and his gentleman friend at Rye, whoever he may be. Aye, dead they all is, if I has to knock 'em all three up alive in coffins at my own expense."

"But the Scarecrow must not die, Mipps, and we must save him," whispered Charlotte. "Think."

"Can't," replied Mipps. "If I could get out of this 'ere without being shot by them Dragoons I would, but even then it would want hard riding to get to the doctor in time, and my donkey's a hearse for speed, unless you loans me your nag 'ere."

"You'd never get through, Mipps. They'd shoot you down. But I can go as I came. You heard my conversation with the captain. I am sure I deceived him, and I'll do better yet. Look here," She undid the bundle of clothes. "I will dress in these, and on my black horse I shall look sufficiently like the Scarecrow to pass through any smugglers' lines. Where can I find the doctor?"

"He'll be waiting now up at Quarry Hill," returned Mipps. "He has a job there before the 'run'. You see, I started this rumour going about Jimmie Bone being the Scarecrow, thinkin' it would clear the doctor, but when the highwayman objects, Dr. Syn promised to clear him of the charge. Well ('ere, Miss Charlotte, oblige me by knockin' that anvil once and again. Thankee). Now, listen, that 'ere scoundrel, Captain Vic, and his friend, are in league with some English traitors in London who are supplying France with gold. Captain Vic and his friend have arranged the transport. Well, what does they go and do? Why, employs Jimmie Bone to rob the coach. And what does Jimmie Bone do but gets Dr. Syn, as the Scarecrow, to rob him. The coach is due when the moon rises, and when he's done, Dr. Syn, or let's say the Scarecrow, rides along the hill line to Aldington and starts the 'run' by firing the beacon. That's the idea. A double haul worth thousands of guineas, this night is, and I'm supposed to be up at the beacon waitin' for the Scarecrow. Damn all Dragoons, say I."

"But Dr. Syn knows you're a prisoner," explained Charlotte. "For Colonel Troubridge told him at dinner about you being watched."

"But he don't know that anyone knows him as Clegg. Some dirty spy on his track from the Americas, no doubt," replied Mipps. " 'Ere, miss, give us that hammer. You get along and change your clothes behind my back in the dark there, while I shuts my eyes, hammers and thinks. There's a coffin stool for you to sit on and a carpenter's bench for your things, and an old cracked bit of mirror what I shaves in hanging up on the wall there."

Charlotte went into the dark corner to change. Mipps shut his eyes tight and hammered at the empty anvil. But between the strokes he talked.

"Miss Charlotte, I'm glad it's you and me as knows, I mean about Clegg. And you needn't fear about loving him. Clegg has killed men by hundreds, I ain't denyin', but only bad men what was better dead. And in all the ships he scuttled, he never left even an enemy to drown. In fact, as we used to say, he didn't deserve success on the high seas because of the chances he took, and the generosity he showed. But he did succeed. Mind you, when he was double-dealt with by a traitor, why then he could be terrible."

"Well, his safety is in our hands, Mipps," replied Charlotte, "and neither of us are likely to prove unfaithful."

"You said a pretty mouthful, and that's the truth," said Mipps. "But damn them Dragoons, say I." He dealt a few lusty strokes upon the anvil.

"You may turn round now," said Charlotte, who had by now dressed herself in the rags. "Will I do?"

Mipps turned and grinned. "Well, miss," he whispered, "you're the best-looking scarecrow I ever see. But that smile of yours would attract the birds, not frighten 'em."

"You must give me some paint or something to make myself look ugly," she said.

Mipps shook his head. "No, that won't do. Out on the Marsh your face will not be seen. It's the horse and rags that will deceive 'em. But you've got to go out as you come in, dressed in a woman's cloak. Suppose them Dragoons want to see your face? It 'ud be like their impertinence. Well, with them black curls you've put in your hat, they'll never recognize the fair Miss Cobtree, but you'll pass for a girl, just the same. Don't forget, Quarry Hill. Go slow till you pass the Dragoons, then ride like hell, excusing the word. I'll burn this letter in the forge."

When the tell-tale letter had turned to ashes, Charlotte took the head of the horse while Mipps opened the doors.

Captain Faunce brought his charger close to Charlotte as she turned to Mipps, saying in a rough voice, "Me 'usband will see to the reckonin' in the mornin' after he's caught this damned Scarecrow."

"Tell your husband not to worry, missus, about the payment. Let him catch the Scarecrow, say I. He ain't the man to be scared of a Scarecrow like some Dragoons I knows of, who's sooner bide safe in the village street watchin' a harmless friend of the riding officers. Your good man will catch him with the help of the village lads and the vicar. As to Dragoons, well—we lives and learns. Fine feathers makes frightened birds, it seems. Good night, missus." And with a snort, Mr. Mipps closed the forge doors and noisily entered the back door of his cottage, which he banged to, and then opened again very quietly, listening.

Captain Faunce walked his horse beside Charlotte's to the corner, where one of his troopers sat mounted on guard.

"Escort this woman to 'The City of London'," he ordered, "and then come back to your post."

Charlotte walked beside her horse round the corner with the trooper close to her. She heard Captain Faunce ride back to watch the coffin shop.

The trooper waited till they were half-way along the straggling street. He knew that he was then safely out of earshot, and he appreciated the fact that the woman who walked beside him was young and virile by her carriage.

"Married, lass?" he whispered.

"Aye," she answered.

"All the better," laughed the trooper, "for you know how to give and take a kiss, and though your hood hides you well enough, I can see you're as pretty as a drum-horse, and here's the moon rising from the sea to give us light. So let's have a kiss, girl, before we goes further or the road grows brighter."

He slipped from his troop-horse with surprising agility and laid hold of Charlotte's hood. The full moon bathed the road.

With her riding switch Charlotte aimed beneath the brass peak of his helmet, and with an oath the Dragoon stumbled backwards with the pain and surprise of that swinging cut. His horse plunged and kicked, so did Charlotte's as she leapt upon his back. Then striking the trooper's horse across the nose with her switch, she set her own horse full tilt down the street. Her hood fell back, the cloak blew wide in the sea breeze, and the discomfited trooper saw that his pretty girl was the Scarecrow. His own horse having galloped away into the fields, he picked himself up and ran back towards Captain Faunce, crying out that the Scarecrow had once more slipped through his fingers.

Captain Faunce set spurs to his charger and galloped away down the village street in pursuit of hard-riding Charlotte.

An hour's riding and she reached the foot of Quarry Hill and entered the darkness of the over-hanging trees. But it had taken time, and the moon, to her dismay, was mounting high.

On the top of the hill two other horsemen watched the moon anxiously.

Jimmie Bone turned to his companion and said: "Scarecrow, there's something wrong with that coach. It should have been here an hour since."

"Listen," warned his companion. "I hear horses. No, one horse and coming up the hill. Wrong way. Let's get to cover."

Reining the horses back into the shelter of the trees that topped the bank, the two horsemen waited to see who rode so fast up the hill. True, there was no one in the neighbourhood who cared to ride slowly on Quarry Hill for it was a place of bad reputation, admirably suited for attack by highwaymen or footpads, and a spot much favoured by Bone himself.

Up the hill towards them thundered the horse.

"We shall catch a glimpse of him in that patch of moonlight there," whispered the Scarecrow.

Into the said patch galloped the horse, and its rider pulled it up on his haunches. Jimmie Bone gasped with astonishment.

The rider was another "Scarecrow"—black horse, ragged black clothes—just the same as he who sat by his side.

"I thought right," muttered the real Scarecrow. "Wait here, my friend. Let me deal with this."

Down the steep bank he slithered his horse, and the two "Scarecrows" met in the moonlight.

"Charlotte," said the Scarecrow hoarsely.

"Beloved," replied the other. "Thank God I have found you."

With their horses close to each other, she told him the threat contained in Captain Vic's letter.

"And you came through the dangers of the Marsh to warn me? Oh, Charlotte."

The sad regret in his voice told her that he was ashamed she knew all, but she quickly dispelled such despair by answering: "I love my three heroes. I love them equally with all my heart—Clegg and the Scarecrow and my beloved Dr. Syn."

"Then since you know all, why, then I can unloose my tongue. I love you, Charlotte. I love you. Oh, God, what am I to do?"

"You mean against this Captain Vic?" she asked.

"No, no," he corrected. "I care nothing for him. I can deal with him. Mipps was right, he must be the red-haired planter who served me so ill. No, I meant with you, dear Charlotte. Never did I think to regret my past. Oh, God, were I only worthy of your love."

"Let me say the same, beloved," she answered. "Oh, God, that I were worthy of this grand adventurer," and she placed her hand upon his sleeve.

Mr. Bone, not understanding this situation, advanced to the edge of the bank.

"Not a word of Clegg before him," whispered Dr. Syn. "That is a secret belonging to you, to me and to Mipps. For the rest, he knows all, but I know, too, when I can trust a man, and Mr. Bone is my sworn friend."

He raised his voice so that the highwayman could hear the latter part of the sentence, at which he also slithered down the bank, and the three black horses stood together.

When Mr. Bone had been told who this new "Scarecrow" was, he swept off his hat, saying: "Then I am more than glad I never stole those pearls. So you have come to warn the Scarecrow that something is wrong. Now, see here. This coach is late, and if the Scarecrow lingers too long to free me, why, we endanger the success of the 'run'. You told me but now that you were anxious about the tide on Jesson Beach. It is time the beacon flared on Aldington Knoll."

"Aye, that's so," returned Dr. Syn, "and no one may light it but the Scarecrow. I did not anticipate this long delay."

"Is your presence necessary—after the lighting?" asked Charlotte.

"No. They all know what to do—but I wished to light the beacon. I wish now I had ordered otherwise."

"Have you hidden a 'flasher' near the beacon?" she asked.

"No, I carry two here in my belt."

"Let me see them, please," she asked.

Obediently the doctor handed them over. Charlotte thrust them in the side pockets of her coat.

"You can stay here and free Mr. Bone, as you promised. I will light the beacon."

"No, Charlotte, no! You will ride back to safety."

"Do you value my love?" she asked.

Despite Mr. Bone's presence, Dr. Syn replied, "You know that, Charlotte, but——"

"Then let me give it you with service," she interrupted. "You can hardly refuse."

"The way down the cup of the valley is free of Dragoons," said Jimmie Bone. "The lady is safe enough under cover on this side of the sky-line. The Dragoons are not to take action till Dr. Syn's lieutenants give the signal, and the Dragoons ride the sky-line with an eye on the Marsh. Of course, they'll not be on the Knoll."

"Aye, it's safer on the hills than on the Marsh," muttered Syn. "After firing the beacon you could be hidden safely if you go back to the Walnut Tree Inn. But no, no, I must find another way. Let me think."

"It is my privilege to do the thinking this time," replied Charlotte, "for *this* time is the first time since you have told me that you love me. Therefore, I claim the initiative as my privilege —this once. I have the flashers. A girl can light the beacon as well as a man, and my dress will pass me through the smugglers' patrols. The Dragoons are on the edge of the hills. They will never catch sight of me. I know the lie of the land—they don't. Besides, I can outride them as I outrode their captain."

"The captain will be taken by our outposts," said the doctor. "Had we known he was to favour us here with a visit, we might have saved ourselves the trouble of taking and disarming two of his regiment. We needed them as witnesses of this hold-up."

"Where are they?" asked Charlotte.

"Dismounted and lashed up," he explained. "Our men who will remove the guinea bags will bring them along to see me rob Mr. Bone."

"It is well planned, but I am glad I am here to help," returned Charlotte. "You would have been forced either to leave Mr. Bone or the others in the lurch. The tide waits for no man. I will ride up to the Knoll, fire the beacon, and then——"

"Wait for me at the 'Walnut'. Ask for Master Awford, and his charming wife will look after you if you say you have ridden on the Scarecrow's business, and that he sends you to await him. But are you sure——?"

"That I love you? Oh yes, yes. You shall see." And turning her horse, she rode on up the hill. Jimmie Bone stayed where he was, but Dr. Syn rode after her and they paused together at the top of the hill.

"And when this night's work is done, will you hold me in your arms?" she asked.

"Until I think disaster is at hand——" he answered.

"And then I shall hold you in mine," she added, "for we belong in safety or disaster." And turning her horse, she waved to him and plunged down the springy turf into the cup of the great valley that headed away behind the old cliff line of Lympne Hill, to the distant Knoll of Aldington.

Dr. Syn watched her as she plunged down into the shadow of that hollow pasture land with every instinct prompting him to ride after her.

Just when the temptation was proving too strong to be resisted, he heard to the right, the galloping of horses, the rumble of wheels and rattle of the coach they awaited! Well, the business would be done quickly now, and he would not be far behind Charlotte at the beacon. He might even overtake her.

Wheeling his horse, he trotted quickly back to where Jimmie Bone awaited him. A few hurried whispers, and then they waited in the darkness with pistols at the ready.

With a great to-do of cracking whips and shouting, the guard descended and put on the skids, and then with much squeaking from the vehicle and much shouting from the driver and guard (which the occupants had no idea was a pre-arranged signal) the four horses, strongly straining backwards, slowly descended Quarry Hill.

And then, a flash of fire from a horse's hoof ahead, and into the patch of moonlight the dread masked figure of the notorious Jimmie Bone.

"Stand and deliver!"

A bang and a flash from the guard's blunderbuss. An answering shot from the laughing highwayman, and the guard fell from his seat down upon the high road. Two gentlemen put their heads out of the window. The driver sprang up on his box, fired a horse-pistol at Mr. Bone, and then leaping down to the road ran to the leaders' heads.

Mr. Bone fired again. The driver cried out, staggered a few yards from the horses and fell against the bank, groaning.

"Now, gentlemen, unless you want to be served the same as the guard and whip," cried Bone, "unpack them guinea bags quick and place 'em at the side of the road. Come on now, I knows all about them guineas. Meant for France, eh? Think yourselves lucky to escape with your necks, then, and think of Mr. Jimmie Bone enjoying your English guineas. Come along, now. Smart's the word. Ten bags under each seat makes twenty. Ten more in the boot. Fifty more upon the roof. Five more under the driver's seat. You see, I am well informed. Look lively."

The two inmates of the coach went to it with a will, unloading guinea bags to the road and whimpering with fear.

When all was unpacked, Mr. Bone told them to cut the traces of the horses, throwing them a sharp knife for the purpose. The released animals, terrified by the smell of powder and the flashes, stampeded off down the road.

"Now, you two can follow as best you can," cried Bone, "and thank God that James Bone's limit for murder tonight is two, but run lively, or it will be four."

"Stand in the Scarecrow's name," cried a hoarse voice. "Very neatly done, Mr. Bone, upon my life, but I have greater need of those guineas than you."

James Bone pretended to be in a terrible rage as he threw up both hands above his head.

"The Scarecrow," he cried aloud, as Dr. Syn rode into the moon patch.

"Your game's up," he cried. "I have men here to remove the bags of guineas, Mr. Bone. Two lumbering Dragoons who rode out here to catch you were first caught by me, and for that you may thank your stars."

Still covering Mr. Bone with his horse pistols, the Scarecrow raised himself in his stirrups and let out three cries of the curlew.

Immediately the coach was surrounded by armed men

fantastically dressed. In their midst were two Dragoons, and Captain Faunce, all three disarmed, dismounted and lashed round with rope.

"Mr. Bone," croaked the Scarecrow, "I have brought these soldiers to witness the robbing you of your prize, since I object to a highwayman setting himself up to be the great Scarecrow. You may now ride away, Mr. Bone, and up the hill, if you please."

He then turned on the two passengers. "You two gentlemen will continue your journey to the 'Mermaid' at Rye on foot, as we have need of those horses, and down the hill, if you please. We will attend to your money bags and to the dead. Quick, away with you."

The two terrified agents, only too glad to escape with their lives after such disaster, took to their heels in the opposite direction to that already taken by the highwayman.

Directly their footsteps died away, the "dead" guard and driver sprang to their feet. They had been previously bribed by the highwayman to fire blank powder and to pretend to be shot. These men quickly captured the horses; the Dragoons were bundled unceremoniously into the coach, and having closed the doors upon them, the party packed the guinea bags upon the horses and made their way across country towards the "Walnut Tree" at Aldington.

The Scarecrow, seeing that all had worked according to plan, waved to his comrades and galloped up the hill to the signpost, where the highwayman awaited him.

"We had best separate," said the Scarecrow, "for it will spoil all if we are seen riding in friendship. Make the best of your way to Mother Handaway's, but keep your eyes open."

"And keep your wits about you, too," replied the highwayman, pointing to the broadsheet stuck upon the signpost.

"Death to the Scarecrow," read Dr. Syn. "Ah, well, they have not killed me yet." And waving farewell to the highwayman, the Scarecrow plunged down the steep bank.

Keeping a sharp look-out ahead, Dr. Syn thundered on until within a mile of the Knoll he suddenly pulled Gehenna up on his haunches and brought him to a standstill. For there had leapt up into the sky the red reflection of the beacon. It was alight. She had succeeded, and he could now ride to the "Walnut Tree" and meet her.

For a moment he watched the great tongue of fire against the sky, and his love for her soared up to heaven with it. And then the silence of the night was broken by three distinct cracks as of musket fire.

For the first time in his long adventurings, Dr. Syn was smitten with the icy sweat of fear. The letter of warning which Charlotte had spoken of—and then Charlotte dressed as the Scarecrow. Was it possible? God—what a fool he had been!

In went the spurs to Gehenna's flanks, and the maddened animal leapt forward, goaded into fury by the demon on his back.

On reaching the Knoll and dismounting, his worst fears were realized, for there, lighted by the flames of the beacon, knelt his faithful Mipps, supporting on his knee the pale face of Charlotte Cobtree.

"Is she dead?" Dr. Syn whispered hoarsely, as he knelt down and took the girl's hands.

His voice recalled Charlotte to consciousness. She smiled bravely and tried to speak in a steady voice. "Not yet, my dear Doctor," she whispered. "If you could carry me down to Mother Handaway's she could help us. Mipps, will you ride for Dr. Pepper and my father? And your clerical clothes are there, Doctor, so it is convenient for all of us. I'm proud that they got me instead of you. I have done something."

"Who was it?" asked Dr. Syn.

"I saw the three flashes as I climbed up here," explained Mipps. "I fired with my blunderbuss, which scared 'em. They ran down that side of the Knoll and by the light of the beacon I saw three men mount on the road and ride towards Rye. I saw Miss Charlotte's horse run away. Then I come here to Miss Charlotte, and then you come along, thank God."

"Make haste," whispered Charlotte.

The doctor lifted her like a child and strode down the slope of the Knoll to where his horse awaited him.

"Take Gehenna and ride for the squire and the doctor," Dr. Syn ordered.

"I have a horse I borrowed from the Dragoons," the little man replied. "I tied it to a tree here."

"I am slipping away from you," whispered Charlotte. "Take me on your horse. Let us ride through the air. It will revive me."

Without knowing how he did it, Dr. Syn found himself with the girl in his arms upon his horse. He knew that Mipps rode just behind them, for when they reached the fields by Mother Handaway's, he cried out to "ware the dyke".

All he realized was that Charlotte kept looking up at him beneath the moon and urging him to greater speed. "Faster, faster, beloved," she cried, and he felt only that she was right and that death could only be beaten by speed.

     •   ‘   •   •   •

It was Jimmie Bone and Mipps who helped Dr. Syn to dismount gently with his precious burden, and they took the horses to the secret stable, bringing back the fat white pony, which they tethered to a ring in the wall of the chicken yard, while the dazed doctor carried Charlotte into the cottage and laid her on Mother Handaway's straw-covered bed.

The old woman, in great distress, busied herself with stopping the bleeding from the three wounds. Within an inch or so of one another, any of the three shots in her back below the shoulder blades might have proved fatal—but together, the end was certain, and the old woman whispered that there was no hope. It was doubtful whether she could live until her father and Dr. Pepper could be fetched.

"This is no time to fear for my own life and liberty," said the highwayman, when he heard the old witch's report. "I ride the faster, Mr. Sexton. I will take the Dragoon's horse for Dr. Pepper, Miss Charlotte's for the squire and ride mine own. I will bring them back quicker than you could, and do you somehow get Dr. Syn into his clerical clothes. If he is taken as the Scarecrow, he will hang. And what will the squire say to his daughter's disguise?"

Although these words were spoken loud enough to be heard by all, they conveyed no meaning to Dr. Syn. His brain could only realize that Charlotte was dying, and for him. But Charlotte understood and called Mipps to her side. Bending down towards her lovely face, Mipps understood too, and his eyes filled with tears as he listened to the girl's last request. She wished to make her sacrifice worth while, by saving her lover's life in good earnest. Mipps saw that here was a way out for his beloved master, and promised Charlotte she should have her wish.

Nodding to the highwayman, he said: "We will keep her alive till you return, if possible. Hurry. I'll look to the Scarecrow's clothes."

The highwayman hurried back to the stables, and in a minute or so they heard the horses dashing away, and Mipps thanked God for Jimmie Bone's honour. He was risking all to bring comfort to the dying girl, and Mipps told himself that he must also risk all to save his master.

"Vicar," he whispered hoarsely, "she has done all this for you. Why will you not help her? Scarecrow."

Dr. Syn showed no sign of understanding. He just knelt on the other side of the straw mattress with Charlotte's hand in his, and he gazed at the pale face with panic-stricken eyes.

Mipps was desperate. He went round to the doctor and clapped his hand upon his shoulder, crying out: "Listen, Captain Clegg. You must play the man for her."

At the word "Clegg" a look of queer recognition came into Syn's eyes as he turned and looked at Mipps.

Mipps went on: "Captain Clegg, she loves you. We cannot save her, but at least you can comfort her by doing what she asks. It is your duty, sir."

"What does she ask?" Dr. Syn spoke mechanically, as he turned back to gaze at Charlotte.

"That you will dress as the parson for the end," whispered Mipps. "You could say a prayer for her then. I'll come with you while the old woman does what she can."

Mipps led his master to the underground stable and helped him to change from the Scarecrow back to the parson, and he certainly felt happier in his mind when the tell-tale clothes were stowed away and the Vicar of Dymchurch was kneeling by the dying girl. At least, he had saved his beloved master. It was obvious that something had snapped in the doctor's brain, and Mipps realized that for his master's safety nothing better could have happened. But at any moment this temporary denseness might clear, and then he would be sent to fetch Charlotte's own clothes from the coffin shop. If the brain lapse continued, however, Charlotte would have her last wish. She would be identified as the Scarecrow by her father and consequently would be shielding the man she loved. So Mipps, determining not to fall under Dr. Syn's vacant gaze, crept out of the cottage door and sat down to wait.

It was not long before he was joined by the old woman, saying that she could do no more, and that the end was very near.

"She is telling him of her love," the old witch whispered. "I have left them together."

"Has he spoken to her?" asked Mipps.

Mother Handaway shook her head. "He is like a man possessed. He is holding both her hands in his and gazing at her face. I think his reason has left him."

For a long time they sat together in silence, listening for the horses, while behind them they heard the dying girl talking on and on. The old woman had left the cottage door open so that Charlotte might have air.

Presently a distant crackle of musket-fire broke the stillness of the night. This was followed by a shouting as of many men, and the words "Death to the Scarecrow" echoed across the Marsh.

"The Dragoons are attacking the smugglers," whispered the old witch. "What will they do without their leader?"

"No cause to worry, Mother," replied Mipps. "The Dragoons are waiting for that. It's part of the Scarecrow's plan. It's the men with the white armlets who are pretending to attack the smugglers. They'll have a fine tale to spin when the Dragoons meets 'em carrying hundreds of captured barrels up to the old 'Walnut Tree'. If it weren't for Miss Charlotte, you'd see me splittin' my sides laughin'."

A mightier shout of "Death to the Scarecrow" sounded behind the cottage from the hills as Colonel Troubridge at the head of his waiting Dragoons charged down to the main Marsh road.

With so many hoofs ringing behind him and the prospect of battle before him, Colonel Troubridge's ear did not detect the soft thud of three horsemen galloping towards the cottage over the fields. With boisterous shouts of "Death to the Scarecrow" they blundered on across the Marsh as Mipps sprang forward to hold the heads of the horses ridden by the squire and Dr. Sennacharib Pepper.

"Gentlemen," cried out the highwayman from his saddle, "according to our bargain, it is here that our ways part. As you will learn tomorrow, it has been an ill night for me. I held up a coach on Quarry Hill and was in turn robbed of its guinea sacks by the Scarecrow. There will be squealing witnesses enough tomorrow for you to learn the truth of it. That misfortune, however, is nothing to the grief I feel about your young lady. You will do well to hasten, gentlemen."

"I shall not forget that you ran this risk for her, Mr. Bone," said the squire, going through the door into the dim-lighted room.

"Get into the stable quick, Jimmie," whispered Mipps. "You must lie low. I'll tell 'em you've rode to the hills."

When the squire stood at the foot of the rough bed and looked down upon his daughter, she smiled at him sadly. "Forgive me," she said. "And remember that the Scarecrow only rode to save the necks of our Marsh men."

Since she was covered by a shawl of the old woman, the significance of this speech was lost upon the squire. He looked at Dr. Syn and asked him what it all meant, and what had happened. But the doctor neither turned to him, nor answered.

From the other side of the bed Sennacharib Pepper made a brief examination, then rose and motioned Sir Antony to take his place.

"I can do nothing," he said. "It is a question of a few minutes at the most."

"You will look after him, Father," she went on. "The shock of what I have done has stunned him. I have not been able to wear his pearls for long. You will give them back to him when he is recovered. I should like to keep them with me, but that would be silly. Their worth is too great to be buried, and I am content with my love for him. Perhaps he will have forgotten that I am the Scarecrow. If he recovers, promise not to mention it."

"That you are the Scarecrow?" repeated the bewildered squire.

For answer she gently moved the shawl and showed the black rags of a man's suit that covered her.

"You? Charlotte? My daughter?" ejaculated the amazed squire.

"The information need go no further, sir."

The squire turned to see who had spoken and met the steady gaze of a very dishevelled Captain Faunce.

"I think we are all your daughter's good friends here, and although she has outwitted me tonight, I bear her no resentment. Above all, there must be no scandal. She has paid a heavy enough price for her adventuring."

The Squire did not answer, for Charlotte moved and uttered a heartrending sigh. With one hand she drew Dr. Syn's head down to her breast, then with a smile she closed her eyes. The lids quivered. The lips trembled, and then she lay deathly still.

Dr. Pepper gently moved the squire away and bent towards the girl. Then he straightened himself and said quickly: "Captain Faunce has spoken the truth. She has paid the price in full."

.   .   .   .   .

In order that Colonel Troubridge should not discover the tragedy, Captain Faunce left Dr. Pepper on guard and walked round with the squire to cut off the soldiers at the bridge. Mipps followed very unobtrusively.

"Well," cried the perspiring colonel, "we have rid the Marsh of the rascals this time. With the help of Dr. Syn's excellent volunteers, we've taken more than fifty prisoners, and hundreds of tubs. Whether we've taken the Scarecrow amongst them we don't yet know, as the villains had to be taken up under guard to Aldington and put under the pump at the 'Walnut Tree'."

"Under the pump, sir?" asked Captain Faunce.

"Aye, sir, in order that we can identify 'em," went on the elated officer. "Their faces were all tarred and painted like a lot of wild cannibals, but I more than suspect we shall discover some worthy citizens under their disguises."

"How many men did you send up to guard them, sir?" asked Captain Faunce.

"Devil take it, sir, not one. I was not sparing a fighting trooper as we heard that a second party of the rascals were landing more barrels between Lydd and Romney. And sure enough it was true. We found the worthy landlord of the Ship Inn at New Romney lashed up in his own bar-parlour, who span a woeful tale of some fifty painted devils who came in and robbed him of his drinks. It seems they've gone to cover somewhere, for we charged up and down the district and never a sight of 'em did we catch. But we'll get 'em. The prisoners we've taken will squeal, you mark my words."

Captain Faunce frowned. "And you sent no escort, sir, to guard the prisoners?" he asked again.

"I have told you no, sir," roared the colonel. "Dr. Syn's capital fellows had proved their worth. I made use of 'em. Besides, they can identify the prisoners—we don't know 'em."

"That's good for our parish boys, that is," chuckled Mipps, rubbing his hands. "I says to Dr. Syn myself, I say: 'I lay our boys will get them, Scarecrow and all.' It will be a great thing if they've got the Scarecrow up there, won't it?"

"So it will, Mr. Sexton," cried the colonel, forgetting in his triumph any antipathy he had felt for Mipps.

"Why, there *is* Dr. Syn," went on the colonel. "Come out with you to hear the news, eh? I must ride over and congratulate him on the work of his volunteers. Yes, by Gad, I must thank him officially for his co-operation."

"I beg you will postpone it," said the squire. "There is an old woman there who is very ill. Dr. Pepper is attending her, and the vicar is waiting to give her religious consolations."

" 'Ere comes the ones to congratulate, sir," said Mipps, pointing up the road. "It's them Upton brothers, ain't it? Fine fellows —all three."

"Ah, now we shall know if they have got the Scarecrow," cried the colonel.

"I think he's escaped, I do," said Mipps. "Them Upton boys don't look their usual perky selves. A bit depressed, ain't they? Or do the moonlight play tricks on their mugs?"

The three horsemen with their white armlets rode slowly towards them and pulled up wearily.

"Did you get the Scarecrow, lads?" asked the colonel.

Monty Upton looked angrily at the officer, and asked another question. "Why couldn't you ride back and lend a hand when you heard the firing?" he demanded.

"What firing?" asked the colonel.

"What firing?" repeated the eldest Upton. "Why, up at the 'Walnut Tree'. You're professional soldiers. We are not. What firing indeed. Can't you hear a battle or are you all deaf?"

"Battle?" ejaculated the colonel.

"Don't be silly, Monty," put in Mipps. "I knows something about firing, having served in his blessed Majesty's Royal Navy, and you wouldn't hear firing all the way back at the 'Walnut Tree'. Be reasonable."

Colonel Troubridge, suspecting that all was not so well as he had hoped, remembered his antipathy to Mipps, and sharply ordered him to keep his mouth shut. He then turned on Monty Upton and rapped: "Well, sir?"

"Oh, tell him, Brothers," said Monty. "I feel sick of the whole business."

"Same here," replied Henry. "You tell him, Tom."

The youngest Upton moved his horse a few paces forward. "Aye, sir," he began, "had you but come along with us to lend a hand, instead of galloping over all the Marsh, things might have turned out better."

"But the prisoners? The barrels?" ejaculated the colonel.

"We stacked the barrels in the stable-yard," went on Tom, "or rather, we made the smugglers do it. We then put 'em one by one under the pump, and every man we cleaned, we found was a foreigner from Sussex. Not a Marsh man amongst 'em, thank God. We then began questioning 'em about the Scarecrow, but they all said different. As each one was washed and identified as Sussex, we'd march him out on to the road, where half of us mounted guard, while the other half made an inventory of the contraband. And then from every bit of cover on both sides of the road muskets began to blaze over our heads. It was a knock-out counter-attack, as you military gentlemen say. Two hundred smugglers, if there was one. They turned the tables on us properly, freed the prisoners and shut us up in the stable-yard after they'd carried off every keg and barrel under our noses. Our men lost heart, and have scattered for home."

What the colonel would have said or done at the awful moment will never be known, for there had suddenly come to their ears a furious clattering of hoofs. Round the bend of the Marsh road came five horsemen all wearing white armlets.

"What now?" demanded Monty Upton, as they drew rein.

"We've just heard tell," cried their breathless leader, "that a second fleet is putting in below Dungeness, and that a string of some three hundred smugglers are already crossing the pebble path-land with the first consignment of kegs. And they say the Scarecrow is there himself."

"Give Captain Faunce a horse," cried the excited colonel. "We'll have 'em yet. Come along, lads. Death to the Scarecrow."

The cry was taken up by the troopers, as Captain Faunce mounted a spare horse, and off they galloped with the five men in white armlets showing the way.

"Death to the Scarecrow," echoed out from the distance as they rode hell-for-leather.

The squire turned sadly and walked back to the cottage. Mipps remained by the three dejected Uptons till he was out of ear-shot. It was then that the Uptons smiled. Mipps winked.

"And now, what's the truth?" he asked.

"All of it, more or less," replied Monty. "The Dragoons will have an uncomfortable ride over all those pebbles at the Petts, and our hundred and fifty 'white armlets' have by now reached home under Dymchurch Wall. There's two thousand guineas' worth of kegs just landed there from sunken rafts. We'll ride down and see that all's safely stowed before the Dragoons get back."

"Death to the Scarecrow," laughed Monty, putting his horse to the canter.

"Death to the Scarecrow," laughed his brothers, as they rode off in his wake.

"Death of the Scarecrow is what they ought to say—and bad luck it is, too," muttered Mipps. "Well, by the time I've spread a rumour or so, the Scarecrow may ride again, and then it will be her ghost. Nothing like a bit of superstition to make affairs like this a success."

He went to the cottage, and producing a tool from his pocket, wrenched off an ill-hung shutter with no difficulty. He carried it

Into the death-room. Dr. Syn got up and mechanically followed him.

"It's a long walk to the village, Mipps," said the squire. "I wish our honourable highwayman had not ridden off. His strength would have been welcome."

Mipps looked at Dr. Syn, who stood dazed and forgotten. He knew it would require all his wisdom to get this madman to the vicarage.

"The vicar's no good, sir. Not just now. No more's Dr. Pepper."

"It seems that you and I will have to manage best way we can, Mipps," said the squire.

"I've a notion, sir," replied Mipps, "that what with all the military about, a sensible highwayman would not ride far tonight looking for trouble. Suppose he's gone to earth close, and I finds him, would you go bail for his safety?"

"I think I would welcome him more than any other," returned the squire. "He knows better than we do how to travel unseen. I'd go bail for his safety with my honour."

"Give me a minute, then, sir," went on Mipps. "I has a wonderful way of sniffin' people out."

He left the cottage and in three minutes returned with the highwayman.

Both he and the squire exchanged a bow of ceremony, as the highwayman said, "I am at your daughter's service, sir."

"You will not regret it, sir," replied the squire.

They placed the shutter by the bed.

"I could make handles," said Mipps. "There are some stout poles in the yard."

"I have carried a wounded comrade to safety before now, sir," said the highwayman. "On horseback we should be there quicker and not attract attention. We could wrap your daughter in a cloak."

But they were reckoning without Dr. Syn. He no sooner saw that Dr. Pepper and the old woman were about to lift the body from the bed to the shutter, than he made a ferocious gesture of disapproval. His arms shot out wide in the shape of a cross as he motioned them away, the physician from the head, the old woman from the feet. He then knelt down and putting his arms around the girl, lifted her like a baby and stood up, glaring at them all defiantly.

The highwayman took Mipps aside. "Bring his pony and the horses. He will do it himself and, please God, it may save his reason. I will ride his Gehenna, and do you ride mine, and we'll hide the white pony between us."

A few minutes later, the old woman, clutching a purse which the squire had given her, watched them ride over the little bridge that spanned the dyke.

The squire, on Charlotte's mount, rode first (for, as he said, who would dare question him on Romney Marsh?) Then came Mr. Bone upon the wild Gehenna, who had had his fierceness ridden out of him that night. On his right, Dr. Syn, clasping his precious burden, sat the white pony, while upon his other side rode Mipps. Beyond them was the physician on the troop-horse.

They fitted their pace to the pony's jog-trot, riding close to screen it from any passer-by. Once only they met a party of horsemen, whom they conjectured to be smugglers hurrying home. Certain it was that they turned their heads away as they galloped past, being none too eager to be recognized by the head magistrate.

Furtive faces peeped out as they passed cottage windows, but Jimmie Bone and Mipps rode close beside the pony and screened the tragic pair who rode it. So was Charlotte brought back secretly to the Court House and laid in her own room.

The housekeeper, having told all she knew of the girl's departure, was pledged to silence, and the tale of her accidental death was spread through the house. Dr. Syn carried the body to the room himself and sat beside the bed, from which no one could move him.

"He must be watched," said Sennacharib Pepper, "but he had best be left here."

Mipps stabled the white pony and Charlotte's black horse, and then led the troop-horse to the Ship Inn field and handed it over to one of the soldiers on guard of the camp.

On his way back he met the highwayman. He was still riding Gehenna. His own horse he was leading on the loose rein. He drew up beneath the gibbet tree.

·"Are you going back to look after your master?" he asked.

"Aye, mate," replied Mipps. "The squire is keeping him there till he recovers, I expect.   He told me to come back. I want to be at hand, in case he should talk silly. I've never known him like this."

"It's been a queer, tragic night," returned the highwayman.

CHAPTER XV

THE CRAWLING DEATH

To the end of his life Mr. Mipps would always maintain that the three days before and after the funeral of Charlotte Cobtree were the worst in his adventurous career. To persuade Dr. Syn from the death chamber was impossible. To get him to take nourishment of any kind was likewise impossible. They gave him a comfortable, backed chair at the side of the bed, but he sat forward on it, with a straight back, one hand laid reverently on the dead clasped ones and the other gripping his sharp knee. When the coffin was brought in, he rose to make room for it, and when she lay in it, he sat once more beside her, but craning forward so as to see the marble face.

On the day of the funeral he still sat with one lean hand resting among the flowers upon the coffin lid, and when it was carried out, he dumbly followed.

After the ceremony, Dr. Syn walked briskly to the vicarage. Mipps followed, and his worst fears were realized.

As soon as they were alone, and the doors were shut, he turned on Mipps sharply. "Brandy. Don't stand staring, but stir your stumps. Brandy, I tell you. We must have clear heads, and warm blood for what we have to do. I can depend on you, Master Carpenter. On whom else? On whom else?"

Once more he gulped down the brandy, and then unhooking an old sea-cloak from a nail upon the door, he wrapped himself in its folds and lay down upon the floor, with the brandy bottle beside him. In a few seconds he was fast asleep.

Mipps raised the head and removed the wig without awaking him, and then put a cushion beneath him. He then took a generous pull of the brandy bottle himself.

While wondering whether he would get help from the Court House in order to carry his master to bed, an unusual disturbance attracted his attention outside the window. While Mipps knew that solemn crowds still filed past the open grave, he could in no way account for what sounded like the ribald jeers of school children.

As he looked through the casement, he saw that there was indeed a crowd of children at the garden gate, while in the midst of them towered the gigantic and majestic figure of a North American Indian, bedecked in full war-paint and feathers.

"Crimes! If it ain't the Blue Heron himself," muttered Mipps. "I forgets his Injun name, but no doubt he'll remember. If this don't make me turn Red-skin and worship the sun and the four winds, I'm no Christian. What's brought him but magic, I don't know. But I'd rather see him now than a barrel of rum."

With such mutterings Mipps rushed from the house and drove away the squalling children, who were disappointed when their wild Indian was dragged by the delighted little sexton into the vicarage.

Shuhshuhgah (the Heron)—for that was the name Mipps had forgotten—had much to tell.

While trading with Captain Vicosa on behalf of his tribe, he had discovered the identity of Colonel Delacourt, as the man whom Dr. Syn had sworn to kill. He discovered more. They were journeying to England, either to send Dr. Syn to the scaffold or to kill him themselves. Shuhshuhgah, having taken solemn blood-brotherhood with Syn, found it his duty to follow, and he sailed to Plymouth by the same ship. In England, however, he was dogged with disaster, through ignorance of the law.

Knowing that his blood-brother's enemies were bound for the town of Rye in Sussex, he saw them depart with Colonel Dela-court's wife by coach, himself following on a horse he purchased from a gipsy. Camping on the road-side as he followed the trail, he was caught in Hampshire cooking a fine deer which he had shot on a gentleman's estate. He was carried before the justices and put into prison, but at length was released and ordered out of the county.

When Mipps in his turn had explained all the circumstances that had led Dr. Syn into his present condition, Shuhshuhgah helped him carry the unconscious man to his bed.

After a careful examination, Shuhshuhgah took from his huge leather belt a sharp pointed knife with a serrated blade.

"You ain't goin' to scalp him, I hope," said Mipps.

The Indian shook his head. "I shall remove a fragment of the bone above the brain. Only thus will our brother get relief. Leave me."

He bound a piece of thin cord round the handle of the knife, then with the flat of his palm pressed the point into the table by the bed. He then pulled the cord swiftly, like a boy spinning a top, the pressure causing the point to bite deep into the wood as it spun. The Indian grunted his satisfaction. The knife was sharp.

"We shall find him again, not lose him," returned the Indian.

"You may trust me. It was thus that I saved my own father for our tribe. I know. I shall not fail. Leave me."

Mipps looked at the unconscious man, and wondered what he would have to say about such an operation. He would certainly trust the Indian's skill. So he took another pull at the brandy bottle, shrugged his shoulders fatalistically and crept out of the room.

At last the door opened and the Indian beckoned him. Dr. Syn lay on the bed as though dead.

"Have you done him in?" asked the terrified sexton, looking at the white face.

"He will sleep the sun round," replied the Indian. "I have given him a drug. He feels no pain. He will wake with his brain restored. When he wakes, give him an egg beaten into milk and then this pellet. He will then sleep again. By that time we will have ready a stimulant to restore him. Revenge."

"Re-wat?" asked the amazed sexton.

"Revenge," repeated the Indian. "There is nothing so stimulating after love. I go to get proof against the men who fired those shots and killed his lover. Then he can help us deal with them as they deserve. I am going to this Rye to trail Colonel Delacourt."

"Well, you can't never go trailing people in all them feathers," criticized Mipps. "I'll have to borrow you some clothes that won't get you stared at. And what if the local doctor wants to see the sick man? He's been here once already with this tonic."

The Indian removed the cork and sniffed at the bottle. He then poured the contents out of the casement.

"I shall return upon my tracks in three days," said the Indian. "You will guard our brother till then."

Mipps explained the way to Rye and pressed a purse of guineas upon the Red-skin.

"I shall have no need of them, however," said Shuhshughah, "for I intend entering the service of Colonel Delacourt. Only as such shall I surprise his secrets."

Mipps watched him stride away, and thought that there were worse things in life than loyal Red-skins.

On the third evening Shuhshuhgah returned from Rye, and Mipps noted the grim smile of satisfaction on the warrior's face. Dr. Syn was sitting up, drinking some hot soup heavily laced with good sherry from the Court House. He recognized the Indian immediately, though showing no sign of surprise at his presence.

"Ah, Shuhshuhgah, my blood-brother. I take this as kind of you," he said in greeting.

With infinite patience the Red-skin dealt with the awakening brain, reminding him that all his life he had been persecuted through the evil of one man, the man who had stolen his wife. He slowly brought back to the doctor's memory all that he had learned from Mipps concerning the wreck of the *City of London,* his dealings with the man Merry, the birth of the Scarecrow, and finally the brave love-death of Charlotte Cobtree.

He then declared that he could put his hand upon the three murderers who had fired the fatal shots. He told him that his wife was dying at the Mermaid Inn. That Colonel Delacourt, none other than Nicholas Tappitt, was drinking, brawling and quarrelling, and threatening to cut the throat of a certain James Bone, who, he declared, had bungled as good a business as he ever had put on the market.

At this information, Dr. Syn tried to spring out of bed, but Mipps held him back.

"It's all right, Captain. He shall not escape us this time. You taught me what to do, and I've put old Gloomy, the Preventive Officer, upon his track. At the first sign of Nicholas Tappitt packing for a moonlight flit, he will be detained till we can get to him."

"Aye," answered the Indian. "That little man sits staring at him. He follows him wherever he goes. Only last night Colonel Delacourt threw a tankard at his head, and told him not to stare down a gentleman. But the little man still watches.

"Aye, he thinks he's the Scarecrow, and he's after proof," said Mipps. "I hinted as much to Gloomy."

"Well, gentlemen," said the vicar, "we must act quickly. Let me think. This news has given me a new cause for life. Let me think."

His thoughts were interrupted by a tapping on the front door beneath them.

"See who it is, Mipps," said Dr. Syn, "for Mrs. Fowey will be abed. It is nearly midnight."

It was poor Meg Clouder that Mipps admitted, and she had a strange tale to tell.

She had been dragged from her bed by her husband, Captain Vic. He had taken her down to the closed bar-parlour where, to her horror, she saw Merry drinking. When she had protested against the man's presence there, Captain Vic had told her that he was tired of her and was passing her over to his friend to deal with.

"And Merry will stand no nonsense like I have," her husband

had said. "Whether he'll tire of you as I have done, is his affair, for I must tell you I married you only to pass you on to him."

When Meg had cried out against this, Captain Vic had struck at her, but overbalancing, had fallen back against the table, and striking his head. Merry had been frightened, thinking him dead, and had run from the house.

"But he is not dead. He is drunk. And what am I to do?"

Dr. Syn, who had come downstairs in a dressing-gown upon the stalwart arm of the Indian to listen to this recital, got from his chair and took the key of the tavern from Meg's clenched fingers.

"My poor child," he said kindly. "And do you love this man still?"

Meg's face set harder as she cried out: "I hate him, sir. I never knew what hate was till now. He has hurt me to the soul. He has trampled on all I held sacred. And he has fouled my clean tavern with his drunken debaucheries. You know he had given my cellars to the slaughtermen. Well, the smell of blood has brought loathsome cockroaches. At night they swarm up into the bar-parlour. Yes, he has fouled the home which the villagers re-built with such kindness. I can never forgive him."

Instead of reproving her vehemence, Dr. Syn looked relieved.

"We will go and visit this Captain Vic," he said. "I do not blame your loathing of him."

The Indian repeated the name. "Captain Vic? Aye, he is the man who so nearly betrayed you to death, my brother. You remember the red-headed planter?"

Dr. Syn looked at Mipps and nodded. "I suspected it was the same. I will call Mrs. Fowey. She will prepare you a room, Meg, to sleep in, for you must not return to 'The City of London' to-night."

Half an hour later, Dr. Syn turned the key in the front door lock of the tavern, and followed by Mipps and the Indian took a look over the whole house.

Merry had gone. The only living creatures were in the bar-parlour. Captain Vic, in the light of two candles, lay on the floor upon his back, his mouth wide open, snoring disgustingly in his sleep. One or two adventurous cockroaches scuttled back to their safety hole as they entered. Dr. Syn marked the spot at the side of the fireplace where they disappeared. Then he turned his concentration upon Captain Vic.

"Poor Meg," he muttered. "He's a handsome beast, I'll say

that for him. Does anything illuminating about him strike you, Mipps?"

"Only that he lies like a pig and the son of a pig," replied Mipps. "What else?"

"His beard," went on Syn. "It is not so red as I thought it. It is the colour of cockroach wings. How he snores, the hog. Get me a pickle cork, if Meg possesses such a thing."

"I brought her some pickled onions last Tuesday," said Mipps. "I'll look in the cupboard here."

Mipps opened the cupboard and produced the pickle jar in question.

"And what is that bottle marked 'Poison'?" asked the vicar, looking at the shelves.

"I concocted that for her," explained Mipps. "A little concoction I made up for her to rid the place of the damned cockroaches. We used it on ship-board, if you remember, sir. Virulent."

"Virulent poison, eh?" repeated Syn, nodding. "That's excellent. But first we must make our enemy secure."

He went to a large easy chair beside the fireplace and turned it over. "Knife here," he ordered.

The Indian handed him a knife from his belt. Dr. Syn cut the webbing from the bottom of the chair's seat. "Now, Mipps, we need nails."

Mipps had dived into one of his side-pockets. A hammer and a fist-ful of coffin nails were laid upon the table. "Coffin nails for printin' initials on the lids," he announced.

"Somewhat prophetic," said Syn, with a grim smile. "I think Captain Vic might be spread-eagled a little more conveniently."

The Indian and Mipps attended to the drunkard's limbs, while Dr. Syn spread the strands of webbing over arms and legs, and fixed them securely, driving coffin nails through the webbing into the oak floor. Throughout this operation, Captain Vic slept and snored, his mouth open and his teeth gleaming white against the wild red beard.

Mipps deadened the sound of the hammer by placing his coat-tail on the head of each nail as Syn struck. Thus it was that Captain Vic did not wake.

"He is like a great tiger-moth on a boy's setting-board," said Syn.

"Got good teeth, ain't he?" muttered Mipps, after the last nail was driven home.

"Will the bands hold him if he wakes?" asked Syn. "He is very strong."

"So is the webbing," replied Mipps. "Besides, nothing grips coffin nails like oak."

"Yes, he has good teeth, as you say," went on Syn. "But I doubt whether they'll bite through a stout pickle cork. Where is it?"

Mipps levered the cork from the jar of pickled onions with his knife. "The cork," he said as he handed it over to Dr. Syn.

Syn bent down over his victim, who most obligingly opened his mouth to lick away the dryness of drink. Syn's sensitive fingers pushed the cork down into the mouth. The sleeper made a gurgling sound in his throat as the cork was forced between his back teeth. He bit down on it, and opened his eyes.

"It is a long time since we four met, Captain Vic," said Dr. Syn. "You will recollect that I was then the captain of the *Imogene,* and this man," and he laid his hand on Mipps' shoulder, "was my master carpenter. You had me arrested for piracy while dining with you, and but for this Indian Brave, Shuhshuhgah, who fired your house and rescued me, you would not be lying like this tonight. I am now going to hand you over to an enemy. Your brutality to your wife, Meg Clouder, forbids me to soil my hands with such a pig's death. I see that poor Meg has a jar of molasses on the shelf there. Hand it to me, Mipps."

Captain Vic tried to struggle, but could not move. His muscles swelled to no avail against the scientific pinning of the webbing. Neither could he speak by reason of the pickle cork. His eyes only moved, shining out red hate and fear.

"Your death will be carried out by your own fouling of Meg's clean tavern. I rather think that no man has ever died before, as you are going to die."

Dr. Syn took the molasses jar and with a spoon trickled a thin trail of the sticky syrup from the little hole by the hearth into which he had seen the cockroaches vanish. The trail led straight across the floor to the pinned-down monster. A fresh spoonful of the syrup was then poured across the red beard to the open mouth and then a generous allowance was dropped upon the wedged cork, from which it slid down into the swallowing throat.

Dr. Syn picked up one of the lighted candles and examined the trail. "Your bestial body, Captain Vic, will at last be put to a good use, for I have turned you into an admirable beetle trap. Your death will be regarded as the hand of God. No blame will fall to us. Your wife reported your brutality at my vicarage. We visit you and find you dangerously drunk. To keep you safe, we nail you to the floor so that you can get sober and do no further harm. We come back tomorrow morning with the beadle, and to our horror we find that you are insect-ridden. The physican will examine you. He will say that these roaches were contaminated with a beetle poison prepared for your wife by Mr. Mipps. They have carried the poison into the body of the dead man. We shall, of course, pour in the poison when the hungry roaches have gorged upon the sweet syrup in your throat. Maybe you will die of their tickling horror before we administer this virulent bottle of poison.

"Gentlemen, we will now sit upon the table and keep very quiet. Give me the dark lantern, Mipps. Presently, we will open its shutter to observe the effect of our living trap. We will sit upon the table back to back and wait in the dark.

"Good-bye, Captain Vic, and may God have mercy on your soul."

The Indian and Mipps clambered on to the kitchen table with their legs drawn under them. Dr. Syn blew out the candles and quietly took his place beside them.

The only noise was the ticking of the handsome Dutch clock upon the wall, and the noise of sticky bubbles bursting from the victim's throat.

But ere long they heard another ticking. It was the tiny sound of innumerable little legs, as the hungry cockroaches fought along the trail, groping with greedy antennæ for a further share of the sweetness.

Presently a strangled gurgle broke into the darkness, but for a long time Dr. Syn refrained from opening the shutter of the lantern. Twice did the big gilt hand go round the clock before he did so, and then without warning the shutter opened silently.

For a full minute the three watchers gazed in horror at their work of vengeance. The red beard was alive. Strong legs and waving feelers stirred and struggled in the hairs. Red-brown bodies crawled upon the grinning teeth, only to fall into the cavity of the mouth.

As they gazed, the Indian grunted with horror. Dr. Syn drew in his breath sharply with a hissing sound of disgust. Only the callous Mipps appeared unmoved.

"Takin' it to wonderful, ain't they?" he chuckled. "Look at that big bloke on his nose. Go on, 'Orace, tumble in, and then take the first turning' to the right and keep straight on."

"Silence," reproved Dr. Syn. "Look at his eyes. He is mad. He has had enough. We must end it."

Keeping the light of the opened shutter upon his victim's face, Dr. Syn told Mipps to get the poison bottle.

Mipps slid from the table and did as he was ordered, uncorking the bottle as he handed it to his master.

"Is it deadly?" asked Syn.

"Kill a sperm whale," replied Mipps.

"Then pour half the bottle down his throat and sprinkle the rest upon the floor."

The task was very congenial to the grinning sexton. He placed the neck of the bottle between the mad man's teeth. Then he paused to flick the large cockroach into the mouth, saying: " 'Ere, 'Orace, you get in and warn your friends that poison's a-comin'!" Then he tilted up the bottle.

Captain Vic shuddered. The great body strained against the webbing thongs, and then the mad eyes glazed. Mipps took the lids and closed them. Then, producing two penny pieces from his pocket, he laid them one on each eye.

"Take them off, you fool," ordered Dr. Syn. "And open his eyes. Don't you see that we are supposed to be at the vicarage? The sooner we are there the better."

He relighted the candles, so that they could burn themselves down to the sockets, and then poured some of the poison around the hole in the hearth. Already many of the foul insects lay dead.

"There are yet two more to die—Merry and friend Nicholas. What does he call himself—Colonel Delacourt? Ah—that is the death I want to see."

CHAPTER XVI

SYN'S SALVATION

In the darkness of the avenue by the churchyard wall, Dr. Syn suddenly stood still. "Listen, Mipps," he whispered. "And look."

It was easy enough to see the only light visible, for Mipps had put out the dark lantern and strapped it to his belt, and there across the churchyard was a supernatural light rising from the ground where the corpses lay. At regular intervals a shadowy wave arose from the ground against the light, and then fell with a rattling swish like hail. A dark solid shadow that cut the light in two moved. It was a man. Something in the movement roused Dr. Syn.

"By God," he cried, "it is my enemy. At last."

The man, evidently hearing the voice, turned and then ran quickly and silently out of the light. Dr. Syn sprang forward, but Mipps and the Indian grabbed his arms and held him back.

"There is another man there," said Mipps. "Keep your voice down, sir. We have not disturbed him. He is digging. Look. He is throwing up loose earth. It is Miss Charlotte's grave. They are for committing sacrilege."

"Charlotte's grave?" repeated Syn, in a low, terrible voice.

"Aye, sir," whispered Mipps. "It is someone after the rope of pearls that are buried with her. I'll lay a guinea it's that rogue Merry."

"By God, I'll kill him; I'll strangle him in her grave," hissed Syn. "Unhand me."

With a great effort he broke from their grip and ran towards the light.

The Indian ran too, drawing a knife from his belt. But the Indian ran past the light in a circle and dropped down amongst the rank grass on the further side of the low churchyard wall.

Mipps trotted after his master, who stood still, now looking down into the open grave. A shower of stones and earth shot up from the digger in the grave and fell upon Dr. Syn. Another spadeful followed, but Dr. Syn did not move. Mipps fetched up alongside him, panting. The noise alarmed the man in the grave. Mipps looked down.

It was Charlotte Cobtree's grave. There were her initials on the

coffin lid, which was all but uncovered. A sharp steel bar lay upon
it beside the lighted lantern. This was the instrument that would
soon have prized the coffin open.

A white, perspiring face turned and looked up, alarmed at the
sexton's panting. Mipps was right. It was Merry crouched over a
spade, and his fear was lighted by the lantern.

Down upon him dropped Dr. Syn with a thud, and wrenched
the spade away. Merry's face was beneath his knees. Mipps saw
the doctor's fingers grasp the top sides of the spade's blade and then
it drove down hard upon the thief's forehead.

"Don't kill him here," cried Mipps. "It's sacrilege."

"Aye. We'll not pollute her sweet grave," replied Syn. "He is
unconscious, and we will not be merciful to him."

Quickly he unwound his great black scarf from his throat and
lashed it round Merry's jaw and neck. He then placed the spade
against the grave side, and using the handle as a stirrup sprang
up and gripped the top of the grave. In his other hand he held the
ends of the scarf.

"You will pull and I will lift," he said to Mipps.

It was a struggle getting the unconscious Merry from the
grave, as it was also a struggle dragging him to the vicarage, but
at last they dropped him on the study floor.

"How shall we kill him when he returns to consciousness?"
asked Syn.

"Wait for Shuhshuhgah," advised Mipps. "He's a fair dab at
deaths. There ain't no cockroaches here, though there's mice in
the panelling."

"And rats in the dyke," said Syn.

"Aye and mud—soft mud in the sluice-gates."

A gentle rapping on the front door interrupted them. "It will
be Shuhshuhgah," muttered Syn. "Rub more brandy on his
temples. He should come round soon. I'll watch him while you
admit the Indian by the back door."

Shuhshuhgah had a strange tale to tell. He had found Colonel
Delacourt's horse tethered to a tree beyond the churchyard. He
had then followed the man's tracks across the grass of the tythe
field and had located him crouched in the laurel bushes by the
vicarage front door.

"He has a pistol in his hand," said the Indian, "and its muzzle
covers the door."

"He is waiting for me," replied Syn grimly. "Well, he shall
have his shot, and the shot will kill. He does not know that I have
returned, but he will soon guess it and then no doubt he will call

up to my window and get me out under some pretext. This falls out very well."

Dr. Syn looked at the clock upon the wall. "Three," he muttered. "We must alter that." He turned the hands on to five, while Mipps wondered why he did it.

A few minutes later Merry opened his eyes, raised himself on one elbow, groaning, and looked round him.

"What is happening?" he asked, looking into the three grim faces watching him.

"I will tell you," replied Syn. "You will see by the clock here that it is five o'clock. Beyond these closed shutters the dawn will be breaking. At three o'clock a villager aroused me with the news that someone was robbing a grave. I sent him to wake the sexton. Meanwhile, I dressed hurriedly and discovered you at your sacrilegious work. You were about to prize open Miss Cobtree's coffin in order, I presume, to steal that rope of pearls you coveted. I seized you and in order to save you from your enemies and your own damnation, I knocked you senseless with your spade and with the sexton's help I dragged you here to safety."

"Safety?" repeated the amazed Merry.

"Aye, safety," went on Syn. "The villager aroused others. Just as I got you here, they arrived. A score or so of armed men, horrified at your deed and determined to have revenge. Miss Cobtree was very much beloved. I refused to give you up to be torn to pieces. I pleaded with them for mercy. All my eloquence, however, has been of no avail, for while they respect the sanctuary of my vicarage they are waiting for you—outside."

"They'll tear me limb from limb," cried the horrified Merry. "What can I do? What will you do?"

"I am a man of peace, Mr. Merry," continued Syn sadly. "I am the shepherd of my flock and must save my sheep, white or black. And there is none so black that cannot be saved by repentance at last. Show me that you repent and I will show you the path to safety."

"How can I show you?" asked Merry.

"By answering the truth to my question," replied Syn. "And let me warn you that I know the truth, so that a lie will not avail you. Who fired the three shots on the night of the last smugglers' 'run' that killed the Scarecrow on Aldington Knoll?"

"The law can't touch us for that," said Merry. "Death to the Scarecrow was the law's order. It was Colonel Delacourt who lies at the Mermaid Inn, his red-bearded friend—the captain who married Meg—and me. They knew you were the Scarecrow. They also told me that you were the pirate, Captain Clegg."

"And you believed them, eh?" asked Syn.

"I did. When you appeared at Miss Cobtree's funeral, we got a fright, I tell you."

"And you don't know whom you killed, eh?" asked Syn.

Merry shook his head. "No, but there's wild rumour goin' round that the Scarecrow was none other than Miss Cobtree, but no one dares say it is so."

"And you three will do well to forget it," went on Syn. "And yet it is quite true that you three killed that lovely girl, and to add to your crime you come tonight to rob her grave. It seems to me that it would only be justice were I to hand you over to your enemies outside."

"But you said you'd save me," pleaded the frightened wretch.

"Aye," nodded Dr. Syn, "and may God forgive me if I am doing wrong. Stand up."

Merry scrambled to his feet.

"We are of a height, we two," he said. "Mipps, on the door there is my cassock, cloak and hat. If Merry wears them he could leave this house in perfect safety. Help him to dress."

The sexton's quick brain appreciated the situation, and he grinned behind Merry's back, as he helped him into the cassock and cloak.

"Now wrap the muffler round his face," ordered Syn. "Put on these glasses of mine and pull the hat down. No, it needs my wig to make it perfect. Put it on, Merry."

The disguise, they all declared, was perfect. Even Shuhshuhgah grunted his approval.

"You will get across the border to Rye," ordered Dr. Syn. "But go by way of Burmarsh. In three minutes the sexton will follow you. Wait for him at the 'Shepherd and Crook' and return my clothes."

"Thank you," muttered Merry. "I have tried to serve you bad, I own. You are returning good for evil."

"It is my duty, sir," replied Syn coldly. "Go, Merry, and I only hope and pray that you will look upon sin—no more."

They led him into the hall and unlocked the front door. Dr. Syn handed the key to Merry. "Lock it from the outside. It will look natural. They will know you are Dr. Syn. I rather think that when you have gone out of ear-shot they will break into the house to get the robber of Miss Cobtree's grave. Go."

They all three stepped back into the darkness while Merry

opened the door, sidled round it, closed it again and fitted the key outside.

Dr. Syn took three glasses from the livery cupboard and a bottle of brandy. He filled the glasses with a steady hand. There was sufficient light from the candles in the study as he had left the door open. He put down the bottle quickly. The three men heard the key turn in the lock from outside. They heard the key withdrawn. Dr. Syn's thin fingers picked up his glass. He looked at the brandy. He sniffed it. One would have thought he had no other interest in the world. Having sniffed it, he held it up against the shaft of light that cut across one end of the hall from the open study door. The glass was held steadily as though in toast. Suddenly there came a noise of rustling leaves, as a man leaped forward from the laurel bush. There followed a sharp cry of fear and then a sharper crack of a pistol fired. A dull moan, then a second shot—sharp—percussive. A gasp. A sound of footsteps, then a crash as of a body falling. Then running footsteps fading away into silence. And then Dr. Syn signed to the others, who picked up their glasses in lieu of "toast". Dr. Syn remarked:

"Perfect safety. Syn's salvation."

"Aye," replied Mipps, smacking his lips in appreciation of the drink. "And that's as neat and as natty a little murder as ever I saw."

"Go and see if it is a murder," advised Syn, nodding his head towards the door.

Mipps opened it and they all filed out, and looked upon Merry's body sprawling on the garden path.

CHAPTER XVII

THE HANGING OF CAPTAIN CLEGG

THE day broke. The Preventive Officer rode hard for Rye. In his pocket he was armed with a warrant for arrest against Colonel Delacourt. It was signed by Antony Cobtree, Lord of the Level of Romney Marsh. By noon, exciting horrors of that night had passed from mouth to mouth, and were discussed in every tavern of the Marsh. During dinner hour when the working folk gossiped most, news spread the quicker, so that by one o'clock it reached across the Kent ditch into Sussex and was re-told by the post-boys at the Mermaid Inn. Although it became time to return to labour in shop or field, the public bar of the old 'Mermaid' kept full house, as the news spread of the wild doings in distant Dymchurch.

To avoid the local physician, Colonel Delacourt crept down into a corner of the bar and listened to the excited whisperings. As he unhooked his sword and slammed it down upon the table, the table was deserted. The cronies gathered at the further end, leaving the dangerously drunk gentleman to his own reflections, his tankard and his sword.

Although Colonel Delacourt was drunk, he could not but help realizing that he was being watched. Were these furtive looks merely the vulgar starings of curious villagers who seldom looked upon so fine a gentleman as himself—or was there something suspicious in the glances?

He called for another tankard and asked the two nearest yokels to join him. When they refused with the lame excuse that they had had enough already, which could be nothing but a lie since they could both stand up, the colonel knew that there was something wrong—in short, that he was not popular. He listened to them whispering behind their empty tankards, and he caught the name 'Dr. Syn'. He comforted himself with the thought that no one but Merry knew of his ride to Dymchurch, and therefore he would never be connected up with Dr. Syn's murder. He would find a means of silencing Merry. Again he caught the whispered name of 'Dr. Syn'. Why couldn't one of them speak out about the murder? The whisperings and the furtive glances got on his drunken nerves. He could stand it no longer.

"Who is this Dr. Syn that the whole town is whispering about?" he asked.

"He preaches over here sometimes, and stays in this house. He's a well-loved man, eh, mates?"

One or two cronies nodded silently in agreement.

"And what's he done," demanded the colonel, "that you should all be gossiping about him?"

"You'd better ask him, sir," answered the yokel. "He's a Dymchurch man. Just been there, ain't you, mate?"

The yokel had turned to address a man who had just entered the bar. The colonel had been irritated by this man for some days. He had a habit of staring at him. The landlord of the 'Mermaid' to whom the colonel had complained, said that the man was the Preventive Officer from Dymchurch, and 'staring' was his trade. He certainly was staring at the colonel now, and the colonel realized that he was expected to say something.

"You're the Dymchurch Customs officer, aren't you?" he demanded.

The officer nodded.

"Come and drink with me," ordered the colonel.

The officer shook his head. "I never drink on duty, sir," he replied.

"On duty, are you?" growled the colonel. "And yet you're a far cry from Dymchurch."

"I was there early this morning, though," was the reply. "But you see, the man I followed last night doubled on his tracks. Went to Dymchurch—then came back to Rye. Excuse me a moment."

He shouldered his way through the gaping rustics to the outer door and called, "Come in, lads." Then he walked back to the centre of the room and faced the colonel, who saw three men enter and group themselves behind the Customs officer. They were the Rye constables. The colonel watched them as he drank.

"You were asking just now, I believe, about the Reverend Dr. Syn," said the Preventive man. "Well, I'll tell you something about him. He raised the Dymchurch men against the smugglers. 'Death to the Scarecrow' was his motto. Well—what happened? The Scarecrow beat him, as he'd beaten me and the Dragoons before. A very successful landing of contraband he had, and a very successful run to hiding. Had he been content with that, he'd have had the laugh of the law. But no, he vows revenge on Dr. Syn. He enlists the service of a rogue called Merry. They go to Dymchurch and their first act against the doctor was to break open the grave of our squire's unfortunate daughter. You may have heard that she was accidentally killed the night of the great 'run'."

"Rumour has it that the doctor was very attached to the young lady," interrupted the landlord.

"And there's no wonder at that," replied the officer, still staring at the colonel. "She was a lovely girl, was Miss Charlotte. Perhaps some day we'll find the man who killed her—then, God help him."

"You said it was an accident just now," sneered the colonel.

"Aye, but there's more rumour than one going on about that affair," said the officer.

"Get on with your yarn," ordered the colonel. "These rascals broke open the coffin, eh?"

"I never said so," retorted the officer. "They quarrelled—for they left a blood-stained spade behind them. The Scarecrow must have chased Merry and lost him. He wants his help to open the coffin and get at Miss Cobtree's pearls, no doubt. As he searches in the vicarage garden the door of the vicarage opens and what does he see? Why, Doctor Syn himself. The Scarecrow fires to kill, and he does kill. He fires again to make sure, and then, afraid of being caught, he mounts his horse and rides away."

"And he never opened the coffin?" asked the landlord.

"No. Afraid," returned the officer.

"Did you see all this" asked the colonel.

The officer shook his head. "Not all. I heard the shots and I saw the body of the murdered man. Then I goes to the church-yard and looks at the uncovered coffin, and the blood-stained spade. I waited around putting two and two together till I makes 'em four. Then I rides back here on purpose to tell the Scarecrow a very interesting fact."

"Then you know who the Scarecrow is?" asked the landlord.

"Aye, I knows that all right," replied the officer.

"And what is the interesting fact?" asked the colonel.

"Just this," went on the officer stolidly. "As I examined the body and unbuttons the cassock to lay my head upon the heart, I hears the voice of Dr. Syn himself, and there he was standing above the dead body right in front of me."

"His ghost?" asked the amazed landlord.

"No, sir," replied the officer. "Himself it was. Dr. Syn himself. The Scarecrow had made a mistake. He'd shot the wrong man. It certainly was the doctor's clothes—wig, spectacles and all—but the corpse was the rascal Merry dressed up in 'em."

"Then Dr. Syn is—alive?" whispered the colonel.

"And kicking," thundered the officer, "with no thanks to you. But Merry's dead, and that's for why we're here—me and the constables. I wants you for running contraband against His Majesty's Customs, but these 'ere constables wants you more pressing. Do your duty, Sergeant."

One of the constables drew a paper of authority from his belt and said, "Colonel Delacourt, I hold a warrant for your arrest on a charge of wilful murder."

"And *that*," continued the Preventive Officer, "is the first and last mistake you're like to make, Mr. Scarecrow."

"It's a black lie," roared the colonel. Both fists came down upon the table and his fingers gripped the long sheathed sword that lay there.

"Now then. Come quiet," ordered the Preventive man, drawing his cutlass and advancing boldly.

With a rasp of steel, the long sword was out, naked. The Preventive Officer leapt like a bulldog. The colonel crashed the heavy table over against him and met the heavy blade with his long sword. The straight steel slid over the curved steel with a sharp hiss, and before the constables could throw themselves upon the colonel, the long sword had passed straight through the neck of the Preventive man.

Down came three heavy truncheons on the colonel's head, as the corpse of the Dymchurch Customs man crashed to the floor.

     .   .   .   .   .

Mipps had filled in the desecrated grave. The Cobtree ladies had reconsecrated it with fresh flowers. Dr. Syn stood above it wrapped in thoughts of devotion when Mipps, leaving Shuhshuhgah at the churchyard gate, crept up to his master and told him what had happened at the "Mermaid Inn".

Dr. Syn turned from the grave and looked at him.

"Where are the parish crutches that we lend to crippled parishioners? Whoever has them—get them. Then order the squire's coach. He has ridden to Lympne Castle and will not need it. I do. I must go to Rye."

"The crutches, Vicar?" repeated Mipps. "Are you lame?"

"No. But I must carry two swords—the ones from my chest —to Rye gaol. I will strap the blades to the crutches and wear my cloak to hide them. Colonel Delacourt must never appear alive in court. I must kill him in fair fight—in his cell."

"Oh, crimes, Captain," whispered Mipps. "It's dangerous. Be careful. Who will believe his word against yours?"

"They must not be given the chance. What I failed to do upon a deserted beach of the Caribbean Islands, I must do in the cell where he awaits justice. Trust me. I have not lost my cunning. Order the coach."

"Shall I come too?"

"You will come too. Also the Indian. We ride together in the coach to Rye."

At sunset the squire's coach drew up at the Mermaid Inn and Dr. Syn, with his crutches well hidden beneath his long black cloak, was welcomed by the landord.

"I was about to send a post-boy to Dymchurch in the hopes of getting you, reverend sir," he said. "Since Colonel Delacourt's arrest for murder this day, his lady has done nothing but ask for you. She is sinking rapidly, and the doctor has given up all hope."

"Many years ago I knew her," replied Dr. Syn. "Indeed, I came here on purpose to visit her wretched husband in his cell. I will see Madame Delacourt first. I should like my usual sitting-room, for I must write to the Mayor for permission to enter the gaol."

The landlord went upstairs to warn the physician of Dr. Syn's opportune arrival, and Dr. Syn thus had the chance of taking off his cloak and wrapping the tell-tale swords that were lashed against the crutches in its folds. He left Mipps to guard the secret while he allowed the landlord to help him upstairs to the sick-room.

The physician made way for the spiritual doctor, shaking his head sadly, and Dr. Syn found himself alone with the woman who had been his bride.

At the sight of that beautiful, sad face, all the bitterness of the years vanished, and he could feel nothing but sorrow for the dying woman.

"Imogene," he said kindly. "It is I, Christopher Syn."

"Ah, Christopher—yes. It is really you. I have always known that we should meet at the last." Her voice was very feeble, and he had to put his ear close to her mouth to catch her whisperings.

It was a strange tale—the story of her life, from the time that she had run away with her seducer. When her boy was born, she knew that her husband was the father, but she deceived her lover into thinking it was his.

"But he was yours, Christopher," she went on, "and as he grew it became only too patent. He looked like you. He developed little mannerisms and tricks of voice that brought you back to us. Nicholas at last suspected, and I confessed the truth. Then he took a hatred for the boy as he had hated you. I had two other children, both girls. They both died. One had the black fever in Charleston at the age of four. The other died at birth. She was born in a convent, for we had no money then, and it was while I was there that your son—our son—Christopher, disappeared. Nicholas swears that the boy broke camp and ran off with some friendly Indians. But we never heard of him again. After that, Nicholas used to leave me for months at a time—oh, and sometimes longer. And then he found out that you were on his trail and he grew afraid. We went to the Indies and he joined the Brotherhood. They were pirates of the worst sort. They quarrelled and fought amongst themselves, but Nicholas was a good swordsman and he prospered. And then came the news of Captain Clegg. I think it was the name of his ship, the *Imogene*, that told him it was you. After that, we were rushed here and there, always on the move, afraid of you. Somehow, we always managed to escape you—and then at last we heard that you had given up the quest of vengeance and had gone back to England. Nicholas was rich then and had changed his name. He had had good trading with Captain Vicosa and they both hated and feared you. They came to England on trading business, but I know that their chief object was to unmask you as Clegg."

"So my son may yet live," said Dr. Syn, and she answered that she did not know whether to wish it so or not.

She told him many things about the boy, and he learnt that Nicholas had become cruel because his children did not live. "Even now I think he hates me," she said, "because of our boy. I think this little girl that was born here will live, but I shall not, and what will happen to the poor mite now?"

Dr. Syn pledged her his word that he would look after the child, which comforted the mother. For some time her mind dwelt on old days, and with almost a happy smile she asked him if he remembered this and that; persons, places and incidents.

At about nine o'clock there was a drumming in the street and the tramp of men's boots upon the cobbles. It was Colonel Delacourt being marched from the Town Hall back to his cell, for cries of "Down with the murderer. Let him hang" rang out with boos and hissings.

The shame of it was her death-stroke.

"Raise me," she said. "Do you forgive me? Can you?"

"I can and do," he answered.

Then she sighed and went to her last sleep in his arms.

Half an hour later Dr. Syn, armed with the Mayor's permit and followed by Mipps and the Indian, who had their own part to play in the coming adventure, accompanied the turnkey to the cell in the town lock-up.

"He is the only prisoner, as it happens," explained the turnkey. "And it's lucky for any others that might have had to share the big cell, for this colonel is a powerful, quarrelsome brute. You've only to look at his great arms and mighty chest all covered with tattooings like a common sailor. He ain't the sort of man to put up with preachin', reverend sir. But I'll watch he don't harm you. I'll keep the grid open."

"It is not necessary," said the doctor.

"But it is, sir," replied the turnkey, "for it's orders."

"Oh, very well," said Dr. Syn resignedly. He knew that he could depend upon Mipps and the Indian to deal with the turnkey.

The door opened and shut behind him, and Dr. Syn was alone with the murderer.

"Good evening, Black Nick," he said.

Colonel Delacourt, or rather Nicholas Tappitt, to call him by his right name, glared his hatred in the light of the dingy lantern.

Dr. Syn glanced back at the open grid, and saw the watching eyes of the turnkey. But only for a few seconds. There was a cry of astonishment, the noise of a slight scuffle and the grid was closed. Mipps and the Indian had dealt with the turnkey, and Dr. Syn would be undisturbed.

"So it's our parson, pirate, smuggler, eh?" sneered Tappitt. "Where have you sprung from to jeer at me?"

"From the Mermaid Inn," replied Syn. "To be more exact —from your rooms there."

"Been kissing your wife, eh?" went on the sneering voice. "A case of 'when the cat's away, the mice ain't afeared to play', eh?"

"She died in my arms within this hour, Nicholas Tappitt," said Syn solemnly. "But she told me of my boy before she died, and I must add his quarrel to mine in dealing with you."

"She's dead, eh?" repeated Tappitt huskily. "Well, God rest her soul. She was a beautiful girl when I took her from you—but plaguey irritating and I think I had the worst of the bargain."

"God rest her soul, indeed," said Syn. "But let us dispense with prayers, for we have very little time in which to settle scores."

"Well, how do we set about it?" laughed Tappitt. "I fear that my cell here is inconvenient. There is no plank to walk, and no sharks awaiting me. Besides, you lack your crew to prick me over the side. There is not even a coral reef for your old trick of marooning."

"We shall fight fair, and the better man will win, as in our pirate days. It was the ruling of the Brotherhood, if you recollect."

"Fight fair?" repeated Tappitt. "With no weapons? Besides, you are on crutches, and I warn you I was never more muscular in my life. But perhaps you have brought pistols under that saintly garb, and think to wing me with the same luck as you winged my uncle, Bully Tappitt, in Magdalen Fields?"

"Aye, something of the sort," nodded Syn. "But pistols are too noisy. They are also chancey weapons."

"Your old trick of knife throwing, then?" suggested Tappitt.

"Which you were never handy at," returned Syn. "No. I said *fair* fight."

"We can hardly kill each other with crutches, Clegg," laughed Tappitt, "and it seems they are the only equal weapons here. Or will you take the stool and I the table?"

"Listen, Nicholas Tappitt," said Syn grimly. "During those long years of death and danger through which I trailed you, my one ambition was to meet you blade to blade on some deserted beach. Well, it seems that the beach is denied us, but our blades can meet, even though they will be cramped for space. Neither can we move the furniture, for I see table and stool are clamped to the floor. Well, we can share these disadvantages, and still be fighting fair. Choose your sword."

Syn whipped the crutches from beneath his cloak and placed their handles from him on the table.

"By God, Captain Clegg, you were ever an ingenious rogue, I'll say that for you."

"Choose," replied Dr. Syn.

Nicholas Tappitt drew one naked blade from the binding round one crutch. Dr. Syn drew the other, and laid the crutches on the table.

"It's a damned cramped fight we shall have of it," growled the prisoner.

"But a better end than hanging, Colonel Delacourt," sneered Syn, sliding his blade against that of his adversary.

The clamped table was between them as they fenced—each seeking for an opening. But they were both experts.

Now one would gain six or seven inches, and now the other, but for a long time neither of their backs touched the wall. An inch forward, an inch back, as the blades pressed and rapped above the corner of the table.

At last the prisoner let out a strangled sob. It was partly due to his bursting lungs, and partly to his rage at not being able to break through the other's guard. Dr. Syn answered the sob with a short little laugh, and it stung Tappitt to the quick. With his last effort he drove Dr. Syn inches back. Then, when he found he could not gain another inch, he slipped back a full foot.

As Syn followed up, Tappitt seized one of the crutches with his left hand, swung it beneath his blade and jabbed it down between Syn's legs, giving it a savage wrench which brought Syn down on one knee. He let go the crutch and lunged.

But the foul was his undoing. As Syn's knee dropped to the stone floor, so did his left hand drop with a crash upon the table. His fingers closed upon the foot of the other crutch. Up went his blade at the same time, and only just in time, for Tappitt's sword shot past over his shoulder but within an inch of his neck.

Dr. Syn's sword gave a wrenching twist and at the same second his left arm lunged up. The scooped head of the crutch caught Tappitt's neck like a collar and jabbed him back against the wall. Tappitt's sword dropped from his fingers while Syn's point pricked his side.

"Don't move," said Syn. "I have something to say to you. This is but foul for foul. Brotherhood rules."

Tappitt could not move. The head of the crutch held him to the corner of the cell like a pillory, and he could feel the point of the sword pricking his ribs.

"If I push this home, you will die a gentleman's death, Black Nick," continued Syn. "Otherwise, you will die upon the scaffold, for I tell you there is neither juryman nor judge in these parts who would dare to recommend mercy for killing the Customs man. Your very cruelty to poor Imogene has been the talk of the town, and you will get no sympathy. Your pirate name, Black Nick, describes you well, for your soul is as black as your beard, and Old Nick has been your master. But you have one redeeming quality and with that I will trade with you. You love your child, the baby girl at the Mermaid Inn. Have you considered what will happen to her? Both her parents dead. Your money squandered. Brought up on the parish. A poor child. The daughter of a murderer. His blood running in her veins. She would have no chance unless you give it to her, in one last generous gesture. You know me well, Nicholas. Even when I was Clegg you will own I kept faith according to the rules. I have always been a man of honour, according to the rules as I interpreted them. Therefore, you may safely trust my word. Then here is the bargain. I will be your child's guardian. I will educate her. I will see she has a comfortable home and as far as lies in my power to give it, a happy life. I will see that she marries a good man, and I will leave her my money when I go to Davy Jones, as though she were my daughter. Should my son, of whose existence I only heard today, fail to make his claim to me, I will leave her all my wealth, which is considerable. I will make her a respected girl that everyone will love in her home of Dymchurch. But for this, there is your gesture to be made in payment. You will go to the scaffold, Nick Tappitt, alias Colonel Delacourt, as Captain Clegg, the Terror of the Seas."

Nicholas Tappitt could not move even to nod his head, but he closed his eyes, which Dr. Syn accepted as assent.

The crutch was released and the sword was lowered.

"You agree, then?" asked Syn.

"Christopher Syn, I have hated you as few men have hated another, but I grudgingly admit that I can trust your word. I also envy you for being the most ingenious rascal I have ever met or heard tell of. Your damned black cloth will be a protection for my little Imogene—yes, I named her after your wife who loved me, as you named your pirate ship. Not even to Captain Vic, were he alive, would I have entrusted my girl, but to you, I do. Give me the proofs to tell the judge and I will hang as you, you lucky devil."

"That will be easy," replied Syn, with a sigh of relief which he did not attempt to disguise. "I shall visit you each day, exhorting you to repentance, and you will sign the confession which I will make out for you. When that is read out in court, at your request, there will be no doubt at all that you are Clegg. You will at least go to the scaffold with a great reputation. Despite your crimes, you will be admired. It will be a great occasion—your hanging."

"By the God I never have believed in, you are, I think, the devil himself," replied the prisoner.

"At least, I will not ask you to believe in God," said Syn. "You can go to the scaffold brazenly unrepentant. It will at least seem more natural in Captain Clegg. But I shall have to exhort you to repentance with all the eloquence I can command."

"The situation will not be devoid of humour, I am thinking," laughed the prisoner.

"I rather think that I agree with you," laughed Dr. Syn, secure in his own salvation.

      •   •   •   •   •

So Clegg died—alias Colonel Delacourt—and despite the vigorous pleading of the eloquent Dean of the Peculiars upon the scaffold itself—Clegg died hard, blasphemous and unrepentant, till he had taken his last kick and the soldiers' drums had rolled. He was hung in chains and later buried without benefit of clergy at a cross-roads hard by the Kent Ditch.

Needless to say, Shuhshuhgah, the Blue Heron, was well loaded with presents from his blood-brother, Dr. Syn, and in return, he promised before he sailed that when he reached America he would inquire most diligently for some tidings of Dr. Syn's son.

For the doctor himself—well, he took his guardianship of the little baby Imogene seriously. But he did not overdo it. He put her out to nurse with a maid-servant at the Ship Inn, appointing Mrs. Waggetts as paid woman guardian. There would be time enough later for him to cultivate the child as he had promised.

On the ride back from the hanging it might be interesting to recount a few words that passed between Doctor Syn and his henchman, Mipps.

Mipps began it. "Well, he looked more like himself with his hair cropped and no beard. That Admiralty man saying he identified him, too. He was doing nothing but repeat what I'd told him myself, for he was the officer on the Royal ship what I served on. And didn't them tattoo marks make the natives stare! A fine show, the hangin', takin' it all round, but it made me sick to see the vanity of that there Black Nick. When you was exhortin' him so nice at the last to show repentance, and he roared out that there oath and then 'No', why, I believe he thought he'd done all Clegg's exploits himself. He took the glory of 'em, anyhow. I never saw a man so swagger his way to death."

"A most fortunate thing for me, Mipps, that he did, for Clegg is hanged now for good and all, and the past is not likely to trouble us."

"Another thing that struck me about the hangin'," went on Mipps, "was the number of folk what think that he was the Scarecrow. Mind you, opinions differ as to that. Some still thinks it is old Jimmie Bone, despite you provin' contrary, and some goes as far to whisper that it was Miss Charlotte—poor lass."

"Does anyone think that?" asked Dr. Syn, amazed.

"Well, you know how rumours get about," said Mipps defensively. "You see, she did ride that there black horse, didn't she?"

"Such rumours must be stopped for all time, Mipps. We'll

ride now by way of Gehenna and have a word with Mother
Handaway."

"D'you want to say 'Hullo' to the old horse? It's some time
since you saw him, ain't it? I mean, what with one tragedy after
another, we've had our hands full lately."

"I like to warn the old woman in good time," said Syn.

"Warn her?" repeated Mipps. "What about?"

"Why, that the Scarecrow will ride again with the next full
moon." And as their horses crossed the little bridge that spanned
the Kent Ditch, Dr. Syn fell to singing the old song of Clegg the
buccaneer:

> "Oh here's to the feet what have walked the plank—
> Yo-ho for the dead man's throttle."

I. you would like a complete list of Arrow books
please send a postcard to
P.O. Box 29. Douglas. Isle of Man, Great Britain.

On the following pages are details of the other books that together make up the Doctor Syn Saga

DOCTOR SYN ON THE HIGH SEAS

Russell Thorndike

Doctor Syn on the High Seas is the first of the Doctor Syn Saga and recounts the early life of this brilliant young Oxford scholar, who throws away the Bible for the Sword in his mad quest for vengeance.

By killing a notorious bully in a duel, Syn wins the hand of the Beauty of Oxford and accepts the living of Dymchurch-under-the-Wall. But his wife runs away with a friend of his, and Syn, abandoning his pulpit, follows them to the Americas. His enemy has hidden himself among pirates sailing under the Jolly Roger. Syn himself follows suit, calls himself Captain Clegg, and becomes the Terror of the Seas.

THE FURTHER ADVENTURES OF DOCTOR SYN

Russell Thorndike

The Further Adventures of Doctor Syn is in sequence the third of the Doctor Syn Saga.

It is concerned with Doctor Syn's adventures as leader of his Night Riders. 'Death to the Scarecrow' is once more the slogan of the authorities hunting him down on Romney Marsh. Syn's audacity in maintaining his double identity reaches new heights when he accepts a challenge to drink with the Admiral on his flagship. Syn, however, remains loyal to his King and assists in the destruction of a French privateer in the Channel. But his first loyalties are to his flock as both Parish Priest and Scarecrow, leader of the weird Night Riders.

THE COURAGEOUS EXPLOITS OF DOCTOR SYN

Russell Thorndike

The Courageous Exploits of Doctor Syn is the fourth in sequence of the Doctor Syn Saga.

Doctor Syn, leader of the Night Riders, is confronted by the most dangerous enemy of his career, Captain Blain of the Royal Navy. The by now exasperated Admiralty decides upon strong action against Syn and his smuggler band. But even this is not enough. The Scarecrow and his exploits make him into a national hero. Syn, as the Scarecrow, grows bolder, and he makes it known that he will hunt with the Prince of Wales.

THE AMAZING QUEST OF DOCTOR SYN

Russell Thorndike

The Amazing Quest of Doctor Syn is the fifth in sequence of the Doctor Syn Saga.

A Welshman comes to Dymchurch to identify Doctor Syn and to inform him that the pair of them, as the last survivors of a Tontine, are the joint inheritors of a vast sum of money. He has been sent on this mission by his landlord, Tarroc Dolgenny, who is an unscrupulous villain and has planned to murder Doctor Syn, get the Tontine fortune paid to the Welshman, and then by marrying the heiress, who was a pretty niece of the Welshman, he could be sure of the money, and could in turn get rid of his wife's uncle. Doctor Syn, who is none other than the Scarecrow, head of the Romney Marsh smugglers, journeys to Wales to pit his wits against his would-be murderer.

THE SHADOW OF DOCTOR SYN

Russell Thorndike

The Shadow of Doctor Syn is the sixth in the Doctor Syn Saga.

Once again Doctor Syn, Vicar of Dymchurch, scholar, wit, friend of the Prince Regent (the only parson who could make him laugh) and notorious smuggler, rides as the mysterious 'Scarecrow' at the head of his Night Riders on Romney Marsh. Despite the Reign of Terror raging across the Channel, and the fact that England is at war with France, his luggers brave the blockade with their valuable cargoes of rum, brandy, sundry spirits and silks, in exchange for shorn wool and English gold.

Here is a tale for all who are fascinated by stories of the exciting, adventurous smuggling days of old. In pulpit, saddle or on deck, Doctor Syn once more fulfils his mission.

DOCTOR SYN

Russell Thorndike

Doctor Syn is in sequence the seventh of the Doctor Syn Saga.

When this story opens there were two things of paramount interest in Dymchurch. One was Romney Marsh—visited, so the villagers whispered, by flaming Demon Riders and Jack O'Lanterns. The other was Doctor Syn, their genial, kindly, well-loved Vicar. To be sure it was a little incongruous at times to hear this godly man break out into the most ungodly refrain:

> *Here's to the feet that have walked the plank,*
> *Yo-ho for the dead man's throttle!*

For that was the favourite song of the redoubtable Clegg. But Clegg had been hanged as a pirate—so it was said—full ten years before.

How Syn's real identity was finally revealed when the King's men came to Dymchurch, and the strange part he played in the mystery of Romney Marsh, make this a decidedly unusual and thrilling story.

Also recently published in Arrow Books

MOON IN SCORPIO

Robert Neill

The year—1679. Many men go in fear of their lives, in fear of a return to the violent days of the Civil War. The Popish Plot has stirred up all the ancient hatred of the Catholics and there are some in the land eager to take advantage of this feeling for their own ends. John Leyburne, gentleman clockmaker, finds his rival in love to be one of the more desperate of these, henchman to the ruthless Lord Shaftesbury, and a man whom he has already encountered at the end of a sword.

Robert Neill weaves a notable story of mystery, action, and romance and creates the menacing atmosphere of London and Lancashire in those troubled times, as we follow Leyburne deeper and deeper among the dark schemes and plots of evil men.